BEYOND THE RAIL

AND OTHER NIGHTMARES

ICHABOD EBENEZER

Cover Art by François Vaillancourt
https://www.francois-art.com/

Editing by
Richard Thomas of Storyville
https://storyvilleonline.com/editing-services

For the members of The Write Practice, who helped make me a better writer, and therefore this a better collection.

For Chelsey Monroe, Kaitlyn Guay, Malachi Maynard, Angela Turner, and Nicki Tate, whose works I intend to see in print very soon.

And for my wife, ever my inspiration, ever my biggest fan.

Welcome, Look-Inside Viewer! May I commend you on your discerning nature. If you are still debating your purchase, perhaps you'd like to join my mailing list and get a free novella you can't get anywhere else. That way you'll know if you like this before you buy it. I'll also let you know when I write the next thing.
Check out https://dl.bookfunnel.com/x3xckjw155

Singalong   *1*

Transplant   *29*

Fertile Minds   *60*

The Permanent Clerk   *90*

Condemned   *113*

The Nocturnal Habits of the Late Derek

Gray   *150*

The Ritual   *165*

The Raven   *171*

Trick of the Light   *193*

Two Hundred Miles   *206*

Agatha Hemsley, Beloved Mother   *226*

Beyond the Rail   *244*

Two Shadows, One Gun   *251*

Singalong

"Hey, check this out," John whispered. He padded past the display cases and bookshelves, and stepped up onto the fireplace, his face inches from a copper mesh box about the size of a child's jewelry box. "What kind of stupid display case is this? Can't even see what's in it."

Crawfish sat cross-legged in front of the tiki statue's case. He paused in his work and shone the beam of his flashlight on John. A tiny screwdriver was wedged between his lips, and his fingers pressed a length of wire across the alarm's contact points.

Aside from the suede reclining chairs and the state-of-the-art entertainment center, the room bore more resemblance to a museum than a living room. Glass cases containing works of prehistoric art stood in each corner, and the bookshelves were dotted with eerie items from a mummified hand to a crystal skull and even a shrunken head, each in its own security case. John had examined each of them before noticing the copper box that currently held his attention.

Crawfish barely spared John a glance before returning to his work, taking the screwdriver out of his mouth. "That's not a display case, it's a Faraday cage. Back when I had that job testing cell phones, we'd put them in cases like that to block electromagnetic signals."

Jobs like this filled John with nervous energy. His responsibility was to get them in the house, and while Crawfish did his thing to get the tiki, John was on security. If someone interrupted their work, John got his hands dirty. Not that he was bothered by that, he just needed something to keep his hands busy in the meantime.

The box didn't seem to be hooked up to anything, so John opened it. "This one's got a set of car keys in it," he said.

Crawfish held the power supply between his teeth while reaching inside with an aerosol nozzle. "Put them back," he mumbled.

Instead, John pulled them out, examining the key fob. "No way! These are for a '65 Shelby GT. If there's a Mustang in this guy's garage, I'm taking it."

"We're here for the Tiki statue. Quick job, in and out." Crawfish set his tools down and pulled the front panel off the Tiki's case. He turned back toward John. "Touch nothing else. That was the deal."

John breathed deeply the scent of the leather fob. "So? You've got the creepy little dude. I'm…procuring a getaway vehicle."

"Whatever, dude." He placed the statue into the foam-filled case and pulled off his gloves. "You did your part. If you're caught, you acted alone. Got it?"

John smiled, clasped the keys tightly, and stole off in the direction of the garage while Crawfish packed his tools.

He found the car under a beige cover. Reflexively sucking in air through his teeth, he walked around, lifting the cover off each bumper, careful around the aerial. This guy kept his belongings in good condition.

The car was a shiny black with a chrome bumper and thick white stripes down the center line. As he peered through the vent window, he spotted the oversized shift handle.

He tore the cover off completely, then unlocked the driver's door. After listening carefully for any sounds coming from the house, he pressed the button on the door handle. It came open on well-oiled hinges, causing John to smile further. He threw the car cover into the back and slid into the bucket seat, caressing the wooden steering wheel. On the visor was the garage door remote.

Anyone who made it this easy didn't deserve a car like this. John sat in the garage a few minutes more. He told himself he was giving Crawfish enough time to make a clean getaway, but really he was building up his own anticipation.

Alright, enough waiting. He put the key in the ignition, disengaged the parking brake, then simultaneously pressed the button for the garage door and started up the engine.

The deep purr of the engine was a work of art. The garage door inched upward. John had the car in gear, one foot on the clutch and the other on the brake, watching the door to the house. If this were his car, he'd be racing down the stairs with a shotgun.

The garage door cleared the height of the car roof, and John popped the clutch, slamming down on the gas. The tires burned, screeching over the garage floor. John slammed the car door and tore off down the driveway, aerial twanging against the still rising door. John laughed maniacally. "Whoo!" he shouted as he fishtailed into the street and was gone.

He relished the sensation, shifting into higher gear and feeling the engine rev. He cranked the window open and pulled out a pack of cigarettes. Pressing in the lighter button, he slammed the pack against his open palm several times before flicking one out and gripping it between his lips.

He approached a stop light, checking the rear-view mirror, but there was no sign of pursuit. The lighter button popped back out, and he removed it with two fingers, cranking the radio on before raising the lighter to his cigarette.

"And Bingo was his name-o!" came blasting out of the speakers.

John fumbled the glowing lighter in his haste to change the station, jabbing his finger at the tuner preset. Registering the burning in his crotch, he dug the lighter out before it touched the pristine seat. "Crap, crap, crap!" he yelled as he patted at the embers in his jeans.

"Grumpy Mr. Bear, he says you can't come in."

Lighter in hand, he hit another preset. The

frequency indicator jumped across the dial.

"Pirate Dan was a helpful man and his crew were—"

"What the hell?" John yelled, turning the volume down low. He hit each preset in order. Every time, another kindergarten song came out of his speakers. Were there really that many kid's stations in the area? Next, he went for the manual tuning dial, sliding through the static between stations. When he finally picked something up, it was a monkey chasing a weasel. A horn honked behind him and he looked up. The light was green.

He switched off the radio and drove through the intersection. The lighter had gone cool, so he replaced it in the dashboard and gave up on his cigarette. Maybe he was having bad luck with the music, but that wasn't going to ruin his night.

Pulling into his apartment's underground garage, he parked it in someone else's spot and put the cover back on, in case the car had a LoJack on it.

Upstairs in his apartment, he tossed the keys onto his kitchen table and switched on his police scanner. For a while, he listened to the garbled voices of bored dispatchers and various units responding. No mention of a two-eleven on Elm so far. Chuckling, he walked to the fridge, cracked open a celebratory beer and flicked the bottle cap at the sink.

There was a lot more interference than usual on the scanner, and the voices were becoming faint. He mucked with the antenna for a bit, settling on a direction that seemed clearest, but when the voices became too low to hear, he turned up the volume.

Still not good enough. The volume wasn't just low, the voices were garbled, like when the microwave ran. He gently nudged the fine-tuning knob. Left went quickly to static again, so he tried right, and the static cut out, only to be replaced by loud music.

"The clock struck one and down he run. Hickory, dickory—" He pulled the cord out of the wall, cursing loudly.

In the silence of his apartment, he calmed himself down. It was past 2:00 a.m. There was no robbery call, and there would have been by now if the old man had heard him tear out of the garage.

He drained his beer, dropped the bottle in the trash, and went to bed.

"—Hi, ho, the derry-o, the cow takes the dog!"

John was startled awake, reacting practically before he knew what he was doing, and slamming his fist down on the bedside alarm radio.

What the hell? This was supposed to be the classic rock station. Was somebody messing with him?

He swung his legs out of bed and sat up. Of course! Crawfish brought them this job. Crawfish had known the car was there and how John loved classic cars. While he was casing the house, he got to the car and reset all the stations. Clearly, he'd done the same to John's alarm. Payback was going to be brutal.

He picked up the alarm radio to reset his station, but there it was, pointing at 105.9—The Classic Rock Station.

That only surprised him for a moment. Crawfish was good with wires, after all. The best around. John had to admit this was a nice touch. He'd have to ask Crawfish how he'd managed to screw with the police scanner, though.

Later that morning, he pulled into his crew's auto body shop, feeling a great deal of satisfaction. He cruised past Marco and Delilah at the gates, letting the silky deep purr of his near idling engine speak for him. He smiled broadly, bopping his head while watching their envious stares.

Same with the boys in the garage. They had music blaring while they worked, so he made sure to goose the engine a few times as he pulled in, to make sure he had their attention.

Scratch and Ink flipped up their welding helmets and craned their necks around. They set down their tools and made their way over as John parked. He gunned it a couple more times to rub it in, then turned off the engine. Only then did he notice what song the team had blaring today.

"—one for my dame, and one for the little boy who lives down the lane!"

Both Ink and Scratch managed to maintain straight faces as they approached the car, but John immediately realized that everyone was in on the joke. Pride and self-satisfaction turned instantly to resentment. He got out of the car, slamming the door. "Very funny guys."

Their boss, Yevgeni, shut off the music as the rest of the crew gathered around the car. Crawfish chuckled as he approached. "You actually did it," he said, looking appreciatively at the car.

"I suppose this was your idea," John said.

Crawfish looked surprised at the accusation. "My idea? I told you to leave it."

"Yeah, whatever. You'd better fix it, though. A car like this needs a radio going."

Crawfish wiped his hands on an oily rag and came closer. "Something wrong with it? You sure it's not just this bunged up aerial?" He hand-straightened the aerial, then opened the passenger side door and slid in.

"You know full well it ain't the aerial!" John leaned in through the open driver side window while Crawfish turned the key to accessory and clicked on the radio.

"Everybody do the Jupiter dance!" came pouring out of the speakers. He hit the presets randomly, each time a different kid's song came up. Finally he turned the key back to off.

Crawfish stepped back out of the car with a puzzled look on his face. "Well, whatever it was, that seemed to fix it."

"Like hell it did!" John yelled, but got a hold of himself when he saw the crew's reaction, more surprised than amused. "Look. Joke's over. You got me good. Now, fix it. I'm gonna grab a smoke."

John was on his second cigarette, which still did nothing to calm him, when Yevgeni stepped out of the shop and joined him leaning against the wall.

At first Yevgeni said nothing, but after a while he pulled back his sleeve and looked at his watch.

"Sorry I blew up back there," John said. "It was a joke. I get it."

Yevgeni shrugged. "That's between you guys. Settle it your way, I don't care. What I do care about is that buyers pay us for the job we do." He scratched at the star-shaped tattoo on his neck, squinting idly at the sun.

"What do you mean?"

"Last night. You were hired to get Tiki statue. Touch nothing else. You got the Tiki statue. Okay. But this morning, the buyer doesn't call. Not okay. Is 11:00 now. He should have called at nine. I'm patient. I wait one hour. He still doesn't call, so I call him. Funny thing: the phone is no longer in service. It was burner. No big deal, lots of clients use burner phones, but the funny thing is, they usually dump it *after* deal goes through. Why doesn't he want Tiki statue? Better question: why the hell would I want Tiki statue?"

"Things happen in this business. Clients get a

whiff of the cops and dump their phone. They usually get back to us with a new one before long."

"Is true. Sometimes things happen. I think something did happen, and client got whiff. I think you stole car you shouldn't have. Maybe statue looks too hot today."

This was starting to sound dangerous. People didn't screw with Yevgeni unless they wanted to end up floating in the sound. Hell, John had put several of them there. Yevgeni was the sort who would make a family member disappear over a simple disagreement. "I'm sure he'll call. It might take a day or two, but I listened to the police scanner, and the theft wasn't even reported yet." He was fudging a bit. He hadn't listened since last night, and it could easily have been reported this morning.

However, Yevgeni nodded. "I listen to scanner too. That's why we only talk for now. But you listen. Tiki worth five thousand dollars to buyer. If buyer doesn't come, I think maybe car is worth five thousand, and you can keep Tiki. Yes? Or you have other way to get me what I'm owed?"

John swallowed, suddenly thirsty. "No, sir. That sounds fair. If he doesn't call, the car is yours. He'll call though."

Yevgeni smiled broadly. "I like your optimism." Quicker than John could react, Yevgeni had one hand around the back of his neck, gripping firmly. "But when client says don't touch anything, you don't touch. Ponimayesh?"

"Yes. I-I understand. It won't happen again."

His boss clapped him hard on the cheek, smiling broadly again before walking back inside.

John had another cigarette.

Going back inside, the music was blaring again, this time something about a short-necked giraffe. Ink was using his welding torch as a guitar and riffing power chords across the gas line like it was head-banging metal.

Enough was enough. "Hey! Turn that crap off! The joke's over."

Heads popped up from around the shop, bewildered expressions everywhere. Ink shut off his torch and motioned toward Liev to turn the music off. "Dude. Smoke on the Water. I thought you liked Deep Purple."

"That was not Deep Purple," John said.

Ink's look was curious, like he was trying to figure out the joke. Scratch spoke up. "Yeah, it was."

Something was wrong. Everyone here enjoyed a good joke, but absolutely no one was this good at keeping a straight face, Scratch in particular. Back in April, John had disconnected the acetylene and replaced the tank with helium to watch Ink try to light it for two or three minutes, fiddling with the mixture. Scratch had to hide his face as he shook silently with tears streaming freely. He finally exploded with laughter when Ink said, "Son of a bitch," in a high-pitched voice.

"What's going on?"

John turned to see Crawfish approaching, scribbling at a clipboard.

"Crawfish, do you remember what song was playing when you flipped on my radio before?"

"Sure, it was—"

"No, don't say it. Write it down."

"This is a customer invoice—"

"Write it on your freakin' arm!" John yelled.

"Dude, chill," Crawfish said, placing the pen's nib against the skin of his arm.

"Ink, do you remember what song was playing?"

"Yeah, but I don't have a pen."

John watched Crawfish until he looked up, clicking the end of his ball point.

"Okay, name it," John said.

"It was Zeppelin. Immigrant Song," Ink said.

John pulled Crawfish's arm over, straightening it out. "Immgrnt Sng" it read.

"No freakin' way," John said, dropping his arm and stalking over to the Mustang.

He opened the door and climbed into the passenger seat. He sat there with the door open, thinking. This was nuts. But he didn't feel nuts. The crew gathered around him, looking concerned. No, it still didn't make sense. He reached across and turned the keys to accessory. The radio came on. "Knees and toes, knees and toes! Eyes and ears and mouth—" He shut it off.

"Everybody know that song?" he asked. Nods all around. "Okay, on three, I want you all to name it. One, two, three."

"Running with the Devil," they all said at once.

"Van Halen," Ink added.

"Shit," John said. He pulled the keys out of the ignition and gripped them tightly, closing his eyes. He needed to think.

"What's going on, John?" Crawfish asked.

"I don't know."

"Did you have a stroke or something?" Liev asked. "My babulya had a stroke and ever since then her words get mixed up."

"It's not a stroke!" John yelled, but caught himself. "I don't think it's a stroke." But was it? His face felt normal, and he spoke without sluring, but *something* had happened. Something sudden, and now he was hearing things. An actual medical diagnosis sounded a hell of a lot better than where his mind was going.

"Should we call somebody?" Crawfish asked.

John stood up. "Do me a favor. Change out the plates and sweep for LoJack? I've got to get out of here, do some thinking. I'll be back in an hour or so."

"Sure, man. I'll cover for you," Crawfish said. He raised two fingers and Liev nodded, went running off. "And I'll call you if the buyer comes through."

He lay awake that night, with balls of wet toilet paper stuffed in his ears. Since driving home, he'd had no peace because the paper-thin walls of this rat trap apartment brought him the sound of every television for three floors. Every commercial jingle, every TV theme song drove him mad until he'd sat in the shower with the water on full.

The sound of the running water drowned out everything else, and the pummeling jets on his scalp acted like a massage. His tension flowed slowly out of him and down the drain. The relief was so great that he remained in the shower long after the water had gone cold. Emerging, shivering, the voices of singing children resumed their assault until he discovered the toilet paper trick.

He still felt on the edge of freaking out at any moment, or start a fight with anyone who bothered him.

It had to be the car. Not a stroke, and not psychology. It was a curse. Was the previous owner some sort of voodoo man? There was that freaky Tiki statue, and other weird things in cases around the room, like a crystal skull, and a mummified hand.

John was interrupted from further musings when the night club a block over started pumping out its music. Only to him, it wasn't the latest bass-thumping dance hit playing, it was "Ain't it great to be crazy."

No sir, it wasn't.

It pounded, even through his makeshift earplugs, so he piled a pillow on top of his head, which only muffled it. His window was still open from his last smoke, so he jumped out of bed and ran to it. "Shut up!" he yelled and slammed it shut.

He scared himself with how out of control he was. He needed sleep. His alarm read 9:04. Not since childhood had he gone to bed so early, unless he was sick.

But he *was* sick.

He was physically exhausted—shivering— and a growing part of his mind wanted to lash out, or collapse crying. Climbing back into bed, one pillow under his head, one over it, he closed his aching eyes.

They flew back open at the sound of an apartment door slamming. He had slept, but didn't feel rested. He'd been curled up in the grass of a forest glen while around him, monstrous teddy bears danced, because today was the day they had their picnic.

He turned to look at the clock. It wasn't even 2:00 a.m. yet. His neighbor had scored and brought a girl home. Any moment now his stereo—

The music came on, all the way up. John didn't know if the guy did it to set the mood, or to cover up the noise they made during sex, but he usually tolerated it because he had once been young. But tonight, it was too much. He could not sit through the adventures of an elephant in the elevator.

He screamed as he leapt to his feet, a guttural, primal sound. He yanked the drawer completely out of his bedside table, and his revolver skittered across the hardwood floor. His nudity didn't occur to him as he scooped up the gun, spun the chambers, ensuring they were full, and rushed out of his apartment.

He stopped in front of his neighbor's door, gun in both hands, breathing heavily. This right here? This is crazy. You are crazy, a voice in the back of his head informed him dispassionately. He didn't care.

He kicked the door open, catching the two of them on the couch, with their shirts pulled up over their head. His neighbor reacted first, whipping it the rest of the way off.

"What the hell?" he said, seeing John, naked, stalking toward him. The guy tried to stand, but got mixed up in the girl's legs.

John picked up a throw pillow, placed a knee on the man's chest and covered his face with the pillow. He fired two quick shots, muzzle buried deep in the pillow, and the man went limp.

The woman screamed, still trying to pull her shirt back on. John covered her mouth with the blood-soaked pillow and fired again, quieting her instantly.

John let go of the pillow, leaving it to cover the poor girl's face. He crossed to the stereo and yanked the cord out of the wall, plunging the room into blissful silence.

A moment of sanity reasserted itself, and John assessed the situation. He was sure no one heard the gunshots, and anyone who heard the scream was probably used to hearing them come from this room. They'd certainly notice the music had ended, but they'd almost as certainly be grateful.

The door jamb had suffered some damage when he kicked it open, but that was only apparent from the inside. He poked his head out the door, cognizant of his nudity, but no one was in the hallway. John pulled the door shut with a knuckle so as not to leave a print, then returned to his own apartment.

He collapsed back into bed and slept with the gun under his pillow.

"Skip to my lou, my darling!" By the time he slammed a fist down on the radio alarm, his dream was fading already, but he had a glimpse of a gumdrop castle.

His fingers touched the gun under his pillow, and he remembered the night's activity.

Pretty stupid to sleep with the murder weapon, right next door to the crime scene. He had priors for chrissakes. Digging the toilet paper out of his ears, he got dressed.

He'd take the gun with him. Of course, he

didn't want to be pulled over in a stolen vehicle with a murder weapon in the car either, so he'd drop it off at the shop. Hell, they could paint the car and etch out the VIN too.

When he left the apartment, dressed this time, he couldn't help looking at his neighbor's door, ever so slightly ajar. Probably nobody would notice by looking at it, but as soon as anyone knocked, it was going to open.

Whatever.

He yawned silently in the elevator on the way down to the garage and got in the car. His car. Despite everything attached to it, the car was the one thing that felt right anymore. Life was good when he was in the driver's seat. He pulled out, reflexively reaching for the radio dial, but remembered just in time.

Even that wasn't going to bring him down, he'd sing instead. "Frère Jacques—" he stopped right there. No. He could do this. Smoke on the Water, they had said yesterday. That's what was playing. He got the lyrics firmly in mind. *We all came out to Montreux.* He opened his mouth. "Sonnez les matines—"

He beat his palm against the steering wheel.

This was not in any way normal. Stopped at a light, he became aware of all the sources of music around him. Radios blaring from open storefronts and cars rolling past. They were all playing kids' music, and nobody else heard it.

The shop was to the right, but instead he went left, not wanting to face the crew just then, and Crawfish said he'd call if they got word from the buyer. Yevgeni was going to want the car, and

John wasn't ready to give it up.

He navigated without thinking and found himself at the lake. Realizing the lapping of the waves against the shore would give him a chance to think without distraction, he found an empty spot and got out, heading straight for the shore.

The cold wind off the lake whipped his hair and felt renewing. The sea birds and the lapping waves were everywhere. A bell rang from a buoy somewhere in front of him. Off to his left, a flag whipped in the wind. No music.

A smile spread across his face. Now, to the problem at hand. His earlier theory still bugged him. If the homeowner had cursed him, he did it awfully quickly. The music started as he was pulling out of the garage. And that copper display case. Crawfish said it was to block electromagnetic waves, and the guy kept car keys in it. They clearly weren't a receiver of any sort.

He pulled the keyring out of his pocket. Were they broadcasting? Was this the source of the curse? Last night when he heard the music, they were with him in his apartment while the car was six floors down. It made sense.

Absently, he turned the keys in front of his face. One for the trunk, one for the engine. Then something caught his eyes. There were little indentations on the fob. Examining them closely, he realized they were bite marks. Several of them—and they were tiny, not a full mouth of them either, four on the bottom, two on top, over and over.

A child had been using this key fob as a teething ring.

The full story flooded into his mind. He had no proof that any of it was true, but he believed it. It made sense.

Some previous owner of this car had a young kid who listened to a lot of music and teethed on this bit of leather. He or she died in some horrible way, and that child's ghost was haunting this keyring. Their favorite music followed them everywhere, and only he heard it!

He spun around. Understanding felt freeing. And at that moment, he saw serendipity. In the middle of a row of shops across the way was a locksmith.

He couldn't help but laugh as he jogged across the parking lot and then the street.

An old man leaned across the counter reading a newspaper. "London Bridge is falling down, my fair lady," came from the old man's ancient radio, accompanied by a xylophone.

"You mind turning that off for a minute?" John said.

The man looked up at him for several seconds without moving, then with the barest of shrugs, turned and switched off the radio.

"Thanks. I need a couple of keys copied. Can you do that?"

The old man looked surprised. "This is a locksmith shop. Now, if you want a donut, you'll have to go next door."

"Right." John handed the key fob to the old man. "Please copy both of these." There was a stand on the counter with dozens of key rings. He picked one out with a Bad To The Bone logo and set it on the counter. "Put them on this. I'll wait."

Five minutes later and twelve dollars shorter, he was crossing the street again. He continued on past the car down to the end of the pier.

He pulled the cursed fob out of the paper bag from the locksmith shop. He bounced the keys in his hand until the Mustang logo was facing up with those tiny little bite marks. "Good bye. Good riddance," he said. He cocked back his arm and threw them as far toward the center of the lake as he could, listening to the satisfying plop as they sunk below the surface. He pulled out the new ones, all shiny and sharp edges where the other was worn and dinged. Bad To The Bone, it read. "Damn right," he said.

He crumpled up the bag, dropping it into the lake, and walked back to the car. Sliding the new key in, he smiled broadly as the engine roared to life and he backed out.

Turning onto the street and feeling pretty proud of himself, he turned on the radio. "Oh where, oh where has my little dog—" His heart fell, but he hit another station preset with fingers crossed, just to be sure. "—where the watermelons grooooooow—" He shut it off.

"I'm too close. That's it. I'm not far enough away from that haunted fob." He turned onto another street, heading toward downtown. He reached for the dial, but stopped himself as he saw the freeway sign.

"Still too close," he said and took the onramp, gunning it.

He passed offramp after offramp, and each one he considered, then dismissed. "Too close," he kept saying.

Thirty miles outside the city, the surroundings became mountainous. A small brown sign advertised Rattlesnake Ridge next right. That sounded about right. He wanted to be as far from civilization as possible.

Off the freeway, it was three miles to the turn off, and another mile and a half on washed out gravel to the parking lot and the trailhead.

He sat in the car, idling for several minutes, building up the courage to switch on the radio. What if this didn't work? What if the distance didn't matter? But it had to.

He clicked it over.

Nothing but static.

He burst out laughing. He hit the next preset. More static. He laughed harder. He hit the next one, and the next and the ne—

"Ooples and Banoonoos! I like to eat, eat, eat, ooples and banoonoos!" He slowly switched it back off.

No, no, no, no, no. He got out of the car and backed away. He had to think. Maybe he still wasn't far enough away. Maybe…maybe the car antenna was picking it up. What if the kid died in the car? Maybe it was both the car and the keys. He had to get away from the car as well.

He turned, finding the trailhead off to the left, and he ran. The keys were still in the ignition, but he didn't care. He ran.

On and on, sweat pouring down his face, he ran until he couldn't go any further, then found some hidden reserve and ran harder. When he could barely lift his feet from the trail, he collapsed in a grassy area. He panted for several minutes, his lungs burning from the effort.

Out this far, he couldn't possibly pick up a signal from anywhere. He closed his eyes and slowly got his breathing under control.

He listened.

The wind whooshed through the trees overhead, then somewhere far off, a bird called out three quick notes. Insects buzzed in the long grass under a spotlight of sun filtering through the trees. A crow cawed, then rolled a long, throaty burr.

Another bird, something predatory, screeched. A couple of squirrels chittered at each other.

He finally relaxed, rolling onto his back. Music to his ears.

Only then did it all come together. Each animal was doing its own thing, like an instrument in an orchestra, but as soon as he stopped listening to each one, he heard them all together.

It was "Twinkle, Twinkle, Little Star."

He screamed at the top of his lungs, getting onto all fours and punching a nearby tree. If anything, the animals became louder, more insistent. He saw mushrooms growing off the side of the tree in a sort of ladder progression, and he pulled one off. Tearing it into bits, he started shoving them in his ears. His screaming continued until he was hoarse and the sound was muted by the mushrooms.

Pausing in his manic work, he could no longer hear the animals. He collapsed again, nearly crying in relief. He was never going to get far enough away from keys nor car. He knew that now. But maybe he could drown out the songs.

Only, there were some songs you couldn't get out of your head, and there on the trail, his was Twinkle, Twinkle, Little Star. But it wasn't just animal sounds blending together to recreate it, no. It was a whole chorus of children and full orchestra. He couldn't just hear them. He could see them doing all the moves.

He tried to scream again, but no sound came out. How did the previous owner cope with this?

That copper cage. It blocked it out, and Crawfish had worked with them before! Maybe he still had one lying around.

John reached into his pocket for his cell phone, but touched instead a small flap of leather. All the hair stood up on his arm. With two fingers, like pulling a month's worth of hair out of a drain, he slowly removed it from his pocket, knowing what he was going to see.

The cursed car keys came out of his pocket. There was no cellphone.

That night, he was back outside the house. He had no choice left. It was either this or go mad.

But something wasn't right.

His instinct was to bolt, as if cops waited in each of the empty cars in his rear-view mirror, as if every dark nook between houses contained creepy black-eyed children in choir gowns, waiting to break into Christmas carols.

He slapped himself, turning the rear-view mirror to stare into his reflected eyes. "Get a hold of yourself, John."

In his state of mind, he couldn't trust much of his own thoughts, but after decades of doing this type of work, he'd built up instincts, and he wasn't going to ignore them simply because of a little madness. Something was wrong. He was still going through with this, but he would cover his bases. Beneath his seat lay the revolver. Three shots left. He picked it up just to feel its cold weight in his hand. He had power back. This was power.

The car's previous owner was going to tell him what he knew about the curse, and if he had cast it, he was going to remove it. Otherwise John would put the first two through the man's knees, and if that didn't work, he had one more.

Still, he had to be cautious. Street lamps stood in a line along the far side of the street while ancient willows darkened his side. One lone dog walker had been the only pedestrian since John had taken his parking spot, and now, two hours later, the children were all tucked away in their little suburban bedrooms, while parents' faces flickered in the glow of late-night television mercifully silent behind well-insulated walls.

No one was watching. No one had reported the familiar car parked across the street from where it had been stolen. The mark's own lights were out, same as last time. Early to bed, early to rise.

Perhaps John was only crazy after all.

He stuffed the gun into his waistband. Looking up and down the street one last time for potential witnesses, he darted across, and quickly picked the lock on the door. The thing that had been eating at his subconscious became immediately obvious.

The heavy curtains that had blocked the windows last time were gone. All the display cases that had filled the room were missing too. Paintings, ornate rug, chandelier—all of it. His footsteps echoed in the empty room. He shone a flashlight through the open door into the empty adjoining room, knowing if he searched the whole house and attached garage, it would all be like this.

Except, there on the mantle, alone among everything that had been there, the copper box still sat.

Screw it. That was all he'd come for, anyway. He gripped the cursed keys in his hand, crossed the room and opened the box. Out fell a folded piece of paper, and a wad of bills. He was so surprised by this that he paused instead of putting the keys away. Picking up the money and riffing through it, he estimated it at several thousand dollars. He stuffed it in the pocket of his hoodie and picked up the paper, unfolding the note.

> *I'm sorry. I'm truly sorry. The keys are yours, and I'm guessing by now that you've tried to get rid of them. I know it's*

going to be awhile before you believe me, but there's only one way that works.

I stole the keys from the previous owner. It took two whole days to regret my decision, and another week to exhaust all other options and try to give them back. The man laughed and said it doesn't work that way. So, I forced the keys into his hands and watched him drive away, but the next morning they were sitting on my kitchen counter.

I've travelled the world, trying to get away from that God-damned music, I've seen psychics and faith healers and hoodoo men. None of them helped.

Someone has to steal them from you. Once I realized that, I spent years trying to find the loopholes. I left them on the seat of the car in bad neighborhoods, and I hired people to steal them. The keys always made their way back to me. Finally, I hired people to steal something else and left the keys out to be found. You were the sixth person I hired, and the first to take the bait.

Last night was the first good sleep I've gotten in four years.

You can't sell them, you can't give them away, you can't leave them somewhere to be found and taken. I had to hire you to steal the Tiki and expressly forbid you from stealing anything else. So, when you did, it was your own free will, and your own fault.

> *Leave the keys here, if you like. They'll find their way back to you. But keep the Faraday cage. It helps. Well, a bit.*
>
> *Good Luck,*
> *-A Friend.*
> *P.S. The money is for the job. You can keep the Tiki too.*

John let the note fall to the floor. He numbly put the car keys in the copper box, closed the lid, and set it on the mantle. A bit. It helps a bit.

He pulled the revolver from his waistband and set it against his temple. The last thing to go through his mind—just before the bullet—was Twinkle, Twinkle, Little Star.

Transplant

Kevin tried to swallow, but something was in the way. His arms were too heavy to lift, and his vision was blurry. He floated in pleasant numbness. Someone spoke, giving him something to focus on, though he didn't make out the words. A blur moved across his vision and he followed it, trying to blink back clarity.

The surgery was complete. He was alive, and he had someone else's liver. He wanted to see himself, assess his own well-being, but he could barely move his head and couldn't tell if that blurry arm of his was even yellow anymore. He blinked again. Sounds began to resolve themselves; a monitor beeping, a nearby conversation, a pump filling his lungs with air regularly.

"Look who's awake." Velcro scraped open, and he felt pressure on his arm. "You are still coming off a ton of Sevoflurane, but you're doing well. The surgery was textbook, and your doctors are delighted with your vitals." The blur moved around to his left again, then he felt pressure on his forehead, and the man pulled tape from his eyelids, relieving a great deal of the blurriness. "Give us a few minutes. We're going to take that tube out, and then, if you like, we can bring your sister in."

His heart rate increased audibly at the mention of his sister. She'd actually stayed. He was overwhelmingly thankful, but couldn't think of a way to signal the nurse, so he blinked again.

The tube removal was unpleasant, and he found he still couldn't put words together and get his mouth to cooperate. They wouldn't give him any water yet, but the nurse came back with some ice chips for him to suck on; Kevin's new favorite thing. They removed the straps on one arm so he could feed himself, but fine motor control was slow to return, and the ice melted half the time before he managed to get it to his mouth.

"Hey there."

His sister was there, squeezing his hand. He smiled at her and slurred some response.

"Looks like you survived this one too. Who'da thunkit, right?"

Unable to speak, he looked down at his hand and raised a thumb.

She moved his cup of ice to a table just beyond his reach and sat down on the side of his bed, still holding his hand. "So that's it? His cirrhosis is gone just like that?"

"So long as he maintains his sobriety. And if he doesn't, cirrhosis is the least of his concerns. The alcohol would interfere with the anti-rejection drugs, and his liver would stop working. Painfully. But that's not going to happen. We wouldn't have given him the liver if we didn't have faith in him. He hasn't had a positive alcohol test in two years."

It was a while before his sister spoke again. "Is he supposed to be so puffy?"

"That's the general anesthetic. He will lose most of that over the next couple hours. You're his sister, right?"

"Yes. Diana."

"Hi Diana, I'm the intensive care night nurse, Stephen. PT will be here in a few minutes, and we'll get Kevin sitting up. You're welcome to stay if you want, but we'll need a lot of room to transfer him from bed to chair. After that we'll see if he can eat something."

Kevin looked up at the clock over the nurses' station. 3:00. If he was the night nurse that meant AM. His sister was here for him at 3:00 AM. Tears welled up in his eyes.

"No, I need to text the rest of the family and sleep. I will try to stop by later. Maybe tomorrow." She squeezed Kevin's hand again. "You do what the nurses say. Don't blow this second chance."

With that, she let go of his hand and was gone.

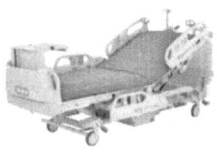

Moving from bed to chair was a weird experience. The physical therapist and the nurse did a complex dance with all the wires and tubes around him, then she helped him swing his legs over the side, and put a belt around him. She rocked him forward, then held most of his weight on the belt with him leaning over a walker. Finally, she lowered him into a chair. There was no pain, but he felt tugging and stretching all along the muscles of his abdomen. As though at any moment it could break open and everything would come spilling out.

She assured him it couldn't happen though, and when the day nurse transferred him back to bed, they showed him his scar. It crossed his entire abdomen, rising a bit in the middle where another incision came down from his sternum to join it.

"You'll carry that scar for the rest of your life. Your Mercedes scar. You know, like the hood ornament."

He fell asleep several times without realizing it until the nurse walked in, waking him. It was probably the drugs combined with the tedium of beeping monitors and daytime television.

Physical Therapy became a regular part of his day. They got him up and walking just hours after his surgery. They brought the walker and the belt back and he pushed his way around the ICU with the therapist lifting the belt from behind. When his victory lap was complete, he was exhausted and shaky, but it was a good kind of tired, and he felt proud of himself for the first time in ages when he collapsed back into bed.

That night, he was well enough to be transferred from the ICU to a recovery room where he would spend the next few days prior to release. They took some blood, started him on a regimen of pills, and offered him some food.

"I would kill for a bloody steak," he said.

The nurse laughed. "I think there's pot roast on the menu."

"Is it any good?"

"Honestly?"

"Never mind. Any statement that starts with 'honestly,' ends with bad news."

The roast was overdone and over-peppered, but at least it was something he could sink his teeth into.

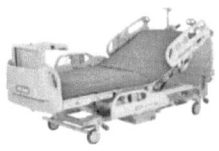

He was sitting at the large table of his parents' house. His sister was seated next to him, but she looked ten years younger and twenty pounds lighter. She was dressed in peach taffeta like it was Easter dinner. The centerpiece of calla lilies seemed to confirm that, but also blocked the view of whoever was across the table from him. All he could see was a painting he didn't remember being there, of a young woman in a red cloak peeking through the door to a cabin.

"Did you hear about Kevin's recovery?"

Kevin turned at the sound of his name. Uncle Dan was at the end of the table where a table arrangement stood, made from what looked like shredded flannel. Uncle Dan held a glass of deep-red wine as though he were proposing a toast. "It lasted three days this time." A smile slowly spread across his face, and laughter spread throughout the table.

"I think that's a record!" It was Uncle Dan's wife. Kevin could never remember her name, but when their eyes met, Kevin was the first to look away. Had they invited him just to talk about him as if he weren't there?

A waiter placed a glass of scotch in front of him, ice cubes clinking invitingly. Kevin pushed it away, his stomach turning. *That's not who I am anymore.*

"What's the matter?" Diana asked. "I thought you enjoyed a little hair of the dog?" Laughter erupted again.

He didn't have to take this anymore. He tried to push his chair back, to get up, but it wouldn't move. The arms of the chair likewise prevented him from escaping.

"I heard Flannery is going to press charges." Aunt Katie was on the other end of the table. He'd always liked her, but now she seemed to be enjoying his degradation.

"Oh, he's just holding out for more of Winslow's money, the greedy bastard," Mother's voice came from behind the lilies. Kevin wished he could see her, even under these circumstances. It had been ages since he'd been allowed in the house.

"That's enough," his father said, unseen. "I don't intend to spoil my supper talking about Kevin. Besides, I just might not pay this time."

Rage was welling inside of him, but he tried to force it down. Two years of sobriety had taught him a bit about people's actions and who's responsible for them. Their mockery said more about them than it did about him. Kevin was only responsible for his own actions, and he would control himself. He forced himself to be quiet. He literally bit his tongue with teeth that felt somehow too sharp. The coppery taste of blood fueled his rage, and it was sheer force of will that muzzled him. But the muscles bulged on his arms and his nails bit deeply into the hardwood of the chair's arms.

Just then, a line of waiters entered the room and encircled the table, laying a cloche-covered plate in front of each of the diners. At a signal from the butler, the cloches were removed. Raw steak sat on his sister's plate, actively bleeding. She picked it up with both hands and tore a chunk off with her teeth. Sounds of gnawing and gobbling came from around the table.

In horror, Kevin turned to his own plate. A raw liver lay atop a plastic bag full of ice. The major veins had surgical clamps cutting them off, but blood pooled at the openings. A label on one of the clamps read "Expedite for McCafferty, Kevin Transplant"

"Bon appetite," the butler whispered in his ear.

Kevin tore into the liver like a starving man.

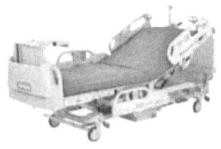

He woke with a start, immediately noticing a change in the way his machines beeped. The red glow from the readout of those same machines was the only light. The hairs all over his body stood out at something he didn't yet consciously recognize.

A new nurse stood in the dark room.

So far, Kevin had seen a great variety of nurses, of all races and multiple genders. They'd been tattooed, they'd been pierced, and they'd had interesting hair colors, but this is the first one that struck him as being out of place.

The man was not just tall, but large, and roughly shaved. His scrubs were too short on him, and his shoulders could burst the seams at any moment. "Sorry," the nurse said, "Must have bumped something."

His smile was friendly, and he pulled up a stool to sit next to the bed, gently shaking several vials.

"They just took a bunch of blood," Kevin said.

"Oh, I'm from transplant specialties. We've got a different set of tests we like to run." He expertly filled the vials and immediately headed for the door.

"I'm really thirsty," Kevin said. "Could I get some water?"

The nurse paused in the doorway. "I'll let your regular nurse know," he said.

When the night nurse eventually came, it was without water, and she apologized, saying she didn't get the message.

Kevin dreamed he was in the woods at night. Shadows of trees stood in stark crisscrossing lines on the blanket of fallen maple leaves where he hid. Something was after him—something that smelled of sandalwood and sweat—and white-hot fear coursed through his veins. His breathing came in gasps and left in clouds of vapor like the dragons of his imagination. He had no plan, there was no safe place for him, but he knew for sure he would be found if he stayed there. He ran, scurrying up a cloud of red leaves, but something was right behind him.

Morning came and along with the nurse shift-change came a pharmacist. She had some paperwork and a long list of new medications to discuss. The pain in his belly was getting pretty bad, but as an addict, he knew better than to ask for more pain meds.

Tacrolimus was the odd one, even ignoring that it sounded like some undiscovered dinosaur, because apparently no one knew how much to give him. "There's an agreement that only you and your new liver can work out, and we can only try something, measure the result, and adjust. By the time you're discharged, we should have the dosage pretty well figured out. But we'll test regularly, and will probably adjust it some more. This is perfectly normal."

There was a second anti-rejection drug that

sounded like it was made from mushrooms, a myco-something-or-other. Then there was a whole slew of other drugs, including an antiviral, an anti-fungal, and an antibiotic. Basically, two drugs to screw up your system so badly it won't notice the foreign liver, and a ton of other drugs to fix the damage those first two drugs did. By the sound of it, he'd be on several of them for the rest of his life.

His sister didn't show up either. The only family member still speaking to him, the only one he hadn't pushed past the point of breaking. She was supposed to be there to go over the meds with the pharmacist because Kevin would need care once he was released and someone had to handle his pills.

But it wasn't just that. He could just use the company. He wanted to spend time with his sister again, let her get to know the new sober Kevin McCafferty.

Lunch offered salads or pasta, both of which turned his stomach. Finally he found chicken noodle, but he didn't end up finishing it. What he wanted was something he could bite.

More blood draws, more walks around the recovery ward, and more daytime TV. Despite the pain in his gut, he had the strength to walk without assistance, astounding the physical therapist. And yet, they make him ask for help to get up and pee. That was his day.

They were concerned about his loss of six pounds since surgery and prescribed more pasta.

That night, his creatinine levels, a measure of his kidney function, were half what they had been, so they put him on a prednisone drip. As much as he wanted to sleep, every time he moved, he clamped the line and an alarm went off. The nurse had to come in and fix it. It seemed like such a little thing to bug the nurse for.

"If you could just show me which buttons to push to silence the alarm and start the drip again, I could take care of this myself."

"It's not a problem. It's what I'm here for," the nurse said, but Kevin imagined some resentment behind the man's friendly tones.

Kevin never quite got deep enough to dream that night, at least he didn't remember any images or sounds. All he could picture were smells, and not of normal things like meals, perfume, or flowers, or even stale urine and cleaning supplies. He remembered the difference between how cotton or rayon would smell. Fake fur versus the real thing. The rubber wheels on these little carts, and the traces they'd leave behind on linoleum floors. The plastic cups in the dispenser near the sink.

He couldn't smell any of that while he was awake, but it was close to the surface as soon as he drifted off.

At one point, he woke up without the alarm, a familiar smell in the air, one that made him want to hide. He looked around to see the transplant specialist nurse standing next to his IV stand with a syringe at the ready.

"That's twice," the man said.

"What?"

"I pride myself on moving quietly. Usually I can get in, draw blood and be gone before the patient knows I'm here. You must have really good hearing."

"Not that I've noticed. But hey, I'm two years sober now, and I'm discovering all sorts of new things about myself."

The nurse finished up with the syringe and dropped it in the disposal. "Two years, huh? Congratulations on that." He sat down next to Kevin and laid the vials out across his leg. "You've got me beat by about, oh, two years or so."

Kevin got the feeling he was being made fun of and changed the subject while the nurse drew blood. "I didn't catch your name last night."

The nurse paused. "Daryl," he finally said.

"Nurse Daryl? Okay, well no offense, but you don't look much like a nurse. What made you choose this field?"

Finished with the blood draw, Nurse Daryl pushed his chair back, rocking the vials as he thought. "My father died when I was young. Right in front of me. For a long time, I obsessed about it, this feeling of powerlessness. If only I'd known what to do, I could have prevented it, or I could have saved him. But at some point, I grew up and realized I could help other people, and maybe stop some other little kid from becoming an orphan. Eight years of hard work later, here I am."

He stood up to leave. "Hey, before you go—" Kevin called after him.

"I've got other patients I need to get to," he said, still heading toward the door.

"I know. Only, could you open the blinds

first? I'm starting to feel claustrophobic in here."

Nurse Daryl looked at his watch. "Okay." He slipped the vials into the pocket of his scrubs, walked to the window and cranked the handle of one set of blinds, then the other.

"Thank you. The room feels bigger already. Hey, look! There's a full moon out."

The nurse stood at the window for a while before responding. "No, that's a waxing gibbous moon. Two more days until it's full."

With that, he turned and left.

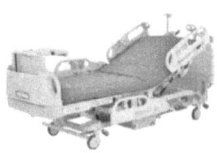

Morning came, and Kevin was allowed to use the bathroom on his own for the first time.

The nurses changed shifts, and the doctors made their rounds. "We're delighted with your progress so far," the lead surgeon said to a chorus of smiles and nods from the other doctors present. "I think we'll lower your Tacrolimus again by point five...Your creatinine looks better, and you've got the highest magnesium I've seen at this stage. What have you been eating?"

Kevin chuckled. "I'm not sure I know, but it came from your cafeteria." The doctors laughed at that. "I've been meaning to ask...Is it normal to...feel different after a transplant?"

"Different how?"

"Well, like food. I used to love pasta, now I

don't want any. I was thinking about the person who used to have this liver. Maybe they hated pasta."

The doctors smiled as a collective. The surgeon responded. "There have been many anecdotal reports like this, so don't feel weird. Though, I would chalk this up to how your subconscious feels about your new lease on life, rather than your liver exerting control over you."

"Uh, huh. And my eyesight? I haven't needed my contacts since the surgery."

"Your cirrhosis led to high amounts of bilirubin and therefore inflammation, which probably affected your eyesight. With your cirrhosis gone, it's not impossible your eyesight has improved."

"Oh, one more thing—you didn't mention the blood tests Nurse Daryl is taking."

The surgeon flipped through Kevin's chart. "Let's see. We've got your whole blood count, which looks healthy as an Olympic athlete, and your EKG is phenomenal, by the way. There's your liver enzymes which have a few outliers, but mainly positive. Your kidney function…Your Tacro, and your CMV."

"No, Nurse Daryl, from the transplant specialties? He's tracking something else, he said. He takes four vials every night."

The doctors looked around at each other. "Margaret, do you have a Daryl on your team?" the surgeon asked.

"No…Are you certain he said transplant specialties?" another doctor asked.

"I'm pretty sure…" Kevin said, suddenly

unsure.

"Tell you what," the surgeon said. "We'll have someone page Nurse Daryl and have him give me a call. Chances are it's the same tests, but we'll get to the bottom of it either way. Sound good?"

TV was too much for him, and he left it off. The pain was building up too. He asked if they could do anything, but they were only willing to offer him Tylenol. It took the edge off of things, but an hour later the pain was back to full strength. All he could do was try to distract himself from it. He texted his sister again, but she hadn't replied to the last four texts.

He pulled up his parents in his contacts list, but couldn't come up with anything to say. Had Diana told them he'd come through the surgery okay? He could just imagine Mother's look of annoyance when hearing the news. There was nothing Kevin wanted more right now than to prove himself a better person, a good son. But how to get there from here? He'd stolen and sold her great-grandmother's silver to feed his addiction. He'd dropped out of college even after Father donated a new research center to ignore his grades a bit. He'd stashed a brick of cocaine in the overflow tank in the master bathroom and subjected the family to the humiliation of a joint FBI/ATF search of the home. Father made it all go away, but it had cost Kevin, every time.

In short, he'd run the McCafferty name into the ground long before he'd run the Rolls into the neighbor's duck pond.

Kevin switched off his phone and set it aside.

When the nurse came around to check on his scar, Kevin asked some of the questions that had been plaguing him.

"I know my new liver came from someone who died, but I wish I knew more about them. Nothing identifying, of course, but how old were they? Was it a man, or a woman? How did they die? Do they have any relatives I can thank?"

"Sure, I get it. I would totally want to know too, but privacy laws and all that. I'll see what I can find out and get back to you," she said.

It was more than curiosity, though. Being in recovery meant examining his life in ways most people didn't. He had worked through the steps of making amends and had some very uncomfortable conversations with people he'd basically betrayed. Mostly, he said his piece, then suffered through a berating from the offended party. His sister came closest to actually forgiving him when she said, "Okay. Is that it?"

This felt like the other side of that coin. Someone had died for him. He couldn't thank them directly, but he needed to keep them in his thoughts. If he could write to their parents, tell them how grateful he was and how he would make the most of the gift their child had given...well, he needed to try.

More time passed, but he couldn't sleep—a mixture of the pain he felt and a fear of the nightmares he'd been having. When the nurse returned, Kevin sat up in expectation.

She stopped midway through sanitizing her hands. "Do that again?" she said.

Kevin bunched up the pillows behind him

and sat up a little higher.

"I'm sorry," the nurse said, pretending to check the number on Kevin's door. "I was looking for someone who just had an invasive surgery! You are doing so well!"

Kevin felt his face warm at the compliment. "Did you find anything out?" he asked.

"Your donor had no living relatives, so isn't covered by privacy laws. Still, I'm not sure how much you want to know."

"I want to know everything. If they had any allergies, I want to stay away from those foods. If they died of a heart attack, I want to watch for that too."

"First off, it was a he. Alex Topher. And he didn't die of a heart attack."

"How did he die?"

"Are you sure you—"

"How did he die?" Kevin said insistently.

"He was murdered. Shot through the heart while he was out camping."

"Oh my God," Kevin said. "Wait, camping? I thought a liver had to be super fresh. How did they get it here on time?"

"It was a drive up camp just off I90. Another group of campers heard the gunshot and found the guy unconscious. One of them started chest compressions while another called 911. Police and paramedics got to him minutes later, declaring him dead at the scene. But that camper kept the blood circulating well enough to keep the organs alive—and thank God they did, because not only did his liver save you, but one of his kidneys went to another patient, and his eyes went to two more."

Kevin thanked the nurse, unable to think of anything to say. His mind was pouring over everything she said though. Mostly, he thought about the murderer. He was apparently still out there somewhere. Kevin hoped they caught the killer, but in a strange sort of way, he also owed them his life.

Then his sister stormed in through the door, jarring him from his thoughts. "You know I still have a job, don't you?" she said, brandishing her phone at him.

For a moment, he was distracted by the oddest thing. She was wearing her favorite hoodie, but Kevin remembered it being red. Seeing it today, it was clearly more yellow. Then her words and tone hit him like a slap. "I'm sorry?"

"You've been saying that a lot, and it's kind of losing its meaning. What was so urgent that you had to text me five times?"

"The meeting with the pharmacist was yesterday. You were supposed to be there."

"Sucks when you need a family member and they're not there for you, doesn't it?"

"I know. I let you down. I let everyone down, and I did it for years. I lied, I stole, and I hurt everyone who cared about me. I'm owning that, and I'm doing better. This liver is a new chance for me, and I'm going to—"

"To what? To change? Do you remember how many times you've said that? Yeah, someone died so you could live, but it wasn't Jesus Christ. He didn't wash away your sins, and you've got a lot to make up for."

Kevin hadn't expected this. He thought he still had a sliver of a relationship with Diana. But she just stared at him like she wanted him to say something, so he did. "Look—"

"No, you look, Kevin. The only reason I signed those papers is because nobody else would. And if I didn't, they wouldn't have allowed the transplant. I guess I wasn't willing to be the one who killed you. And let me tell you, I've regretted that more than once. When they release you, I'll come and pick you up. After that, you're on your own. If you need someone to care for you, find someone you haven't screwed. It's a short list."

Diana turned and hurried out of the room. Unreasoning rage built inside Kevin again, though he wasn't sure whether he wanted to direct it at his sister, or at himself.

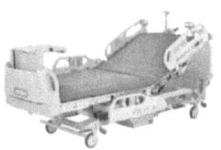

When the pain returned, Kevin welcomed it. He deserved this pain for twisting his sister into that. She had once been sweet, and now she was jaded. Hateful. And the pain was acute. There was no sleeping, no finding a comfortable position to lie in. It stretched across his stomach and down the length of his spine. Every little sound brought more pain. The squeak of a wheel in the hallway outside or the ding of the elevator sounded as if it were right in his ear. It was hard to draw breath, and it showed up in his blood pressure that evening. The nurse looked at him strangely and asked him what level his pain was.

"About a three," Kevin lied. It was an eight at least.

They drew blood, gave him insulin, and delivered dinner. He had no interest in eating, though. The broccoli smelled like swamp gas, and the tomato sauce turned his stomach. The tray was eventually cleared, untouched. Kevin lay on his back, shivering despite the warmth.

He was still awake when Nurse Daryl arrived. "I just had all my tests. Unless you want to tell me what's so special about yours, you aren't getting any more blood out of me."

"No blood draw today," Nurse Daryl said, holding up his hands defensively. "See? No vials. It's just an MRI tonight."

"Whatever," Kevin said, turning away.

The nurse paused while moving Kevin's drip bag to a stand attached to the bed. "Everything okay?"

Kevin sighed. "It's like Freddy said all those years ago. Nothing really matters. I screwed up my life, and I didn't start trying to fix things until it was too late. But I woke up with a new liver, and it felt like a new start, a clean slate. I had a chance to do better. It took just one visit from my sister to remind me that I'm the same old piece of crap I was before. Only now, I'm a sober piece of crap. I don't know what the point of sticking this liver in me was. They should have just let me die."

Nurse Daryl came around and took him by both shoulders. "Hey! There is always a point to life. And you don't have to let anyone else define you. Your sister is family, and family has a habit of crapping all over you when you need support. Don't you listen to her. You are the one who decides your fate. And if she considers you a burden, screw her. I'll be your ride home if you need one."

Kevin didn't respond. He couldn't. He just covered his face while his shoulders bobbed in silence.

Nurse Daryl squeezed Kevin's shoulder and went back to his task, turning off the monitor and disconnecting everything he couldn't take with him. "Alright. We'll be heading toward the freight elevator."

The bed moved, but Kevin, still embarrassed by his tears, had his eyes covered. They stopped again, and Kevin lifted his gown to wipe at his eyes.

"You okay, buddy?" the nurse asked, patting his shoulder.

Kevin nodded.

The elevator dinged, and the doors opened. Nurse Daryl pushed the bed inside and pressed a button. As the doors closed behind them, the nurse said, "Turn your head to the right for me?"

Kevin did so and asked, "Why?"

There was a pinch at the left side of his neck, and he heard the injection. Less than a second later, the world went black.

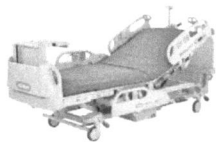

When Kevin woke, he was still in bed. He wondered if he'd dreamed the whole thing. He was about to reach up to rub at the sore spot on his neck when he noticed the rest of the room.

This wasn't a hospital room. The sloping ceiling was made of rough-cut pine, the wall nearest him was a stack of logs with clay for mortar. Windows, chopped from the bare logs, were covered in newspaper. He was still pretty groggy, but somehow this didn't feel like a dream.

"Hey!" came a whispered voice. "Hey, are you awake?"

Kevin turned to his right and saw a boy no more than seventeen laying in a gurney, velcro straps holding his arms to the rails. His eyes were of two different colors. "Hey, can you get out?" the boy asked.

His meaning wasn't immediately clear to Kevin. Instead, he looked around at the rest of the room. The floor where he could see it was concrete. All four walls were logs like the first, but there was a door cut into the wall closest to his feet. A ten-drawer rolling tool cabinet sat at an odd angle between him and the boy, and shop lights hung over both gurneys, orange extension cords stapled to crossbeams above them.

Pegboard covered a large portion of one wall,

but rather than tools, it carried a variety of firearms. A support column held up the peaked roof at midspan, and a pole resting against it connected to a wide panel in the angled ceiling.

He tried to reach for his neck again, but his arm wouldn't move. Thick black bands across his arms secured him to the bed. "What's going on? Where are we?" Kevin asked.

"That guy's not a nurse! I knew there was something sketchy about him! He's going to kill us if we don't get out of here."

The firearms suddenly registered in Kevin's mind. This was some sort of torture cabin! The fog lifted a bit from his mind, and he started pulling more frantically at his straps. The pain in his stomach flared up again. "I can't get my arms loose!" he said.

The kid was also tied down. Kevin looked for anything else that might be helpful. "The beds are on wheels! Can you move yours closer? Maybe I can undo your straps."

He started rocking back and forth on the bed, but it only swayed a bit. "I think the wheels are locked."

Kevin craned his neck to see behind them. The tool cabinet was on wheels too. If they could get to that..."Hey! Your legs aren't strapped down! Can you get them under you? Maybe you can reach the cabinet and push it toward me."

The boy cocked an ear toward the door for several seconds, then shimmied into a sitting position and bent first one leg back, then the other. "I think so..." He stretched one leg back, unable to see what he was doing.

"A little to the left," Kevin said. "Now back…Back…"

He had to adjust his other leg to get any further back, so he tried again, and Kevin guided him through it until his toes touched metal. He kicked, and the cabinet moved a couple inches, then toppled over.

WHAM!

The kid's odd eyes widened, and he scurried to get his legs out in front of himself.

The door flew open, and Nurse Daryl rushed in, then stopped when he saw the cabinet. "Sorry. I was worried that one of you had knocked your gurney over and maybe hurt yourself." He walked over to the cabinet and set it upright, a little farther from them.

He had abandoned the scrubs and lab coat of a nurse in favor of the denim and flannel of a back-woods survivalist.

"Please, don't kill me," the kid said, his voice rising and tears flowing. "I'll do anything you want. Even if you like it rough! I'll be good, just don't kill me."

"Shut up, Terry. I'm not into any of that."

"What about what you said?" Kevin demanded, suddenly furious. "About there always being a point to life? Why'd you even say all that if you were just planning on killing me?"

"I meant every word I said. I wish things were different. I really do. I wish those people had camped a little further away that night. I wish I'd checked him against the donor registration. I wish you'd gotten someone else's liver, and you, someone else's eye. Or that you'd been like the other two. The lady who got the kidney shows none of the signs, and the other one's system rejected the eye right off. I got into this business to save people. Believe me, I don't want this."

"Signs? Signs of what?" Kevin pulled on his restraints again, the adrenaline giving him renewed strength. The velcro crackled and popped as it strained, but it did not loosen.

Daryl didn't immediately answer. Instead, he opened one of the drawers in the tool cabinet and pulled out a gleaming saw, examining the blade.

Terry started crying again. "No, no, no, no."

"The State Forest starts just past Issaquah, and there are some great spots out there to just park your car and dip your toes in a mountain lake. That's all Tracy and Imogene Watts and their friend Stephanie Ayers wanted, but Tracy suggested a short day hike, and the three of them were never seen alive again. A search began when a ranger spotted their car past closing, and soon after, they were found. They'd been torn apart. It was blamed on a cougar attack, and a hunt was called that ended with a dead, albeit innocent, animal. It never struck them as unusual that a cougar was able to kill all three of them within feet of each other. They didn't think it strange that the animal ripped them apart, but was only interested in eating their hearts."

He set the saw down and picked up something that looked a lot like an ice pick. "There were other signs they missed, like what was going on in the sky, and the sorts of prints found around the murder site. I tracked the real killer, knowing he would be back on the next full moon. But he caught my scent and ran, throwing off his shoes and changing into the wolf. I shot him through the heart from one hundred fifty yards. If only I'd followed up and taken his wallet, we wouldn't be here now."

"A werewolf? You're saying our donor was a werewolf? You realize that's insane. What you are doing is insane," Kevin said.

Terry spoke up quickly. "Not insane, um, troubled. You need help. We can help."

"He wasn't the first. Since one of them killed my father, I've killed dozens of them. But the curse has always been transferred through a bite. And that means there must be an infection. I looked through all the medical websites I could find, but there was nothing to tell me whether human organs could carry the infection, and which ones. So, I had to figure it out for myself. I devised tests. I put silver nitrate in one vial, wolfsbane extract in another and introduced your blood into each, carefully watching the results. I gave you both a dose of wolfsbane hoping it would act like an antibiotic. It looks like it worked on Drew, but both of you have some blood abnormalities, and I don't know what they mean."

"You can't go killing us just because you don't know what a couple blood tests mean!" Terry said.

"I'm with him. If you really are thinking clearly, you have to see that's murder," Kevin said.

"I told you. I don't want to kill you. But I couldn't just sit back and see if you killed a few hospital staff before doing anything. So, this is the test. The last test. If you're going to turn, it'll happen when the light of the full moon first hits you."

He set the icepick back in the cabinet and pulled out a knife with a sweeping blade, serrated on one side and filed to razor sharpness on the other. He brought that with him to the center post, and the pole attached to a panel on the roof. "If nothing happens, I'll bring you back to the hospital, and you'll never see me again. But if you change…" He didn't bother finishing the sentence.

"Moonrise was about half an hour ago. It should be cresting the trees any minute now." Daryl lowered the pole, swinging the panel open, and reset the pole in a higher spot, propping the panel open. He switched off the overhead lights.

Moonlight threw a rectangle of silver against the far wall. It crept downward, directly toward Terry.

"Wait, wait, wait," Terry said, he yanked at his restraints, eyes wide in panic as if he believed the moonlight would hurt him in some way. He sat up and shimmied back like he had when trying to reach the cabinet.

"Hey! No, kid, don't do that," Daryl said. He started toward the boy, but Terry just pulled harder, now in a kneeling position. "Those restraints are there for your own good!"

The moonlight touched his neck and shoulder, and instantly his back arched. Terry froze in a visage of pain and shock. Hair speckled his face, then grew to an amber brown. His jaw shot forward and his nose rounded over the end, turning black. His ears lengthened and shifted backward. Muscles swelled across his body, filling out the hospital gown, and thick, coarse fur sprouted at every opening.

Kevin watched the transformation with unblinking eyes, his mouth involuntarily open in a scream without breath. Ice ran through his veins and for a moment, he forgot the pain in his stomach. His bladder loosened, and urine ran across the plastic bedding, dripping over the side of the gurney.

"Ah, hell," Daryl said. He flipped the blade around and stalked toward the creature.

Terry's thumbs shifted up his arms, becoming small nubs while his palms shrank nearly to nothing, and his fingers became paws with large black nails.

The velcro cuffs slid easily off him.

Daryl swung the knife, aimed at Terry's back, but the dog launched to the foot of the gurney, spinning around to face the hunter. His lip curled back in a snarl, showing teeth as long as Kevin's fingers. Daryl feinted forward, and the massive wolf leapt for him, gaping jaws dripping saliva.

The wolf missed his mark, and Daryl brought the knife down, catching it behind the shoulder. The monster yelped, and smoke rose from the gash on his back, but his reaction speed was much faster than Daryl's. He sprang from the floor and wrapped his jaws around Daryl's thigh.

Daryl cried out in pain, but stabbed the wolf repeatedly in the side, right under the shoulder. The smell of burning flesh nauseated Kevin, and the sight of all the blood, human and wolf mixed together, threw him over the edge. He dry heaved. The pain in his stomach was excruciating, and he wished he had something to bring up.

His nausea was forgotten as Daryl stood up. "Damn. That one got me," he said, looking at the flap of flesh spraying the room with femoral blood. He tore off his belt and wrapped it around his leg, yanking it tight and screaming in pain. He tied it off and pulled the knife back out of Terry's ribcage. The boy had returned to human form in death.

"I can't die until we know about you, kid," Daryl said. He leaned on the side of the gurney and kneeled on the wheel lock. The bed drifted sideways.

"No! Don't! I can avoid the moon! I can stay in on full moon nights! I can keep track of the calendar and lock myself away. If it never touches me, I'll never turn." Kevin yanked at his straps repeatedly. His stomach was on fire, and he'd never be able to shimmy up the way Terry had.

"Sorry, kid. The full moon is out in daylight hours too. A city kid like you can't go three days without stepping outside. You'd never hold down a job."

Desperation filled his voice. "But you said the animal needs to come out, and no one's strong enough to hold it back! But that's like addiction! The need is strong, and no one can hold it back without support! I *have* that support, and I'm proof that people can win against addiction! You don't have to kill me! Please don't kill me!"

"Kevin, I'm dying here. I have to make sure

you're not a threat." He pushed the gurney into the light.

Kevin felt the moonlight on his skin like a soothing balm. The pain he'd felt since the surgery disappeared, replaced with the song of primal being. He felt his spine lengthening and his heels moving up his legs. Hair sprouted across his cheeks and nose, and it was right. What looked so painful in Terry felt like liberation. This was his true form, awakening for the first time. His teeth lengthened and his jaw grew forward.

"Noooooooo," he said through clenched teeth. As good as it felt, he rebelled against the change. He balled his hands into fists, trying to keep his thumbs where they were.

He smelled fresh blood, heard a beating heart as it slowed in the final minutes of life. The saliva flowed in his mouth, and his vision narrowed. He was hungry.

"Nooooooo," he said again, but it came out like a howl. He saw the bar on the side of his bed and clamped down with his jaws, refusing to let go. He would not give in to the animal. He would not feed.

Daryl pulled himself up on the side of the bed. Their gaze met as Kevin continued biting anything within reach. "Poor kid," he said. He plunged the knife between Kevin's ribs. Smoke and blood poured from the wound. Daryl slipped on the blood flowing down his own leg, pulling the gurney on top of himself. His makeshift tourniquet slipped and loosened.

Kevin's eyes were all wolf now. He turned them on Daryl, jaws still holding the bed rail, even while gasping for breath. The light faded from both their eyes simultaneously.

Fertile Minds

Thomas Mansfield was collecting his freshly annotated newspapers when he heard the hansom stop outside. Moving swiftly, he poured water from the kettle into the teapot, set the newspapers atop the red cedar box, then the tray with pot, cup, and saucer on top of that. He took a scant second to compose himself, then hurried to get to the door before Chelsea Pepperdine arrived on the front steps. Seeing her distinctive silhouette through the shaved glass, long hair piled high and impeccable posture, he opened the door.

"Good evening, Mr. Mansfield," she said as she moved past him. "Cup of tea, how did you know? By the smell of things though, it will need to steep a bit more. Anything interesting in the news today?"

"Two further boroughs have been announced to replace gas lighting with Mr. Wexley's electrics."

"About time London comes into the nineteenth century. Anything else?" she called over her shoulder as she left the entry hall for the sitting room. Thomas hurried to keep up, careful not to spill a drop of tea.

"Brougham announced plans to sell family-sized dirigibles. He claims he'll put the horse out of business within ten years."

"That's exactly the sort of news I warn you to ignore, Mr. Mansfield," she said, removing her coat and hanging it up. "It's the banal passed off as extraordinary." She sighed as she put one booted foot up on her lacing stool. "Is there anything at all of interest going on in London today?" she asked, using a pick to rip at the laces of her boot.

He flipped through the edge of the newspapers wedged between box and tray. "Perhaps not this evening, Miss Pepperdine." He tried changing the subject as he poured her a cup of tea. "How did things go at the Hellfire Club?"

She gave him a crooked smile, easily reaching her deep blue eyes. "As usual, a flash of lacy underthings will get me in the door," she said, lifting her skirts to knee height as if to demonstrate, but then she reached beneath and retrieved a gun made of copper, glass and fresh solder. "But it was up to my hypno-darts to get me back out unmolested."

Thomas slid the tea tray off the cedar box and onto the vanity table. He opened the box toward her, revealing the velvet interior, custom molded to the shape of her gun. She set it inside, and he closed it back up. As he turned to set the box down, she stopped him, pulling one of the newspapers from the middle of the stack. "You entirely failed to notice the most interesting event of them all."

She held the newspaper toward him, indicating an article near the bottom of the front page. "Famed Botanist Returns from Peru with Remarkable Specimens," read the headline.

"Read it to me," Chelsea said, then turned and crossed the room to step behind a dressing screen. "I'll want something more comfortable, I think, for tonight's activities," she mumbled, removing the pins from her stylish hat and allowing her dark tresses to shake free down to the small of her back.

Thomas quickly read through the article, then returned to the top for the salient information. "It says here that Lord Humphrey Atherton timed his London return so that he could put his plants, particularly his 'crowning specimen', on display at the Great Exhibition."

Chelsea poked her head around the side of the screen, a pale shoulder exposed behind the corset she clutched to her chest. "Excellent! Then I shall break in tonight, get a private viewing before it opens tomorrow." She disappeared again, and moments later, her skirt came to lay over the top of the screen.

Thomas turned away. "If I may ask, what is your interest in this botanist and his plants?"

"I'm surprised you need to ask. I'm not just an inventor and adventurist, I'm an alchemist after all. Undiscovered plants are the source of all sorts of new tonics, tinctures, remedies and soporifics. Oh dear, is the brown dress not ready yet?"

"Sorry, Miss. The bullet holes are proving

difficult to mend seamlessly."

"Pity. Try lacing over them. But it will have to be the blue one today. A fantastic job you've done on the mercury stains. Where in the Crystal Palace will the plants be located?"

"Actually, according to the article, his request was rejected. The organizers are quoted, saying the exhibit space was full, and it wasn't right to ask anyone else to give up their spot."

"Well, that will certainly make it more difficult to observe and sample the new plants. I wonder where he will be housing them instead…" She stepped out from behind the screen, lifting the skirts of a blue, floor-length dress with a low-cut bodice. "More than likely he has a greenhouse on his manor's property. If I were him, after such a disappointment, I would want my specimens close to me, so that is where I will start."

She paused in front of the mirror, pulling an ivory brush through her curls until thoroughly tamed, then crossed the room to join Thomas, tapping him on the shoulder with her matching fan. He turned to face her. "How do I look?" she asked.

He looked her up and down, eyes wide and mind searching. "Entrancing," he selected.

"Oh, Mr. Mansfield, you always know *just* the word I'm looking for." She reached past him to pick up her clutch purse and the cup of tea. She quickly drained it, pinky in the air, and headed for the door.

Thomas rushed to get there first, opening it for her. "Thank you, Mr. Mansfield," she said, transferring items from the bureau near the door to her clutch. "Don't wait up. Wish me luck," she called over her shoulder, and headed up the cobblestone without waiting for his reply.

The hansom cab left Chelsea Pepperdine off at the foot of Lord Atherton's drive. The lights in the front windows shone invitingly, and several coaches waited near the entry. Lord Humphrey had company this evening.

She strode up the drive with all the confidence of one who resided there. Her attention was drawn to the large orangery at the left side of the house. Not much could be made out at this distance, but the greenery did have a decidedly tropical look about it, and beads of humidity ran down the windows facing her on this cool and cloudy evening. As she approached the doors, a valet stepped out of the shadows and bowed toward her. "Miss…?"

"Pepperdine. Lord Atherton is expecting me." Confidence in all things. That was a credo that served Chelsea well in this society, so dominated by the rougher sex. Even if this valet believed he knew she wasn't invited, her confidence would make him doubt himself before he ever considered she was wrong.

"Yes, Miss Pepperdine. The other guests

have all arrived. If you'll wait in the foyer, I'll summon the butler to guide you." He opened the door and ushered her inside.

"Thank you," she said, and waited politely for the door to close before bolting out the doorway to her left and up the adjoining corridor.

The rubberized soles of her boots made little noise on the marble floor as she walked along. When she approached the first door on the left, she paused to listen against it, reaching into her clutch for a small metallic box. The upper half of the box was dominated by an inset glass lens, while the lower half was a mess of switches and dials. She heard nothing, so she placed the box against the door and flipped a switch near the middle of the box. The lens glowed amber, and she twisted a dial until a monochrome image formed and came into focus. A table, vase and flowers.

She slid the box along the door, and saw a chair, and further along a chesterfield. She lifted the box past the door jamb and continued along the wall until she saw what she was looking for. A fireplace against the far wall meant that the room beyond did not open out onto the orangery.

She continued down the corridor until she reached the next door and repeated the process. This time she had to scan the entire room before she was assured it would not lead where she wanted to go. The background of the third room was a solid bright orange, nearly white, and she knew this was the room she wanted. The only things her intrascope couldn't penetrate were lead and glass, and Lord Atherton was unlikely to have a wall made of lead in his manor.

Trying the door handle, she found it locked. No matter. She switched off the intrascope and returned it to her clutch, removing a tiny pistol with a wickedly sharp barrel. A thin needle fit neatly into the keyhole, then she looked up and down the corridor before pulling the trigger.

Rather than a shot going off, there was a mechanical whirring as if a small wind-up train were inside the pistol. It chugged and popped in fits and starts, then with a click, she released the trigger, stood up, and opened the door.

Through the glass of the far wall, Chelsea Pepperdine could see the glow of the clouds that hid the full moon, and dimly illuminated the room she stood in. Her night vision was still compromised from staring at the back-lighting of the intrascope screen, but her peripheral vision had always been most acute, and she used it to identify the room. The wall she'd come through and the two to the sides were filled with books. One large section cut from the bookshelves, the sort that would normally contain a portrait, contained instead a magnificent map of South America. Chairs built more for study than for comfort were arranged around two tables, one flat, and one draftsman style, both littered with papers. A globe, larger across than she could reach, dominated the center of the room. Of course Lord Atherton would have his study in a location he could observe his subjects.

As she finished scanning the room, her vision was very much improved, and she approached a set of double doors in the center of the glass wall ahead. Once more, she found the door locked. This time, however, she chose to observe from this distance. She placed the pistol in the clutch once more, and retrieved a third item, a pair of opera glasses.

She peered through the glasses into the orangery. She slowly twisted a ring on the handle of the glasses, and a secondary lens clicked into place, throwing light and shadow into stark contrast. The sharp outlines of footprints in the soft earth popped out, and she followed them with her eyes to an area of newly turned soil. The plants were entirely camouflaged with this filter though, so she continued to twist the ring until it changed again.

With a sharp intake of breath, Chelsea looked over the top of the glasses, then quickly through them again. There were six newly planted specimens in a ring with a larger plant in the center. Each of the outer plants would have been a remarkable find, if not for the fact that all her attention was drawn to the central one. It was a cactus, but unlike any she'd ever seen. There was a central stalk that tapered and then rounded again, such that at first it looked like the head and shoulders of a spiky man. Several bulbs budded off the crown, giving the impression of curly hair. Inch long needles covered the stalk from crown to base, and from the "shoulders" grew fronds in all directions that arched upward, then grew down to trail along the ground.

She wished she could see it in the light. In the artificial brightness provided by her glasses—the stalk, the needles, and the fronds were all in different shades—giving the impression of colors she could only guess at. And the buds on top of the crown…

She twisted a second ring on the handle of her opera glasses and the buds grew larger in her field of view. They were fruits! The curled and blackened remains of spent petals remained on the tips. She simply had to liberate one.

She returned the glasses to her clutch and felt the grip of her lock pick gun against her fingertips when she heard a polite cough from behind her. She froze in place.

"When I found the foyer empty, Miss Pepperdine, I thought you might have found your own way here," said a baritone behind her.

Chelsea closed her clutch and forced a smile, turning. "I couldn't resist the mystery."

The butler smiled knowingly. "Lord Atherton intends to present the new finds to his guests after dinner. If you'll come with me, I've had a place set for you at his table. I'll save you the embarrassment of having to admit you ruined his surprise, and perhaps you'll save me the embarrassment of having entirely forgotten that you were invited this evening."

Chelsea's smile became quite genuine at this point. She crossed the room to join him. "Your sense of propriety is matched only by your tact, Mr…?"

"Harrison, Miss Pepperdine. Thank you, Miss."

Harrison locked the door as they left the study and placed the key in an inside pocket. He led her through an adjoining corridor to a large and noisy dining room.

The soup course was being cleared while a rotund man with remarkable muttonchops was regaling the group with an amusing anecdote which broke off as she came into view. She suppressed a smile, wondering whether the subject was too delicate for any member of the fairer sex, or because he had a specific objection to her presence, given their recent run-in at the Hellfire Club.

Seated around the table was a who's who of the scientific, industrial, and noble communities.

Lord Humphrey Atherton was seated at the head of the table, and to his left she recognized Lord Geoffrey Mayfield, the noted anthropologist, by reputation only. Next were Professor William Dane and Sir Benedict Upton, who were the chairs of chemistry and mathematics respectively at King's College, and she had debated both at one time or another in the past.

Past them were two men who carried themselves like royalty, though she did not know them. The man with the fabulous facial hair, who watched her walk past with a look akin to fright, being one of them. Beyond them sat Henry Chesterton, distiller of gasses both flammable and buoyant and Andrew Wexley, supplier of the city's recent addiction to electricity.

Next were Arthur MacKenzie, who owned hundreds of acres of hothouses, supplying the nation with off-season fruits and vegetables and Aiden Kelly, the shipping giant. Coincidentally, she'd had adventures on both men's behalf—the

Irishman quite recently.

At the far end were two men she felt she should recognize, but their identities escaped her momentarily. Nevertheless, she nodded politely to each as she was brought to the foot of the table and seated between the two men.

"This is outrageous!" She smiled, having wondered since the moment she entered the room who would have reacted first. Her money would have been on Professor Dane, and her money would have doubled.

"Professor?" said Lord Atherton, a hint of amusement in his voice.

"Lord Atherton, you have been away these last eight years, but this...lady," he said the word with contempt usually reserved for vermin, "has been making a mockery of the scientific establishment with her theories and politics."

Sir Upton added, "Here, here. She has been a rather vocal nuisance, and I for one would prefer not to be seated at the same table with her."

Several people coughed nervously, and everyone seemed suddenly fascinated by the table settings. Chelsea busied herself straightening the silver and unfolding her napkin. She was neither unused to nor uncomfortable with such a reception. However, when she looked back up, Lord Atherton was meeting her eyes with some curiosity. But there was something else in his gaze that sent a chill up her spine. If she had to put a name on it, it would be hunger, and not necessarily of a lecherous nature.

"You're Oliver Pepperdine's daughter, aren't you?" he finally said.

"That's right," she said. "I remember as a child, he told me such amazing stories of your first expeditions. They truly inspired me toward an adventurous life. Tell me, did he really bankroll those early voyages, or was he exaggerating?"

Lord Atherton smiled by way of response. "Any child of Oliver's is always welcome at my table. I was saddened to hear of his passing. Professor Dane, Sir Upton, I shall understand if you feel it necessary to hasten your departure, but I'll have you know you are missing out on a truly ravishing dessert this evening, and the unveiling of my recent acquisitions will only be for those who remain through dinner."

What an odd choice of word for a dessert, Chelsea thought. Not delicious or delicate, not even exquisite, but ravishing.

The men of King's College harrumphed about it, but in the end chose to stay.

The main course was set down, a roast in a heavy sauce alongside tiny purple potatoes. "You must forgive the gaminess, but I rather developed a taste for wild boar with so few other protein sources to be found in the jungle. Lord Whittaker, was just regaling us with a recent experiment into the reanimation of severed body parts."

Lord Whittaker. Of course, the famous anatomist. Now she had a name to put to the face. And other parts...

Whittaker cleared his throat uncomfortably. "No, that's all right. Suffice to say that rigor had set in again, if you know...well, you know." He filled his mouth with a large chunk of boar meat and chewed conspicuously.

The table lapsed into uncomfortable silence once again.

The gentleman to Chelsea's right cleared his throat. "Perhaps, Lord Atherton, you can tell us a little about the specimens you brought back with you?"

Humphrey smiled and wiped a bit of gravy from the corner of his mouth. "Or perhaps, just the one I'm hoping you'll allow at the Exhibition tomorrow?"

"The way the paper described it, that didn't sound possible," Chelsea said. "Is that not the case?"

"Quite impossible," said the gentleman to Chelsea's left.

The one on her right added, "What Mr. Henry means is that it is simply out of our hands. We only came here this evening to pay Lord Atherton the respect of telling him in person."

Instantly, Chelsea knew where she'd seen the two. On her left was Francis Henry, and on her right was Sir Charles Wentworth Dilke. Along with Prince Albert, they were the primary organizers of the Great Exhibition.

Atherton set down his napkin. "I remain certain that after this evening, the two of you will change your minds. I named it after the queen, you know, Pseudorhipsalis Victoria. A truly remarkable specimen of cactus unlike any I've ever seen. Much as the platypus of Australia exhibits qualities unique to any other mammal, but common amongst other classes, P. Victoria displays qualities only found in Droseraceae, and a symbiotic relationship with jungle animals that suggests true intelligence."

"Intelligence? In a plant?" Chelsea asked.

"Poppycock," Lord Mayfield said. "He's pulling our legs."

"Not a bit of it. You shall see, all in good time."

"Perhaps if the bar isn't set too high," Lord Whittaker said. "A leech could be said to demonstrate a certain...cunning, shall we say?"

"I estimate the plant's intelligence to be far higher than that. Surpassing that reported in chimpanzees, but I will let you be the judge of this soon enough."

Chelsea pushed her plate aside, leaning over the table. "Yes, but, perhaps you can describe to us, how a plant would display signs of its intelligence?"

"I'm afraid that would rather be giving away the surprise."

"Well then, what are we waiting for?" Chelsea said. "Having been forced to spend time among members of my own species with intelligence far less than a chimpanzee, I find myself wanting of intelligent discourse with this cactus."

Several of the men around the table chuckled knowingly, which was a pity since Chelsea had been thinking of them at the time.

Lord Atherton slammed a fist down on the table. "No one sees the plants until we've had dessert," he said.

The table went silent again. Chelsea knew full well that men can change, and the jungle is certainly the sort of thing that can change them, but this was not the unflappable and jolly explorer that had been so often described. She had to assume that others at the table knew him personally, and based on their reaction, his outburst was uncharacteristic.

Lord Atherton seemed to read the sudden change in social temperature, and he smiled. "But there's no reason we can't hurry that along." He reached for a small silver bell and rang twice.

Mr. Harrison arrived presently.

"Have the roast removed, Harrison, and skip the salad. We'll go straight to sweets."

The butler bowed and left. The serving girls followed shortly after to remove the plates, and the diners were left again in uncomfortable silence. Finally, Chelsea asked what they were all clearly wondering. "What is so special about tonight's dessert?"

"It is a unique treat, and the reason I arranged this gathering. When I came upon the Pseudorhipsalis Victoria, it was guarded by rodents and birds that nested in its root system and atop its crown. They fought off my expedition team with a ferocity that was at odds with their small size and their natural disposition. We retreated initially, and I made my studies at a distance. Rabies, of course, could have explained the rodents, but there was no frothing, and none of my men took ill. It also wouldn't account for the birds' behavior."

"You have a theory, no doubt?" Lord Mayfield asked.

"Naturally. I believe it to be the symbiotic

relationship that I spoke of before. The cactus needles protect the creatures from their natural predators, and the animals return the favor, becoming a nuisance for larger animals. In return, P. Victoria provides food for these creatures in the form of its fruit. These fruit grow quickly, and the majority of them fall off to be picked up by the rodents, but just enough remain to feed the birds that defend it. After a week of studying P. Victoria, I realized that the cactus produced exactly enough fruit on a daily basis to feed its defenders. No less, and no more."

"That is quite remarkable," said Professor Dane. "Is this the reason you came to believe the plant was intelligent?"

"That was the first indication. I needed to learn more, so we approached the cactus again, prepared for the onslaught with nets and other precautions. Having done away with the majority of its defense, the plant overproduced fruit, and I collected several of them. That evening, my guide volunteered to sample it, and pronounced it 'the best thing he'd ever eaten.' After suffering no ill effects over the course of two days, I tried it myself. I shall not describe the taste, as each of you will now have a chance to taste it for yourself."

"What a remarkable story," Whittaker said. "In your further exploration, did you find more of this species?"

"I was reluctant to leave the one we did find, having slaughtered its defenders. We waited a week to see if other animals would take their place. In the end we decided to dig it up and take it with us, but being such a massive specimen, it was impossible to explore further while bearing it along, and it became necessary to return to our ship with it."

Harrison and the serving girls returned with their desserts, and Chelsea tuned out the remainder of the discussion. A pink fruit, cut in half and drowned in warm cream, slid onto the table in front of her. The other diners all received theirs simultaneously.

Atherton picked up his spoon, but continued speaking. To his left, Lord Mayfield dug in to the translucent flesh of the fruit while watching Atherton with rapt interest. His eyes closed, and he smiled briefly before going back for another spoonful.

Professor Dane and Sir Upton began eating as well, and the three men swallowed simultaneously.

Chelsea watched, but as her hand strayed toward her own spoon, certain parts of the evening's conversation came together.

Atherton believed the plant to be intelligent. His latest expedition has brought about a change in his personality. He also brought the organizers of the Great Exhibition here, expecting to change their minds. The creatures they found eating the fruit defended the plant with their lives. Atherton and his men even felt the desire to protect it in their absence, going so far as to bring it to London. He said the cactus displayed characteristics of the Droseraceae family, which, if she recalled correctly, referred to carnivorous plants.

Mayfield, Dane, and Upton developed a tremor in their spoon hand. Moments later, it disappeared, and the three men gasped.

Lord Mayfield spoke as if their actions had been perfectly normal. "I say. I do hope Sir Dilke and Mr. Henry reconsider. Everyone should have an opportunity to taste this exquisite fruit!"

The cactus fruit had mind-altering properties, and Atherton was feeding it to them.

Chelsea dropped her spoon with a clatter.

The noise drew the attention of the entire table, and she placed a hand on her throat. "Pardon my interruption, but was there rosemary, by chance, in that gravy?" she asked, knowing full well that there was.

"Yes, Miss, there was," Harrison replied.

Francis Henry looked at her with concern. "My dear, you've gone all white and sweaty. Are you alright?"

"No, I'm not. I have a terrible reaction to rosemary. Please excuse me." She pushed back her chair and held her purse to her chest.

"But you haven't had your dessert! I'm sure you'll feel much better after a spoonful or two."

"I'm afraid I'll require my medicine, which I have unfortunately left at home. I must bid you all goodnight." She stood up.

"Wait," Lord Atherton said, pushing back his own chair. "Perhaps we have the same medication here?"

Chelsea ran for the door, not bothering to reply. Though she had no such allergy, she was distraught. She felt a strong desire to warn those men she left behind, but she would never be taken seriously, and doing so would certainly put her in danger. As it was, she felt as if she were being chased all the way down the drive.

Chelsea felt a paranoia she was not accustomed to. It was as if eyes were upon her at every turn and she did not want to stop long enough to hail a cab. Furthermore, she was uneasy with the idea of going straight home for fear of someone with faster transportation waiting there.

Instead, she spent the night roaming the streets of London. She visited Hyde Park and looked upon the Crystal Palace. She looped around Buckingham Palace, and as the sun came up to the east, she finally returned to Kensington and her home, peering closely into each remaining shadow before committing to the front steps of her residence.

As she reached for the latch, Thomas Mansfield was there to open it for her. She smiled, her mood lifting instantly, then grew serious again. "Have the papers arrived?"

He swiveled around, bringing his left arm forward. He held a tea tray with a stack of newspapers and a steaming cup.

"I do not pay you enough." She traded her clutch for the cup and drank deeply, feeling the warmth run through her. She then traded the cup for the stack of papers and stalked past Thomas into the main room, glancing at each story he had circled, and discarding each paper in turn. She found the one she'd been dreading and collapsed into a reading chair.

Thomas brought a table close to her, setting the tea tray on it and refilling her cup. "What is it?"

"The Exhibition organizers have reversed their decision and given Atherton's cactus a place of prominence at the center of the vast transept. It will be hidden behind a curtain and visitors will be charged tuppence apiece to see it."

"All's well that ends well, then. That's what you wanted, right?"

"Not after the events of last night. I believe that plant is controlling Lord Atherton, and by feeding its fruit to his guests last night, he put them under its influence as well. Francis Henry and Sir Charles Wentworth Dilke were in attendance. That is why they changed their minds and allowed Lord Atherton's exhibit to go ahead. I believe he is limiting access to the cactus so that he can get people alone in there and control everyone that comes to visit."

"How does a plant control a person?"

"You've seen how my own hypno-darts will render a person vulnerable to suggestion. The plant's nectar seems to contain a similar compound. It is also constantly blooming, meaning it releases pheromones into the air, attracting pollinators. Once the mind is suggestible, the pheromones make the victim feel...well, I don't know. Something stronger than love, I would guess. Devotion? Fervor? From Atherton's description of the symptoms, they were positively rabid. I would have to study it further to truly understand it and getting close to that plant is dangerous."

"Then what can we possibly do about it?" Thomas asked.

"The solution is alchemical in nature, as it is so often. But to concoct an antidote, I'll need a sample of that plant's nectar. And that means getting in close, unobserved. Aside from the aforementioned dangers of approaching the plant, the exhibit is expected to be quite the spectacle, making it difficult to approach covertly. With limited time, they are likely moving the plant as we speak, and it will certainly be under constant guard between now and opening, at which time tens of thousands of people will be watching."

Turning the paper around, Thomas tapped on the article. "Not to add stress to the urgency, but Queen Victoria is opening the Exhibit in a couple hours, and she's expected to get a private showing."

Thomas Mansfield stood in the main transept of the Crystal Palace, turning an opaque and stoppered globe in his sweaty hands. Workmen were in the midst of cleaning up, having spent the night on final preparations for a number of exhibits. The dove-white curtains of Atherton's pavilion lay directly in front of him. Only the butler, Harrison, was standing outside the pavilion, but Chelsea and Thomas knew there were two guards inside.

Chelsea Pepperdine watched from a spot between two booths, brow furrowed with concern. Their plan involved a lot of improvisation, and while she was quite good at it, Thomas was abysmal. He was just as likely to drop the globe as he was to throw it, and accuracy would be a matter of luck.

Thomas's lips moved as he practiced his lines. She closed her eyes, unable to watch any more. If he was suspected before he played his part, she was going to have to do even more improvisation.

The closest group of workmen finished loading their cart and wheeled it toward the exit. Thomas cocked back his arm and shouted, "Exploration is colonialism, and colonialism is cruelty!" With that, he lobbed his globe of squid ink at the frame of Atherton's pavilion. It pillowed into the curtain, missing the metal frame, but then fell to the hard floor and shattered.

The white sheets were sprayed with viscous black. Atherton's guards pushed through the curtain, crunching on glass and slipping on the mess. They looked up from the puddle and spotted Thomas, who bolted. They gave chase, running down the length of the transept.

Well done, Mr. Mansfield. Chelsea opened her clutch again, verifying the small vial of her nullifying liquid, before removing the extractor syringe and hiding it behind the bag. She broke from concealment and approached the opposite end of the pavilion, lifted the curtain, and ducked underneath.

Chelsea stood up to see the cactus. Lit from above, it again gave the impression of a person standing there. The fronds that draped from the shoulders trailed along the floor to the edges of the curtains, and the fruit had been picked clean. Chelsea had to hope that the sap in the cactus would contain the same chemicals as were present in the nectar of the fruit, or else her nullifier would have no effect. She approached the barrel of the cactus, intending to take a sample.

A figure stepped out from behind the cactus, startling her. It was Lord Atherton. She took a step backward onto one of the fronds and simultaneously felt an impact on her chest. She looked down to see she had been struck by a tight grouping of cactus needles.

Chelsea pictured Lord Mayfield and his transformation from the night before.

"Oh, dear. So close to your heart as well. As I've always been an optimist, I'd like to think that if you survive the dosage you've received, you'll be joining us any moment now. I had a feeling that your hasty departure last night might turn out to be a problem for us this morning."

"And just who is this 'us' I will be joining?"

"The loyal subjects of Victoria, of course," he said, carefully stepping around the cactus fronds. "Not the queen though, rather the plant. A remarkable species. These fronds that spread out around the cactus head are actually trigger leaves, much like on the Venus flytrap. So much as brush up against it, and the head shoots out quills in the precise direction of the intruder. Did you imagine we would force-feed every visitor who came here today? The serum contained in both the needles and the fruit makes one feel overwhelmingly protective of the plant. We found that the army of birds and small rodents were little more than a nuisance, distracting us so we forgot our footing around the fronds. The story I told about the tasty fruit was only half-true. We discovered it only after many of us were already under her spell and we went back for those who remained in camp."

"But you're a scientist. You know you are being controlled by this thing and you're doing it anyway," Chelsea protested.

"I think you'll find that doesn't matter as much as you'd imagine. I actually find comfort in its control. My greatest worry at the moment is that the effect may wear off without daily doses."

She looked down again. "How long before the effects take hold?"

"Why, I imagine it's already taking hold. Tell me, do you still feel like injecting P. Victoria with that concoction you have there?" He inclined his head toward the syringe still partially hidden behind her clutch. His cautious eyes never left hers.

She turned it over in her hand and returned it to the purse. "No, I…I don't suppose I do…"

"Good. After all, the plant isn't dangerous, is it? Shouldn't everyone get a chance to see it?"

"Of course not! I mean, it's not dangerous. It only wants to protect itself, after all. And it is so beautiful, it should be protected!"

"And naturally, the more people who protect it, the safer it will be…" His eyes drifted toward her right arm, which had begun to twitch.

"Naturally! And we should grow more like it! But that's why you had Mr. MacKenzie and Mr. Kelly at dinner last night."

"Good girl. Now, unfortunately, there was someone who declined my invitation last night, and he's rather important to our plans. Harrison!"

Harrison entered the pavilion carrying a wooden box. He walked carefully around the fronds and opened the box facing her. On a velvet lining rested a cactus fruit, three needles, and a blowgun.

Chelsea gasped.

"You are to bring this fruit to the Archbishop of Canterbury, and offer it to him. Use my name to get in the door. Be friendly, be charming, be convincing. But in the end, if you do not witness him eating the fruit, use the blowgun. I imagine an adventuress such as yourself will have no trouble with it. You must not fail in this. Sacrifice yourself if you must. Understood?"

"Of course. He would be a far better protector than I ever could," she said.

Harrison closed the box and handed it to her. As they walked her carefully to the pavilion entrance and parted the curtains, the two guards returned.

Atherton gave them a stern look, and one of them said. "He won't be back."

"Good," Atherton said. "Keep watch from out there to be sure there aren't any others."

Chelsea left them, heading toward the exit, but keeping an eye out for Mr. Mansfield. She was concerned about the guard's comment and hoped he hadn't been hurt. She glanced up at a clock. Eighteen minutes before her majesty, Queen Victoria was to arrive and officially open the Exhibition.

Rough hands pulled her into a space between two stalls. Thomas had found her instead. "You were in there so long. Did you get it?" he asked, looking past her for any witnesses.

"They actually handed it right to me. Here. Hold this." She put the box in his hands unprepared, and opened it.

"Why did they do that?" he asked, looking over the lid at the box's contents.

She thrust her shoulders back, drawing his attention to her chest. "Because I was struck by these cactus needles just dripping with the same compound contained in the fruit and naturally, they believed I had become one of them."

"But you're not...Why aren't you?"

"Thomas, my dear. Underneath the lace and frills, a bustier is all whalebone and brass. You've pounded bullet impressions out of this. Did you really think a few cactus needles would get through?" She pulled the syringe from her clutch and inserted it into the fruit, drawing back the plunger slowly.

Thomas looked back toward the exhibition floor again. "Are you sure this is wise? We don't know how many of them there are, and we've no way of telling who is already under P. Victoria's control."

She continued her work, adding the nectar from the syringe to the vial of nullifier. "You have an excellent point. My darts are a limited supply, and I can't shoot everyone. My best hope is to get Lord Atherton and his guests from last night. Stop the spread of this plant's influence."

She clicked the vial into place in her homemade dart gun, lifted the barrel and shot Thomas.

He looked down at his chest, then up at her in shock. "You shot me!"

Chelsea cocked an eyebrow in response.

Thomas's arms dropped to his side. "You knew I was under the plant's effect?"

She waved the gun nonchalantly. "Let's say eighty percent sure. I figured the guards would likely be armed with a similar blowgun, and they were awfully certain you wouldn't return."

"But your dart will neutralize the nectar? I'll be free of its influence?"

"Yes. Don't worry. It should take no more than a minute, and you'll be able to think for yourself again."

"But, then I won't want to protect her anymore! I must act quickly!"

He pushed away from her, dropping the box and stepping out onto the exhibition floor. "Guards! Guards! Miss Pepperdine faked her devotion! You have to stop her!"

Chelsea hurried to see the reaction of the other exhibitioners. Several of them were heading toward her, including Atherton's two guards.

All pretense was gone now. Chelsea dropped her purse and detached the skirts from her dress, running toward Atherton's pavilion in only a short skirt and bustier. She fired two quick shots at the guards, then chastised herself for the waste. It would take too long to have any effect, and their natural inclination even without the plant's influence was probably to do Atherton's bidding. Now she was down to three darts.

She ducked as the guards neared and rolled past them. She came up sprinting, and made it to the pavilion, pulling back the curtain, only to be blocked by Lord Atherton. He held a pistol pointed at her.

"I had truly hoped not to use this, Miss Pepperdine."

Chelsea looked around at the guards and exhibitors gathering around her, blocking any option of escape.

"You can't shoot us all, Miss Pepperdine. Not before I am forced to put you down."

She returned her aim to Lord Atherton. "Perhaps not, but one does what one must for queen and country." She adjusted her aim just off his left shoulder and fired three darts, hitting the plant each time.

"No!" Lord Atherton yelled. He turned and rushed toward the plant, and the group behind Chelsea shoved past her to join him.

Lord Atherton plucked needles from the cactus, unable to tell Chelsea's darts from the plant's own spikes.

Chelsea grabbed Thomas as he pushed past her and forced him to the ground. Needles shot past them as the crowd trampled the cactus fronds trying to pull out the darts before the nullifier had its effect.

"Let me go, damn you!" Thomas said, but with little conviction. Her dart was starting to work.

Atherton turned toward Chelsea, the entire front of his body covered in cactus needles. She remembered what he had said about the grouping in her chest being a potential overdose. He fell to his knees, then flat on his face.

The rest of them were mindlessly ripping out needles, oblivious to their own state or to the damage they were dealing the cactus.

Thomas had stopped struggling and was watching the scene with horror as the plant's protectors dropped one by one.

"Are you yourself again, Mr. Mansfield?" Chelsea asked, easing her grip on his arms.

"I am, Miss Pepperdine. When there is time, Miss, my apology will be detailed and lengthy."

She smiled, and patted him, pushing herself to a kneeling position. "No need, Mr. Mansfield. Your actions weren't entirely your own, and the good you did today outweighed the bad. But be a good lad and retrieve my skirts. Rumor has it the queen is arriving shortly."

Over the course of the day, Chelsea paid a visit to each of the men in attendance the night before. She managed to collect the remaining fruit, primarily from Mr. MacKenzie, who had already cleared out one of his hothouses to make room for P. Victoria sprouts. His temporary devotion would cost him, and the country's supply of citrus would waver until he could bring new orange trees to harvest.

She considered destroying all the fruit, as she had done the plant, but in the end secured them in her laboratory. After all, her own hypno-darts were by no means perfect, and the sense of devotion that this plant had inspired in its tragic victims was truly impressive.

The Permanent Clerk

"Do you believe in ghosts?" It was officially the strangest interview question Martin had ever been asked.

It was tough to guess what someone wanted to hear when they asked a question like that, but his answer, "No, I don't find them scientifically credible," seemed to work for the interviewer, because later that evening he got a call and the job was his.

Morris and Tennyson's file clerk position was as low as a white-collar job got. It was repetitive, boring work, but Martin needed it. He had gone through his savings and had nothing left to pawn and no way to pay his rent come Friday. Now he'd be able to make rent, stock up on ramen noodles, and maybe save enough to buy his bed back in a couple months.

Monday morning, he was at the receptionist's desk at 7:30 sharp, wearing his only tie and one of two business shirts. She directed him to Sandra in HR, who had some forms for him.

Once the paperwork was out of the way, Sandra took a key from her desk and held it out to him. "The file room is in the basement," she said. "Follow me, and I'll introduce you."

"Introduce me?" Martin repeated, taking the key. His understanding was that he'd be working alone.

"To the file room," Sandra said over her shoulder as she walked swiftly down an aisle between cubes. "And...well, we'll see," she finished enigmatically.

At the end of the row, there was a fire door, and a staircase leading down. Sandra held the door open, and the two went down side by side.

"Mr. Edison, did anyone ask about ghosts during your interview?" Sandra asked him.

"Yes," Martin replied warily.

"An odd question, right? But we prefer to hire file clerks who don't believe in ghosts. Statistically speaking, they're less likely to see him."

They'd reached the bottom of the staircase, and there was a small landing before another metal door. Martin stopped and turned toward Sandra. "To see whom?"

"We call him Mr. Kent, but that's just a name we made up because he haunts a clerk's office. Clerk Kent, get it?"

"You're saying this office is haunted?" he said, ignoring the joke.

"Yes. But don't worry, it's not like in the movies. He goes about his business like he can't see you. And not everyone can see him either—I've never seen him myself. I guess it's like those pictures where you cross your eyes and you're supposed to see a sailboat or a teapot or whatever, but all I ever see is a bunch of dots."

"Wait, you hire people who don't believe in ghosts, and then you tell them you have one?" He started looking around for hidden cameras. "Is this a joke of some sort? A haze-the-new-guy sort of thing?"

"Just open the door. Either your world view will change, or you can go about your job like I said nothing. But if you do see him, you mustn't let him touch you."

He stepped up to the lock, a simple one set inside the handle, and inserted the key. He turned back to Sandra. "If there's a guy in there in a mask…"

"Go ahead, Mr. Edison."

"Martin," he said, then with a puff of breath, he turned the handle and pulled the door open.

The well-lit room beyond had a concrete floor and lime green walls. It was divided into rows of metal filing cabinets with one aisle bisecting the rows. On top of the cabinet just inside the door were two wire baskets, marked Incoming and Outgoing. The only other feature was a pair of pneumatic tubes at one end of the central aisle.

As far as he could tell, no one else was in the room. He took a cautious step inside.

"Excellent," Sandra said. "You'd have seen him by now if you were going to." She came in to stand next to him, looking at her watch. "Now, it's nearly eight o'clock. In a few minutes, it's going to get very busy in here with all the calls over the weekend. You're going to get B14 requisition forms, either in batches delivered by one of our couriers, or through the tubes there. Fill those first. I have an example here."

She walked him through the process of locating the file and bringing it to the outgoing basket. She then did the same for an example folder and showed how to file it.

"Remember, fill outgoing requests first, and incoming as you have time, okay? You get half an hour for lunch, that's strictly twelve o'clock to twelve thirty, and you get two fifteen-minute breaks, one at ten and one at three. Use those to go to the bathroom and to smoke if you need to. Now, if you leave this room, lock that door. There are a lot of people out there who would love to burn it to the ground, and you are responsible for any files that go missing. Are we clear?"

Before he could answer, there was a *thunk* from behind him, causing him to jump. A small plastic cylinder sat in the incoming pneumatic terminal.

"Great! Now, you know where I sit. If you have any questions, just use one of your breaks."

As she left the room, he walked across and grabbed the cylindrical carrier, popped it open and retrieved the requisition form. He found the corresponding cabinet and started picking through the folders inside.

"Hello, hello," came a man's voice from the doorway. Martin looked up to see a tall man with short brown hair and a soul patch smiling at him. "New guy, eh?"

"Yeah. Martin. How you doing?"

"Can't complain. I'm your new worst enemy, Aaron Raleigh," he said with a little wave.

"Why worst enemy?" Martin asked.

"Because every time you think you're just about caught up, I'm going to bring you more of these." With that, he set a stack of folders a meter thick into his incoming basket. "Oh, and here are my B14s from the weekend. I'll be back to collect those in a bit." He set the forms down on top of the cabinet and waved again. "See you around."

Martin pulled the requested folder and set it in the outgoing basket. Then he picked up the stack of B14s Aaron had left, around twenty or so.

Before he'd gotten halfway through Aaron's requisitions, another man, this one with thinning gray curls of hair, piled on more folders and laid down several more B14s. He left like he had to be somewhere.

They kept coming too. They started piling file folders next to the incoming basket so as not to risk a collapse. Out of all the people who dropped off forms and picked up folders, Aaron was the only one who stayed any longer than the job required, or indeed ever spoke to him.

Martin was so busy, running back and forth between the pneumatic tubes and the outgoing basket, that he completely forgot all the earlier nonsense about the ghost.

At the end of the day, Aaron came down without his typical load of files. "How was your first day, new guy?" he asked, idly riffling the stack of folders still in the incoming basket.

Martin let out a long sigh, only then realizing it was past five o'clock. "A lot more frantic than I thought it would be."

"Well, that's just Monday. It gets easier from here on." Aaron's eyes kept darting off to the left. Martin couldn't help but follow his gaze, but saw nothing there except another row of filing cabinets.

"How'd you get along with your…roommate?" Aaron asked. A smile played across his lips.

"Oh, the so-called ghost? I didn't hear a whisper from it."

"No, you wouldn't. He never says anything."

"I take it you can see it?"

"Him. And yeah, he's over there right now," he indicated with a lift of his chin. "He's heading slowly this way."

"Right. So, how do I know where he is? Does he tussle papers or open cabinets or anything? Wait, aren't ghosts supposed to create cold spots?"

"Yeah, I've heard that, but I don't know much about them. I've never seen one aside from Kent—in fact, I never believed in them until I started working here. Anyway, he doesn't do any of that stuff. He just wanders up and down the rows. He always goes around the cabinets, never through them, and sometimes just kind of stands there. He doesn't touch anything or move anything."

"A-huh. Well, no offense, but I'm not convinced. This feels like an odd practical joke or something."

"Cool. Well, I just came down to let you know it was quitting time. I know it can get kind of timeless down here. You probably want to get a watch with an alarm or something." He turned and headed back up the stairs. "See you tomorrow, new guy."

"It's Martin," Martin mumbled. He pulled his last file for the day and set it in the outgoing basket, locking the door on his way out.

When he first came to New York, Martin set unreasonable expectations for himself—he knew that now, learned it the hard way. He'd had some savings, and he'd graduated top of his class. His expectation was to get a job straight away, and in that vein, he wanted to live close to work. Like an idiot, he'd rented a two-bedroom in the city and posted Roommate Wanted on all his social media.

He did get a job pretty quickly, though not at the pay rate he'd wanted. Between that and the scarcity of roommates, he ate through his savings in no time.

New York was nothing like in the *Spiderman* comics either. There was no making of deals with a cranky landlord—two days after he missed his first rent payment, he was evicted, his belongings were in boxes in the hallway, and half of those had been stolen. The super's only response to his complaints was to hand him a bill for rent he still owed.

Two days later, his company announced the

decision to outsource a number of positions, including his. At least they paid him two weeks ahead.

His new apartment was two trains and a bus ride away from his old one. The bathroom door wouldn't swing all the way open because it collided with the toilet. His bedroom had a kitchen sink in it, and that was the tour. With little money and fewer possessions, he snapped it up even after seeing it.

Martin dreamt of filing cabinets, laying on the bare floor of his bedroom, covered in his winter coat, while his downstairs neighbors shouting over their crying child.

In at work early the next day, he was nearly finished with the previous night's stack of folders when the new ones started coming in. Throughout the day, he noticed more people acting like Aaron had. Some would stop and say hello, and maybe even mention how many B14s they were leaving, but others dropped their files and basically ran. Those people always looked nervously at some random spot around the room rather than at Martin.

He figured the relaxed ones couldn't see Kent, and the others were too scared to spend any more time in the room than they absolutely had to.

Aaron was different though. He could clearly see the ghost, but it didn't seem to bug him at all. The next time he came to visit, Martin decided to ask him.

"You say you can see the ghost, but it doesn't seem to bother you. Why?"

"I got used to him. I was the file clerk a while back. But I remember opening the door on that first day. Scariest damn thing I ever saw. Part of me wanted nothing more than to run screaming, but I needed the job. So, I swallowed the lump in my throat and told the guy I didn't see anything. Eventually, I got promoted out of here, and in the meantime, I got used to him. He went about his business, and I went about mine."

Without a break in speaking, Aaron stepped to one side and flattened himself against the cabinets, turning his head in a slow arc as he did so. Then he re-adopted his casual pose and continued, though he kept glancing the other way. "But if you don't have anything else, I've got my own work to do."

Tuesday turned out to be a much slower day, just as promised, but that left Martin with a lot of empty time, and he thought about the ghost more often than he liked.

Multiple times he shook himself, ashamed of where his mind was, and forced himself to think about something else. Family was the next thing to come to mind, and that held its own baggage. At what point did he give up and call his parents for money?

No. If he'd worked things out properly, he'd

have a paycheck before his landlord came for his kneecaps.

Left to its own devices, his mind returned to the ghost.

On one of those occasions, he was snapped out of his thoughts by a phone ringing. He hadn't even noticed it before, but against the wall, under the pneumatic tubes, a phone sat on the wall. He set down his current folder and picked up the handset. "Hello?" he said, then added, "File Room."

"Mr. Edison. I need a file brought up immediately. Andi is on the way down now with the B14. Drop everything you are doing and grab that first. Alright?"

"Yes, of course, sir."

"Good man, Mr. Edison. I knew I could count on you."

Martin hung up the phone and turned. He saw a figure standing in the doorway and jumped. Rather than a ghostly old man, though, it was a nervous young woman in huge glasses and a tight skirt.

"Can I help you?" he asked as he recovered.

"Yes. I need a file for Mr. Morris."

"Oh. I was expecting a dude. He said Andy was coming."

"That's me. Andi with an 'i'. Andrea really, but no one calls me that." She waved the form at him without leaving the doorway. "Here."

"Alright," he said cautiously and crossed the room to meet her.

"Oh my God," she said and threw her hands over her mouth.

Martin stopped in his tracks. "What?"

"You can't see him? You nearly bumped into him!"

If she was faking it, she was a good actress. Her look of fright and disgust was truly convincing.

"Is it still there?" he said, staring into the air in front of him, looking for any kind of ripple or heat-haze effect, but there was nothing.

"Right in front of your face," she said.

Martin still didn't see anything, but he reached out his hand and slowly swept it across the space in front of him.

"Oh God," Andi said again.

"Right through him?" Martin asked, though he didn't feel a thing. No static, no drop in temperature, nothing.

"Could you just take the form so I can get out of here? Please?" She waved her paper at him again, looking the other way.

"Sure, hang on." He ran to grab it, then looked up the file and brought it to her. "Here you go," he said, holding it out to her.

As she reached out for it, a thought occurred to him, and he held it away for a moment. "If I'm going to spend every day with a ghost, I ought to know a thing or two about it. Would it be okay if I asked you a few questions later? Over coffee?"

"Yes. Coffee," she agreed. She snagged the file and rushed up the stairs before Martin could place any more conditions on her.

After work, he stood at the entrance to the building while the other employees streamed out.

Andi paused in her stride when they made eye

contact, then changed directions and made for him, though her expression was that of a student who'd been volunteered by the teacher.

They made their way to the roasters across the street in silence. Martin was mentally counting his cash. Honestly, he couldn't afford his own coffee, and he ran through several conversations in which he asked her to buy her own. He needn't have worried though, as she walked straight up to the counter with her card in hand.

"Okay, let's make this quick," Andi said once they each held steaming cups of coffee, hers a hazelnut mocha, his a tall drip. "I've got hot yoga at 7:00. What do you want to know?"

She kept looking across the street as she spoke, as if she could still see the ghost and he might at any minute enter this establishment to order a flat white.

"I'm sorry if this is too creepy, meeting like this. You seem put off, and I don't want you to be," Martin said. "Maybe we should just…go."

Her expression changed to sympathy. "No. I'm sorry. It's not you. Not really, anyway. It's just, Kent gives me the willies. And you…"

"Guilt by association," Martin said. "I work in his room, and any time you come to visit me, you'll be seeing him too."

"Exactly." She rolled her neck and breathed deeply, then smiled a genuine and endearing smile. "Go ahead and ask. I'll tell you what I know."

"Well, first off, how can there be a ghost in the basement? Did a former employee die down there?"

"The way I hear it, the ghost was there when Morris and Tennyson moved in. Maybe even a long time before that. The file room used to be full of crates of textbooks, and before that, it was medical supplies, and before that, war rations. I couldn't tell you what was there before that, but rumor is, the ghost was already there."

"Huh. I wonder how old the building is. Someone had to dig that basement out, and they would have stopped digging as soon as they saw the ghost.

"The building's cornerstone reads 1901. The rations were from World War II. But Kent's clothes are from somewhere in between. He has one of those high-collar shirts that you see in really old photos."

A picture was forming in his head. "Cool. What else does he look like?"

Andi shuddered, nearly spilling her coffee. It took several attempts before she got any words out. "He's disgusting. His skin is gray, and dry. Like some sort of mummy. And it's come off in a bunch of places. You can see his skull through his stringy hair, and half his nose is missing. Oh, and his clothes are fraying and covered in dust. It's like he's been collecting dust since he died and watching you put your hand through him— it's like...you got it on you." She shuddered again.

"Okay. I won't do that again, then."

"Now that you mention it though, at the last holiday party, I remember Sandra talking to some of the older employees about him. Don't quote me, because I wasn't paying too much attention, but I think one of them said when they first built the place. He looked like an Indian—like a Lenape tribesman, or whatever? And later they said he looked like a doughboy, whatever that is."

"That's what they called World War I soldiers. That's really weird—so he changes how he looks as time goes on?"

"I don't know. Anyone who saw him like that is long gone. It's just rumors from previous companies." Andi looked at her watch and quickly downed half her coffee. "Look, I've really got to go. You should ask Sandra if you have more questions. She knows a lot about the building, and she's a total buff when it comes to the ghost." She was backing toward the door even before she finished talking, giving him no opportunity to do more than wave goodbye.

Later that night, waiting for his kettle to boil before making his nightly Cup Noodles, he searched the web for "Morris and Tennyson Ghost." Oddly enough, nothing came up. Assuming this wasn't still a prank, they had real proof of the supernatural, and no one was talking about it?

Martin wasn't going to ask Sandra, though. He far preferred Andi's company.

The next morning, Martin unlocked the door to the basement, flipped on the lights, and had to stifle a scream.

There, shuffling slowly down one of the rows between cabinets, was a rotting corpse in a business suit ninety years out of date.

Martin stared, not even daring to breathe for fear he'd scream again. But a moment later he realized it must be a guy in a mask. First, Aaron set him up, then Andi knocked him over with that description. And here was the coup de grâce.

It was too short to be Aaron, but whipping off the mask would reveal who it was and put an end to the nonsense. He made for the aisle that ran across the rows.

Suddenly the HR woman's words came back to him. "You mustn't let him touch you." He stopped. He didn't want to be wrong. What happened if he did touch it?

How could he prove this wasn't a ghost without touching it?

He took several steps backward as Mr. Kent took a turn down the aisle and headed toward him. Glancing behind himself, he saw the pneumatic tubes.

The shambling figure paid Martin no attention. The cataracts of his eyes were pointed down and to the left. Martin took a chance and reached behind himself for one of the plastic pneumatic carriers, then he gently tossed it at the so-called ghost.

It went straight through Kent and clattered on the concrete floor behind him.

Martin wailed, and ran down the closest row

to the far end, turning to watch the ghost. It turned down the same row, coming straight for him again. He remembered the way Aaron had squeezed against the cabinet, but Martin didn't think he could bring himself to do that. He watched Kent approach him, hoping he'd just stop or even turn around, but he just staggered forward. Martin panicked and climbed up onto the nearest cabinet, then swung over into the next row.

The ghost continued, oblivious to Martin's actions, until he reached the wall, where he stopped, just staring down at it. Martin stood panting and staring until he heard someone clear their throat.

It was the curly-haired guy. He gave Martin an odd look and slammed a load of folders down on his incoming basket. "Three B14s," he said and headed back up the stairs.

How was he supposed to get any work done with this thing wandering around?

But he desperately needed the job.

At the moment, the ghost was clear across the room. Martin ran and grabbed the requisition forms.

The ghost still faced the wall, its head bobbing around like a drunk trying not to fall asleep. The top form was for a file in the middle of the room. He ran across, pulled out the drawer and thumbed through the files, glancing up constantly to be sure the ghost hadn't moved.

He had the first one. He held it under his arm and shuffled the forms to get the next one. It was in the same row as the ghost.

He looked up. The decayed old man was still staring at the wall. Maybe he could get it while it was distracted...

He shuffled the form to the back. The next one was near the stairwell. That one he could collect. He ran across the room, pausing to put the first folder in the outgoing basket, then searched for the new one. When he found it, he looked back up and nearly dropped the folder. The ghost was on the move again.

He quickly put the folder in the basket and edged carefully down toward the other end of the room. He had no reason to believe the ghost could hear him, but better safe than sorry.

He could collect the second folder now. He slowly pulled himself onto the cabinet.

"What the hell are you doing?"

Martin quickly jumped down, but it was only Aaron.

"That's what you've been seeing?" Martin demanded, pointing at the creature shambling down the center aisle.

"Wait, you mean *you* can see it?"

"Hell, yeah!"

"But yesterday you couldn't."

"I know! I thought that meant...I don't know, that I was immune or something! Why can I see it today?"

Aaron stepped into the room, paused while the creature passed him, then walked over to join Martin. "I don't know. I didn't think that was supposed to happen. What changed since yesterday?"

"I don't know! I had coffee with Andi, we

talked about the ghost…"

"Did she describe it to you?"

"Yes, I suppose—"

"And you believed her?"

"What?"

"Did you believe what she was telling you?"

Martin thought about it for a moment. "She was very convincing," he finally said.

"Maybe that's the difference, then. Yesterday you didn't believe in it, today you thought it was possible."

"Then how do I unsee it?" Kent was coming back their way, and Martin started to climb up onto the cabinet again.

Aaron grabbed him by the belt. "Relax, Martin. Relax."

The ghost was coming closer. "Let go, Aaron!" he said, struggling to get away.

Aaron yanked on Martin's belt. "Stop it, Martin. Just relax. He'll go past you, you just have to relax. Aaron held him against the cabinet, then just before the ghost got there, pressed himself against it next to him.

Martin bit his lip to keep from screaming, his eyes wide with terror. Cold sweat covered his forehead.

The ghost shambled past them, an inch from his face. Not even a whisper of air stirred.

It continued on until it got to the wall again and stopped, as if checking the boundaries of his cage.

"You okay?" Aaron asked, loosening his grip on Martin's belt.

Martin batted his hand away. "Are you crazy?

He could have turned at any moment! He could have touched us!"

Aaron held up his hands and backed away. "I did you a favor, Martin. You're going to have to get used to him, to stop thinking he'll come after you. You have to learn to get along. Kent doesn't notice you, he just goes about his business. Just stay out of his way and don't let him touch you. You'll be fine. I worked in the file room for two years and never had a problem."

He stopped in the doorway and ran his finger along the stack of files in the incoming basket. "But what you have to do is get your work done, or you're going to get fired."

Then he turned and climbed the stairs.

Martin was alone again, with the ghost. He needed this job. He spent the rest of his day waiting for the ghost to move, then going into a flurry of activity. He'd find several files at once that were in a different section from the ghost, and he'd file all of them quickly, keeping one eye on the ghost's wanderings. Several times the ghost came down his row, and he forced himself to step aside to let the ghost pass rather than scramble over the cabinets.

Toward the end of the day, he had three folders that went in one drawer. He spent too long getting them in their proper order and didn't notice until the ghost was nearly upon him. He threw himself against the cabinet and watched the ghost pass straight through the open drawer.

He decided to start looking for another job in the evenings and during lunch, but until he got one, he'd do his best here. Quit or get promoted—

those were his two options, and he couldn't quit until he had somewhere else to go.

The next day Martin opened the door, wary of the ghost, and when he reached in and flipped the lights on, he found himself standing face to face with Kent.

He drew his hand back like it was spring loaded, but kept his coffee from spilling. The ghost stood just inside the open doorway, blocking any entry. It stared straight ahead, and at first, Martin thought it was staring at him, but when he backed away, the ghost continued looking up the stairwell.

Martin stood just out of arm's reach, waiting for the ghost to move, but ten minutes went by and Kent was still standing there. He could think of nothing else to do, so Martin locked the door back up and went upstairs.

He came back down a few minutes later accompanied by Aaron and pulled the door open. Kent remained in the doorway, staring straight ahead and exercising his jaw like an old man trying to set his dentures.

"I don't know what to tell you. I've never seen him do that before."

"So, what should I do? I have to get past him."

"You're going to have to squeeze. You can make it. He sort of sways a bit, and you can get by on the right side if you time it."

"I'll never make that. What if I just jump through him really fast?"

"No!" Aaron said, fear showing in his eyes for the first time Martin had seen it. "You can't touch him, you can't even brush past him!"

"But, I reached through him the other day when Andi was there. She watched me do it." Martin said.

"I don't know why, but I think it's different when you can't see him."

Kent chose that moment to turn and shuffle back down the row, making it a moot point.

"What happens if you do touch him?" Martin asked.

"I don't know," said Aaron. "Just…don't."

It turned out nobody knew. During his ten o'clock break, he stopped by Andi's desk and asked her since she seemed to know so much about it. He even talked to Sandy from HR. "The ghost was here when the company moved in. Whoever first gave us this admonishment is long gone, and since we know the ghost is real, no one ever questioned the rest. But you don't have to worry since you can't see it."

Martin wasn't ready to admit that he did see it.

But Martin did question it.

He went back to his basement and watched the ghost as it wandered the aisles.

Maybe the reason that it's been down here all this time, unable to leave, is because nobody has made contact with it.

He collected a folder that was in the same row as Kent, and when the ghost turned and started back toward him, Martin stood his ground.

At the last moment, he chickened out and got out of the way.

Eventually closing time came around and Martin grabbed his coat and headed for the stairs. He noticed the ghost was following him, and he backed up the stairs, but the ghost stayed at the bottom landing, just inside the open door.

He wondered what magical force bound him to this location. What kept him from shambling up those stairs and home to his ghost-wife at closing time? He watched the ghost for a few moments, knowing he was supposed to lock that door. The ghost didn't move from the spot, and Martin decided he was just going to do it. Just one quick swipe of the arm.

He got ready to slam the door in case it reacted in some way as his arm passed through it—or if instead, God forbid, his hand made contact with the thing's shoulder.

The next morning, Aaron discovered Martin's body just inside the open door to the room. He called 911, and by the time the EMTs arrived, there was a group of employees standing on the landing at the bottom of the stairs.

Aaron looked up to see Andi approaching with tears in her eyes, and the two stood together watching the paramedics attempt resuscitation. "You told him not to let the ghost touch him, didn't you?"

"Of course I did. Everyone did. I don't think he believed us, though. He wanted to know what would happen if he did."

"Well, now we know," she said, looking past the EMTs at the figure wandering the aisles. She shivered. "There's no way I am ever coming down here again."

"Come on, Andi. You'll do what you have to do so you won't get fired. You know how to be safe. Just don't let Martin touch you."

Kent was no longer in the file room, and yet a ghost wandered the aisles. His expression was glassy, his suit cheap but modern, he suffered none of the peeling skin or dust of the ages. Andi and Aaron watched as Martin's ghost shuffled directly through one of the EMTs as well as his own body, seemingly unaware of their existence.

Condemned

The bulldozer was poised to go. The neighbors were out in bathrobes and business suits in the early morning hours to watch the eyesore's destruction.

"No, that's what I'm trying to tell you, he's still in there!" the foreman said.

Officer LaThanya Barber looked at the dates and signatures on the forms he thrust in front of her. So far as she could see, everything was in order, and the man should have been out last week. The large Notice of Eviction sign was pasted across the man's door alongside one with bold red letters proclaiming Condemned.

"Alright, sir, I'll have a talk with him. What did you say his name was again?"

"Antonín Kučera. He's old, and he speaks with an accent, but don't let him fool you, he understands English just fine."

"Alright, sir, just step aside." LaThanya pulled out her flashlight and waved it toward her partner, who was taking notes with one of the neighbors over by the squad car. He flipped his notebook shut and came to join her.

"The resident refuses to leave; one Antonín Kučera. He no longer owns the property and should have vacated a week ago." She said as they set a brisk pace for the front door.

Officer Harry Stilton nodded his understanding and put a hand on his cuffs. "Do you think we'll need to arrest him?"

LaThanya had only been on the force for a little under four years, yet she was the one they chose to break in the new guy. "I hope not. Usually just the fact of a police presence is enough to get them to cooperate, but sometimes it depends upon whether they have somewhere to go."

The screen was laying against the door, the hinges having rotted out long ago. LaThanya set it aside and rapped on the door with the butt of her flashlight.

"Mr. Kučera? This is the police. Open up," she said.

A heavily accented voice came from the other side of the door. "Then you can tell these thieves and vandals that they cannot take my house!"

"Sir, I'm going to need you to open the door," she said.

Locks clicked, and the door cracked open. A prodigious nose and a pair of bushy, gray eyebrows poked through the gap.

"Are you Antonín Kučera?" LaThanya asked. The nose nodded, briefly bringing into view a pair of sky gray eyes. "Sir, your house has been condemned, and you haven't kept up with payments. I'm afraid it no longer belongs to you, and it is unsafe to stay in. Now, I don't want to, but we will force you to leave if you make us."

"Unsafe!" He said something in a foreign language that clearly translated as vulgar. "Then let the house fall down on me, if that is His will. Why is it his concern?" The door opened wide enough for an accusatory arm to jab out toward the foreman.

"Sir, it is too late for you to lodge your complaint. Please come outside, sir."

The man's face darkened, and the accusatory finger tucked into his fist. The door flung open, and the man shot under LaThanya's arm, a five-foot-nothing blur of gray hair, wrinkled skin and dark flannel.

"Grab him, Harry!" she yelled, but the old man was faster than Harry, as well as the stunned foreman. The old man hit him full force and began clawing at the foreman's chest, yelling a string of foreign profanities with the word bastard thrown in for good measure.

Harry pulled him off the man, tucking his arms behind his back. "Calm down!" Harry said. "You don't want to get arrested, old man. Calm down!"

"No, I want him arrested!" the foreman said, righting his displaced hard hat. "You saw him! He assaulted me!"

"Cuff him," she told Harry, then she stepped between the old man and the foreman. "Look at him. He's pushing ninety, and you're in construction. Think about what that's going to do to your image, claiming that frail old nothing could hurt you. You're already taking his house away. Don't you think that's enough?"

The foreman looked away from her. "Fine."

The old man continued to struggle, nearly getting an arm free before Harry got it cuffed. "LaThanya! A little help?"

LaThanya got in the old man's face. "Hey! Antonín! Stop this nonsense right now, or you're going to spend the night in jail! Is that what you want?"

The man went limp in Harry's arms, but he held LaThanya's gaze. "You can't just take away a man's home. That's my...church."

LaThanya wasn't sure whether that was an error in translation. The boarded-up, warped-wood structure didn't look like any kind of church she'd ever seen. At this point, she didn't care. She turned to the foreman. "Alright. Go ahead."

The foreman smiled and waved to the bulldozer. The diesel engine roared, and the tracks moved forward as the blade raised to head height.

Antonín tore out of Harry's arms, rushing forward. LaThanya caught him this time and wrestled him to the ground. He tried to bite her, but she caught his forehead and pinned it to the ground.

"That's it. You're under arrest." She grabbed him by the elbow and forced him onto his chest. "You have the right to remain silent."

The old man stared wide-eyed at the bulldozer. "Lesovij!" he yelled. Flecks of spit flew from his mouth. "I have failed you, Lesovij!"

LaThanya flipped him around to face her.

"Who did you fail? Is there somebody else in there, old man?"

The old man scrunched his eyes closed. "Lesovij!" he yelled again.

"Stop that bulldozer, Harry! There's someone inside!"

Harry ran forward, waving his arms and shouting. The foreman pantomimed not being able to hear him, and Harry ran past him, onto the porch. The bulldozer's brakes screeched, and it came to a stop, inches from the porch's support beam.

"Mr. Kučera, does someone live with you?" The old man's only response was to break down in tears. "Oh, forget this," LaThanya said, flipping him onto his chest again and finishing with his Miranda rights.

Harry was in animated conversation with the foreman. LaThanya lifted the old man to his feet by his shirt collar and marched him to the squad car. She pushed him into the back seat and depressed the button on her radio. "Officer Barber, ten-alpha-six. I'm at one-one-two Pestle Street. There may be someone else in the house. Officer Stilton and I to investigate, over."

The radio on her epaulette crackled, then the response came through: "Roger ten-alpha-six. Do you want backup?"

She clicked the button again. "Negative. We can handle this. Be prepared for a complaint from the construction folks, though. Over."

"Copy that."

She closed the door and approached the bystanders. "Anyone know if Mr. Kučera lived with anyone else?"

There was some muttering and general shaking of heads, then a frumpy woman in a flour-stained apron said, "He had a son, but he moved out a long time ago."

A young woman with long, stringy hair said, "I've heard yelling, but I thought it was just the TV."

"The power's been out for over a month," said a man in a suit and glasses.

LaThanya turned and walked back over to where Harry was still arguing with the foreman. "Sir, we're going to have to search this place before you can continue," she said, interrupting whatever the foreman was saying. "The man's wife may be inside, bed-ridden for all we know. This will just take a few minutes, okay?"

The man fumed, but stepped aside for them to pass.

LaThanya pulled her flashlight back out and nodded to Harry. She pushed open the front door and stepped inside. "Police! Is anyone in here?" she called.

The room inside looked worse than the exterior of the house. The olive green carpet was decomposing in many places and burnt in others. Grease-stained newspapers and old takeout containers littered the floor. A ruptured beanbag chair sat in one corner, spilling its beady white guts, and a chair that was more duct tape than vinyl sat in front of a cracked cathode ray television on a stack of bricks.

Stepping through an open doorway, they came to the kitchen. The smell was unforgivable, and a cloud of flies buzzed around them, angry at being disturbed from their week-old feast. Piles of broken linoleum chips were everywhere amongst rat droppings and cockroach specs. "Police!" she called again and began coughing to keep from gagging. "Is there anybody home?"

A short hallway ran from the kitchen toward two rooms at the back of the house. LaThanya snapped on her flashlight, shining it toward one brass knob, then the other. "Hello, Bay Town Police," she called again.

She swept her flashlight in the other direction, where a door led outside. "Check the backyard, maybe it's just a dog," she said to Harry, then headed toward the hallway.

The linoleum gave way to creaking plywood boards. Ancient wallpaper was torn in broad sheets, and small nails poked out of the drywall. She stopped in front of the first door, noticing for the first time a handprint shaped stain on the brass. It could have been ketchup, or even chocolate, but it may have just as easily been dried blood. She placed thumb and forefinger on the only two clean spots and turned.

She immediately shut the door back up. The toilet had clearly not been flushed in weeks, but that hadn't kept the old man from using it. The bathtub had a couple inches of congealing mud at the bottom and smelled like a particularly pungent swamp, but what she cared about was that no one was inside.

Turning to the last door, she prepared herself for the horrors within, but it turned out to be suspiciously clean, livable even. A brass bed was pushed against the north end of the room, and gauzy curtains swayed in the breeze from an open window. The closet door was open, revealing neatly hung shirts and pants, and a pair of slippers placed against the far wall.

No sense letting the bulldozer have those. She clicked her radio again. "Officer Barber, ten-alpha-six. The house is clear, over."

"Copy that, ten-alpha-six."

LaThanya gathered all the hangers in one hand, then bent to pick up the slippers with the flashlight still in hand. She turned and gasped at the sight of a figure in the dark hallway.

"Sorry," Harry said, turning on his flashlight. "The backyard is clear."

"Forget about it. Here, take these. Put them in the trunk. Mr. Kučera can have them back when he gets out."

"Copy that," he said, taking them from her, and heading back down the hallway. She followed him, taking a deep breath before they entered the kitchen.

The foreman was standing just outside the front door. "Well?" he said.

LaThanya was about to answer when she stepped on a board that sounded different from all the others in the house. She looked down, shifting her weight from one foot to the other.

"What've you got there?" Harry asked.

"Don't know. Loose board maybe? Trap door? Give him the clothes for a moment." She swept her foot in a wide arc, clearing a spot of all the trash until she could see a seam. "It's a door alright."

She got a couple fingernails under the edge and pulled up a square section of floor. Homemade stairs led down to a dirt floor roughly cut from the earth.

"He's not supposed to have a basement," the foreman said over the top of the clothes pile in his arms.

"Thank you, sir. Please stay back, okay?" She leaned down and clicked on her flashlight once more. "Hello?" she called, waiting a few moments for any reply. She shone the light around, but couldn't see more than rock walls and a clay floor leading off in one direction. A heavy smell of rot hit her. She looked up at Harry, sighing. "I'm going to have to go in there."

Harry nodded, and LaThanya lowered her feet over the edge and started down the protesting stairs. The light didn't do much good; there was a fair deal of dust in the air, trapping the beam like fog. The smell of rotting meat came to her, somehow fresher than before.

"Hello?" she called again, but still there was no response. Finally, her flashlight beam reflected off something other than stone walls. There was a silver tray on the clay floor, with dark fur on top. Another step closer. It was a cat, sliced open from neck to hind legs, with its intestines displayed next to it.

LaThanya turned away, but as she did so, her light caught something else and she had to go back. On the far side of the tray was a skeleton splayed out and chained to the wall. Vines wrapped around the bones and dried strands of meat and skin clung to the skeleton like jerky.

The abdomen was a soupy mess of larva-infested innards. Somehow, worst of all, bolted to the skull were a pair of deer's antlers.

She turned and stalked back to makeshift staircase, burying her nose in the crook of her elbow. "Harry!" she said, "Tell the workmen to go home. We've got a crime scene."

LaThanya chose to stay at the site while forensics finished up, letting Harry take the old man in for processing. She felt a responsibility toward the victim, having discovered the body, and wanted to make sure they were treated respectfully.

Portable flood lamps bathed the scene in light. Evidence markers were laid out, and a thousand photographs were taken. Swabs were run across the skeleton's mouth as well as the bones of its arms and hands. Larvae were placed in vials. A ground penetrating radar was brought down to look for any evidence of other victims, and samples were taken of every stain in the room.

The body was never disturbed.

"Don't see that every day."

LaThanya turned to see Dr. Pegah Jahandar, the medical examiner. She was dressed all in white, with a painter's mask over her mouth and nose, and cloth booties covering her shoes. In one hand she held a tackle box, and in the other, a body bag.

"Do I have the scene, LaThanya?" she asked.

"Yes. Forensics finished with the body a few minutes ago. Just be careful around the cat."

"Roger that," she said, shaking her head. She squatted over the body, set the bag on one side and her tool box on the other. She opened it up and pulled out a camera. "Looks like the blowflies have been and gone." The flash on her camera went off once, and she leaned in closer, taking two more close shots. "Could you grab my specimen net?" she said without looking back.

LaThanya found the net poking out of her tool box and handed it over. Pegah waved it over the body several times, then collected the netting in one hand and examined her catch. "And these flesh flies are proud grandparents. This body has been here for a month, at least. That wriggling in the pelvic cavity is going to be millipedes. Hang onto this net and don't let them escape. I'm going to see if I can capture a couple."

"What about the cat, doctor? Why isn't it covered with crawlies too?" LaThanya asked.

"Oh, it is. You just can't see them at this distance. Thousands of blowfly eggs. The cat's only been dead a few hours. It needs to marinate awhile before any of these guys are going to be interested." Pegah withdrew her forceps from the soupy mass of organs, pulling with them a wriggling ichor-covered millipede, which she dropped into a sample container.

LaThanya turned away from the revolting work. "What the hell is going on here? The old guy chains someone up, kills them, then brings them dead cats like it's some sort of shrine?"

"I'm afraid you're going to have to figure that out. All I can get you is cause of death. The edges on the skin and musculature look more consistent with predation than tool marks, and I see no cuts on the exposed ribs. Your victim is male, by the way." She ran her gloved hands over the skull. "I'd say early twenties. As soon as I get him back to the lab, I'll run toxicology, but I see no signs of trauma. These organs are going to tell me something."

Pegah took the net back from LaThanya and returned her camera and samples to the toolbox. "Help me lift?" she asked.

LaThanya's nose wrinkled. "Got another set of gloves?"

Pegah handed over a second pair from a pocket of her jacket, then laid out the body bag.

"How are you planning to get him out of the manacles?"

"I'm not," Pegah said, producing a long screwdriver. "There's skin on them. I'm taking the cinderblocks." With that, she started working on the grout between blocks.

LaThanya had nothing to help out with, so she went back to examining the body. Between the leaves and ribs, she could see the withered heart and lungs, apparently intact. "What's up with the ivy, do you suppose?"

"First thought? Structural support. Mr. Kučera looks to have wanted the skeleton intact, and the vines are the only thing holding it together. But that just brings up a more interesting question."

"Which is?"

Pegah paused in her work, pointing the screwdriver around the room. "The only lights down here are the ones we brought in, right? Since the ivy would need light to grow, where are the grow lamps?" She pulled the cinderblock from the wall and set it next to the corpse. LaThanya couldn't help but feel her own left shoulder stretch and relax.

"There hasn't been electricity in this place for weeks," she said.

Pegah paused with the blade of the screwdriver against the grout of the second cinderblock. "Huh," she said, and started chiseling.

"Huh," LaThanya agreed.

They ended up digging up the plants as well, and LaThanya helped Dr. Jahandar lift the corpse and move it to the body bag, sloshing as little as humanly possible. The vines and the cinderblocks went in okay, but the zipper wouldn't go up over the antlers. They rolled the body out past the frenetic cameras, and LaThanya got a ride to the station in the Medical Examiner's van.

Once they got there, she took a moment to wash the stink off herself, then proceeded to the interrogation room.

"Can I go home now? I am very sorry I tried to hit you. I promise not to do it again."

LaThanya turned toward the two-way mirror, not even sure there was anyone there, but needing to share her incredulity with someone. She turned back to the old man cuffed to the table.

"Mr. Kučera, assaulting a law enforcement officer is the least of your problems right now. Would you like to tell me about what you've got going on under your house?"

The old man clenched his hands into fists. His lips became a hard, thin line. "How dare you trespass on my property?"

"There is a body under your house, Mr. Kučera!"

"Bah," the man said. He turned around in his seat, coming up short at the end of his manacles' reach.

"You've killed someone, and all you can say is, 'Bah?'" LaThanya said.

"It's a cat. Who cares? Those little vermin have it coming."

"It's still a crime, but I'm not talking about the damn cat! There was a person in your basement, a real-life dead person chained to the wall in your basement!"

Someone knocked on the door. LaThanya watched Mr. Kučera for a few moments, but his expression didn't change, and no response was forthcoming, so she answered the door. "What?"

"Sorry, Officer Barber," the nervous rookie said. "Dr. Jahandar said she had cause of death for you."

LaThanya took another look back at Mr. Kučera, then stepped outside and closed the door. She read the name off his badge. "Thank you, Wilkins. Has Social Services been contacted? I'm starting to think this man might need a psych eval."

"I'll check, but I don't think so. His only living relative is a son, and we're still trying to contact him."

LaThanya thanked him and took the stairs down to Autopsy. As she approached the double doors, she heard Pegah cursing in Farsi.

"Should I come back?" LaThanya asked over the sound of the complaining power screwdriver.

Pegah pushed up her face shield and smirked at LaThanya. "No, come on in. Either someone Krazyglued these antlers on, or the bone had time to grow around the screws. I'm going to have to saw them off just to fit him in a drawer."

"You had some news for me?"

"Cause of death was starvation. There were multiple layers of scabs in the skin around the manacles, suggesting he'd been chained up there for months, and the state of his remaining organs means he wasn't fed in all this time."

"Jesus. And the dead cat just out of reach, was that just adding taunting to torture?"

"Forensics is searching the grounds for more cat skeletons, but if he just dumped them in the trash, then who knows? This one was put there long after the poor guy was dead, and it doesn't have a collar, so we don't even know if it's going to be missed. There are a lot of feral cats in this city."

"Any idea who he is? Have you run DNA?"

Pegah laughed. "Are you kidding me? It's taken me years just to get a PCR machine for the lab. I still have to send the results out, and that's going to take at least a week before we'll get any matches out of CODIS. But—" She pulled off her exam gloves and tossed them in the trash. "I can tell you exactly who he is. Wanna see a magic trick?"

Without waiting for a response, she walked to the film viewer and flipped on the backlight. "That's the victim's DNA. This one over here was collected from Mr. Kučera at booking. Now, abracadabra!" She snapped the second film in back of the first. The alleles lined up almost perfectly.

LaThanya stared. "They're related."

"Closely related. Based on his age, I'm thinking son."

"Well, we can tell Wilkins to stop looking. The son of a bitch killed his own kid."

"Enjoy your interrogation. I've got a date with a bone saw." Pegah flipped the face shield back down and selected a new pair of gloves.

Dates! LaThanya thought. She pushed through the Autopsy doors and pulled out her phone. She had to climb the stairs before getting a signal, then quickly dialed home. After two rings, her boyfriend answered.

"No, you're not," he said.

This wasn't the first time she'd had to call him about working late, but it was the first time it fell on poker night, and he clearly knew what she was going to say. "I'm sorry, but I have to. I've got a murder case, and this one is weird. I need you to stay with Shanie, but I am so going to make it up to you later."

"I've got a better idea. I'm going to take Shanie with me. We'll teach her how to smoke cigars and cheat at cards."

"You're the best, honey," she said with a smile. "Kiss her for me."

"I will. Call me when you leave."

She hung up, standing for a moment with the phone in her hands, a picture of little Shanie on the lock screen, then she occupied her mind with the bastard in Interrogation Room Two and set her jaw.

"Your son!" she said as she threw the door open. It bounced off the wall, causing the two-way glass to shake. "You starved your own son to death! How could you do that?"

"He is not dead," the old man said calmly.

LaThanya wasn't sure what kind of response she expected, but it definitely wasn't that. "I don't pretend to be a doctor, but people without skin don't tend to live long!"

"But now, he will live forever. He has become Lesovij. It was his calling."

"His calling? Is this some sort of religious thing?"

"He was born with the mark of the forest. Right here, on his chest. We knew from childhood that he would one day host Lesovij. He does not live on meat and plants like you and I, but on the souls that are sacrificed to him."

"What exactly is this Lesovij you keep talking about?"

"Lesovij is lord of the forest where I grew up. He walks the land and enforces its laws. He calls the wolves and makes trees to grow in the smallest cracks of rocks. In his name, the deer graze free, and the water runs pure. He that never dies looks over everything that lives and crushes whoever disturbs the balance."

"So, you bolted antlers to your own son and starved him so he could become this thing?"

He slapped the table. "Now you see. People of this town have turned their backs on nature and forgotten how to live with her. So, we bring him back. Now that we understand each other, I have to get home. It will be dark soon and I have to feed him before sunset." The little man stood up as far as the manacle chains would allow.

"Sit your ass down, little man! You are not going anywhere! It is against the law to starve someone to death—I don't care what it says in your religion."

"But he must be fed."

"Your boy ain't home, anyway! He's in our autopsy having his antlers removed!"

"You *what*?" The man said, baring his teeth. He stood up and started yanking on his chains, cursing in his native tongue.

"Calm down, sir. And take your seat," she said, but that only made him more aggressive. He continued yelling in rapid-fire Czech and tried reaching for her throat, but the manacles stunted his reach. He tried lifting the table next, but of course it was bolted down, and he finally settled for throwing his chair. She easily ducked it and put a hand on her taser, trying again. "Sir—"

There was a knock on the glass, pulling her attention away, then two other officers entered the room, followed by her supervisor. "Antonín Kučera, you are being charged with the murder of your son, Lukas Kučera, improper disposal of a body, and criminal trespass. You've already been read your rights, but you are allowed a phone call, and I highly suggest you use it to retain a lawyer. I'd like a word with you, Officer Barber."

The two others were switching his manacles for cuffs and leading Mr. Kučera to a holding cell. The old man was struggling and yelling the entire time. LaThanya and her supervisor waited until they left, but they could still hear his voice all the way down the hall.

"What purpose did you think it would serve to feed his delusions like that? You got him to confess that he knowingly did this to his own son! That's when you advise him not to speak and take him to his cell. Now we've got this whole bit about the blasted 'forest lord' right there in his taped confession, and it's just begging for an insanity plea!"

"Sorry, sir, it just seemed there was more to the story. But we did learn this was an isolated incident which means there aren't any other bodies out there."

"Human bodies, Barber, maybe. So far, they've found eight cats, three dogs, fourteen raccoons, and countless rats. The entire back yard is full of them."

"Sir, I know the state doesn't like the insanity plea, but I think this guy actually may *be* insane. He seemed convinced that his son wasn't dead and only got upset about feeding time." Something clicked in her head. "Sir, I just had an idea. Perhaps if we tell him we've fed this Lesovij, he may calm down. We don't want the cell block up all night with his yelling, and a sedative might be a bad idea if we don't have a diagnosis. His brain chemistry might be abnormal."

"We'll see what the results of the psych eval say. For now, you can consider this case closed. I want you and Officer Stilton fresh in the morning and ready for the next case. I've already sent him home, and I'm telling you the same. Go home."

"I understand, sir. I will."

Her supervisor left, and she checked her watch. Too late for her boyfriend to get to his game. But he was going to be extra-pissed she made him miss it for half an hour of overtime. Maybe she'd stop for some chocolate strawberries.

She took the elevator down to the parking garage and walked to her car. She fished out her keys and happened to glance up at the exit ramp. The last light was fading from the sky. With one hand on her car door, she considered her options. Her baby girl was waiting for her, and today might be the day that second tooth broke through. On the other hand, the sun had already set. Would Mr. Kučera calm down on his own, or would he yell all night? Would they end up giving him a sedative if he did, and if so, what would it do to him?

It was going to nag at her all night, how one simple statement could reassure the old man and keep him calm until tomorrow's psych eval, but she didn't get the impression that her supervisor was going to pass it along.

"God damn it." She clipped her keys back onto her belt and got back into the elevator. Four bangs rang out, distant, muffled. LaThanya was used to the clanging noises of the Eisenhower-era box, but damned if those didn't sound like gunshots.

Her ears strained for any other sounds as the elevator door opened. The way to the holding cells took her past the morgue, but the light coming through the double doors was blinking sporadically, pushing a jolt of ice through her already tense system. She blamed it on Mr. Kučera's story. Campfire bullshit to be sure, but now her cop's intuition was buzzing, so she approached the morgue with caution.

Just outside, she noticed a smear of red across the threshold. Possibly a footprint, and it looked enough like blood that she drew her service weapon.

"Dr. Jahandar?" she called, pushing the door open. The swivel-arm lamp used for autopsies was thrust up through the fluorescents, throwing sparks and occasionally lighting the one remaining bulb. "Oh, *hell* no," she whispered. The instrument tray was lying on its side, and near her feet was a chrome bowl filled with what looked initially like fingers, but as the bulb flashed again, she saw they were chunks of antler. There was no sign of either the body or the doctor.

"Dr. Jahandar?" she called again. Still no response. "If there's anybody in here, announce yourself, so I don't shoot your ass!" The lights kept flashing. Smears of blood covered every surface, illuminated in strobe light. Arcing across the ceiling tiles, spattered along the counters, and in large droplets on the floor near the examination table.

He's not dead, the old man had said. As his words echoed in her mind, the scene unfolded in front of her.

Pegah cut through the antlers with the bone saw, eventually getting down to something vital. The corpse on the table twitched; a pain response, but Pegah convinced herself she was seeing things and turned the saw back on.

The corpse grabbed her by the arm and broke it. Blood dripped onto the floor. She screamed with only the recorder as witness. The creature rose from the table and threw her across the room, snapping her spine against the cabinets.

No. LaThanya forced those thoughts out of her head, replacing them with something more rational.

Pegah was sawing through the antlers when a chunk broke off, flying at high speed, and cut her. Maybe cut her bad. She jerked, knocking the swing-arm lamp hard enough to crash into the ceiling. She went to the cabinet looking for medical supplies, but she was losing a lot of blood by then and ran out of Autopsy leaving that smear by the door on her way for help.

That was far more plausible, and she felt a little better having thought of it.

Only, *where did the corpse go*?

Her eye went to the morgue drawers. Without

the antlers, he'd fit in there. She just about had herself convinced, when a rattle came from behind, and she spun in place, gun at the ready.

The door swung closed, and the bowl of antler chunks spun, empty.

Another noise came from behind the autopsy table, this time a wet popping sound. She made sure her body camera was on and called out, easing her way around the table that blocked her view.

"Police officer! I am armed! Come out with your hands up, or I will fire!"

There was no direct response, just a sound like her stomach after Brussels sprouts. She continued around the table, and a dark shape came into view low to the ground.

The light blinked on for a moment. A wolf, drenched in blood, licked its lips. It was standing over a puddle of human remains and Dr. Jahandar's lab coat.

LaThanya nearly fired, and then nearly ran, but her rapidly shrinking rational side stopped her from doing either. *Keep your cool and don't go slipping on all this blood. Just back away and call animal control.*

The wolf looked at her, disinterested, and loped off, pushing between the doors like it knew where it was going.

LaThanya quickly recovered and pressed the button on her radio. "Central, this is Officer Barber. I'm in Autopsy. Dr. Jahandar is down, and there is a wolf in the station. Say again, this is no joke, there is a wolf in the station!"

She took one more look down at the body. No

wolf caused this; all that was left of Pegah were ragged flaps of skin as if she'd burst open from neckline to navel, no sign of a ribcage or any internal organs.

LaThanya couldn't look any longer, so she went after the wolf.

The bloody paw prints headed off in the direction of the holding cells, and she followed. Halfway down the empty corridor, the hallway lights began to flicker. She heard a *tickity* sound before she saw the source of it. Those chunks of antler from autopsy were rolling down the corridor to disappear around the corner.

"Oh, *hell* no."

Every instinct told her to run and don't look back. This was too weird, and someone else could deal with it. But she was a cop. The lights steadied, the antler pieces were gone, and she continued.

Blam! Blam! Blam! Blam! She was certain it was gun fire this time. At the T-junction ahead, the wolf prints and the antler pieces had gone left, toward the break room, the lockers, the showers, the gun range, and the armory.

Central still hadn't responded to her earlier call. She clicked the button again. "Central, where are you? Did you hear what I said about the wolf?"

Just off the right side was a staircase leading up to Central, Booking, Dispatch, and Interrogation.

She tried the radio one more time. "Central, get your ears on! We've got a dead coroner down here!"

Still no response. Had those gun shots come from upstairs? LaThanya poked her head around the corner. The fluorescents were out along the corridor to her left, showing no trace of the wolf in the darkness. She reached behind her for the stairwell door, finding it ajar. She threw it open and whipped around, sweeping the inside with her gun. English ivy grew from a crack in the floor and up along the hinge of the door. Otherwise, the stairwell was empty. Her heart was pounding, and her arms were covered in goosebumps. If someone didn't respond soon, she was going to start screaming.

She stepped into the doorway, keeping an eye on the left-hand corridor, and clicked her radio three times. Three bursts of static came from upstairs. Was no one manning the desk? She needed backup!

The wolf could wait. Unless it learned how to push the arm-bars on the doors, it was trapped down there. She ripped the ivy away from the hinges so the door would close and climbed the stairs to ground level. Emergency lights cast a red glow through the tiny window. Something propped the door open. Probably more ivy. She clicked on her flashlight in the darkened stairwell, finding instead the body of another cop. Boneless, just like Pegah, a wedge of skin and pulp squeezed between door and jamb. A moan escaped her and she bit it down. Concentrate on the job. Find survivors, get backup, get a hold of the situation.

She pulled the door open, leading with her gun.

The roll-down shutters were deployed, cutting off the front entrance. Someone had initiated Lockdown. But the steel shutters were covered in English Ivy, and sprays of blood covered them like graffiti across their length. Bullet holes littered the walls, and there were more bloody smears looking like drag marks in all directions. "Officer Barber here! Are there any survivors?" What the hell had happened up here?

Just across the hallway was the open door to Central Communications. More ivy grew up both sides of the doorway. She crossed quickly and looked inside. The bodies on the floor meant that she couldn't deny it any longer. This was what the old man was talking about. Lesovij.

Of the officers on comms duty, one had his throat torn out, and the other had vines wrapped around her limbs, looking much like the corpse in Mr. Kučera's basement, but constricting her throat and turning her face purple. Both had their guns drawn for what little good it had done them. The radio equipment also had vines running through it. There went her option of calling out.

That thing had woken up in Autopsy, and it had been bringing in wolves and killing cops. The guns were useless against it. How do you kill a skeleton? If anyone would know, it would be Kučera, and he was down in holding.

Shots rang out downstairs. Someone was still alive!

LaThanya turned and ran back down the stairs. As she rounded the halfway point, movement caught her eye through the half-open door below. The empty eye sockets and screwed-on antlers of Lesovij glided past. She ran the rest of the way and pressed her face against the opening in time to see two wolves follow along behind the skeletal figure. With each step he took, English ivy grew from the floor beneath his feet. It wrapped its way up his leg to the femur, then broke off as he took his next step.

Gunshots rang out nearby, and she slammed against the push-bar, stepping into the ivy carpeted hallway. Officer Wilkins was sitting with his back against the wall some thirty feet down the corridor with a dead wolf in his lap. His leg and both hands were a mess of blood. He was trying to reload his weapon, but his shaky hands kept missing.

LaThanya fired a burst of three rounds into the second wolf charging at Officer Wilkins, and three more into the back of Lesovij's skull. The first went wide and shattered his clavicle, but the second two hit dead on, forcing its head forward.

She watched as the shattered bits of bone flew together and re-knitted. The creature didn't so much as turn in her direction.

Wilkins finally slammed his clip into place and panic-fired at the creature slowly approaching him. A bullet whizzed past LaThanya's head after threading harmlessly through the thing's ribcage. She fell to the ground and covered her head. "Watch your fire!" she shouted, but shot after shot tore through the air overhead.

After the clip had emptied, and the trigger clicked impotently, she looked up. Lesovij had reached Wilkins. "No. No, don't—" the rookie said. The creature reached out and placed one skeletal finger on Wilkins' head, then continued on down the corridor toward Holding.

Once Lesovij turned the corner, LaThanya got up to run. Something caught her leg, and she looked back to see the ivy creeping up her calf. The vines that had been planted with every step it took were continuing to grow. The entire corridor behind her was a green carpet. More lights went out as vines curled around the fluorescents and popped them out of their sockets. She tore away from the thickening vines and sprinted toward Wilkins.

"Hey! Are you alright?" she said, looking over him. His pant leg was torn up, and blood flowed from several puncture marks. He'd need a rabies shot, but nothing was life threatening. She put pressure on the wounds. "Look at me. What did that thing do to you?"

"He—he touched me. That's all. But I feel…" A gurgling sound came from his throat, and he clamped his mouth shut to keep from throwing up.

"It's okay. We're gonna get you help."

"But I feel…" He made that sound again. LaThanya prepared to dodge if he went projectile.

"You're gonna be okay. Try not to talk, just breath."

"It's not like that. I feel…hungry," Wilkins finally managed. And he looked hungry too. By the look in his eyes, he could just about take a bite out of her.

"Wilkins?" she said, backing away. He bared his teeth, but made no move to come toward her.

Instead he arched his back. His stomach bulged like he was ten months pregnant, and the buttons tore from his dress blues.

LaThanya found her back pressed against the far wall where the vines once more tried to grow around her. "Wilkins!" she said, eyes wide in horror.

His bare abdomen distended further, the shape of a snout pressing against it from the inside, and a moment later it snapped, tearing him from neckline to crotch and spraying LaThanya in gore. A wolf, dripping Wilkins' lifeblood stepped out of the skin left behind and shook, further covering LaThanya with tiny droplets.

A voice in her head was screaming to shoot the damned thing, but she physically couldn't raise the gun to fire. The wolf had the same blue eyes as Wilkins, and there was a feeling of recognition there.

The wolf turned away from her and loped off down the hallway after its master. LaThanya watched it go with unblinking eyes, until its tail disappeared around the corner, then started clawing at her face, trying to get the blood off. A sound escaped her as she worked, half moan, half scream. It rose in volume until LaThanya caught herself and clamped her mouth shut.

She held herself for countless seconds, not trusting her arms unattended, not trusting her mouth not to scream if she didn't hold her lips tight.

Eventually, she relaxed her arms and stared at her trembling hands. "Come on, girl, get a grip here." There was a chance, however slim, that police officers made it out before the lockdown, but the prisoners in Holding had no way out. Some of them had done nothing worse than being drunk in public.

She batted away the probing vines and stood up. She ran down the hallway, checking how many rounds remained in her clip before slamming it back in. *What the hell use is that? Bullets haven't done a thing to that creature so far!*

Yeah. But they sure do a number on those wolves.

She turned the corner toward the holding cells. Lesovij would be stuck at the far end, because there was a secure door. If you didn't have a physical key, someone had to buzz you in.

The lights were already blinking by the time she got there, the corridor overgrown. Still, she could make out the antlered figure with his hands pressed against the security door.

"Stop right there, you paranormal murderer!" She fired a warning shot through its skull. The lights blinked again. Wilkins the wolf was heeling next to it.

Great. Now what could she do? She was trying to keep that thing away from the prisoners, but her gun was no threat to it, and she had no idea how to contain it. If what Kučera said was true, it woke up at sunset and started prowling for sacrifices. Did that mean that it would die again on its own at dawn? But that was ten hours away. All she had to do was survive until dawn, just her and that thing. And the wolf. Would the wolves turn back to people at dawn?

The fluorescents went out entirely. LaThanya grabbed for the flashlight at her belt and clicked it on. In the focused beam the skeletal figure still stood with its back toward her, head bowed toward the door, but the wolf had turned in her direction, its eyes decidedly less friendly than Wilkins' had been. Its lip curled, and it lowered its snout.

"Oh, Wilkins, don't make me shoot you," she said. The world was going mad—she knew that—but some sort of magic was at work here, and if she didn't kill that wolf, she could hold on to hope for getting Wilkins back. But the way the wolf burst out of him, the skin left behind, and all that blood, none of it seemed reversible. But that wolf was her partner. Wilkins was a rookie, and a screw up, and almost all her interactions with him was reminding him of protocol or when he was spilling coffee on her. But he was her partner. He had a good heart, and that was the makings of a good cop. But he was more than that. In a way, he represented her old life. Maybe if she didn't have to kill him, everything could go back to normal, where the dead don't rise, cops don't burst into wolves, and her biggest worry was finding a private space to express her milk and finding room in the fridge for it.

Wilkins didn't currently share her worries, nor her optimism.

Lesovij lifted its arms in a mockery of the position she first found him in, chained to the wall. At his urging, the plants surged in growth. Vines wrapped around her legs like grasping skeletons. The concrete structure popped and ruptured with roots growing down from above. The solid steel door in front of Lesovij screamed as the hinges twisted and lifted. Trunks a foot thick grew from the foundation, crumpling the eight hundred pound door like tin foil until the hinges snapped and the door fell forward.

The creature stepped over the threshold and into pandemonium. Prisoners reached through their cells, and toilet paper streamers floated in the darkness. The two guards stood facing Lesovij, shotguns in their hands, but thoroughly unprepared for what they were seeing.

"Herbold! Planck! Don't let that thing touch you!" LaThanya yelled.

The two guards broke free of the fear that held them, and they each fired. The creature's ribcage exploded in a cascade of bone chips, then a chunk of skull and antler disappeared.

The creature took a step closer, and the wolf ran at them.

"No!" she shouted as Herbold lowered his shotgun and blasted the wolf mid-leap.

Her face hardened, and she walked swiftly forward, pulling out of the twisting vines. Her service weapon didn't have the caliber to do any real damage to this thing's skull, so she took careful aim its right leg instead.

Two more shotgun blasts, and pellets whistled past her unnoticed. Close enough, she fired. *Blam!* Just missed. *Blam!* Its fibula snapped in half. *Blam, blam!* A crack formed in its tibia, and the creature fell forward, its foot left behind. Its ribcage and skull were reforming as the three officers watched, but it was on hands and knees and missing a foot.

The guards took aim at its skull, and LaThanya flattened against the wall. *Blam!*

The skeleton, now headless, sat motionless. The bits of bone that had been stitching together, lay where they fell.

LaThanya stepped through the ruined doorway to Holding. "Are you two alright?" she asked, eyes on the wolf, that lay still, but breathed shallowly.

Planck ripped his leg away from the vines wrapped around it. "What was tha—"

The skeleton raised its arms and brought them down, pounding the floor with its fists.

Vines burst through from all directions, surging up around their legs and shooting up around the bars of the holding cells. The men inside, no room to escape, were wrapped in the thickening vines and crushed to death. A thick trunk dropped from the ceiling and looped around Herbold's neck.

Planck started screaming, and he dropped his weapon, ripping at the vines with both hands instead. Moments later, the screams choked off, and vines crept out through his open mouth, and still more exploded through his uniform shirt, tearing the man apart from the inside.

Bits of bone rattled along the ground, then shot back toward the figure, rapidly filling in all the missing pieces. It stood, turning toward LaThanya for the first time. A chunk of skull containing the right antler clicked into place as she tried to back away. The vines around her legs, too thick to break, bit into her leg. She screamed and dropped her gun, ineffectual against this creature.

Its eye sockets flared a deeper black, something darker than she'd ever seen, and the creature reached a finger toward her forehead.

LaThanya leaned back, desperate to get away, and fell over, laying in a pile of twisted, worming vines, eager to wrap around her.

"Quickly, Officer Barber!" It was Kučera's heavily accented voice. She located him, pressing his face between the bars of his cell at the far end of the corridor. "Say that you will die for him!"

"What?" She was staring death in the face, she wasn't going to die for the creature!

"He will not rest without a sacrifice! Say the words!"

"There's been plenty of death around here! None of that made him stop!"

The creature loomed over her, bending to reach for her head again.

"Death is not the same as sacrifice! He will kill until he receives one! You must say, 'I die for you, Lesovij!'"

The creature paused, its skeletal fingers inches from her head, its hungry eyes boring into her.

It turned and stomped off toward Kučera.

"No! No, my son, not me!" Kučera backed away from the bars. "I live for you! I worship you! I bring you sacrifice."

LaThanya ripped at the vines, twisting them until they broke, and unwinding the ones that wouldn't. More vines grew to replace the others, but they were fresh—easily broken. She stood, looking for her gun, dropped earlier and covered now in vines.

Herbold's shotgun still dangled from his lifeless fingers, and she grabbed that instead, stalking after Lesovij.

"Take her! She's the one you want," Kučera screamed from the back of his cell.

The creature reached his cell and gripped the bars. Smoke rose from the fingers curled around the cold iron bars, and it let go. Vines grew up in his place, and more snaked up through the toilet behind the old man.

"Lesovij!" LaThanya yelled. The creature turned its cold gaze toward her. "I make this sacrifice for you!" She leveled the shotgun and fired.

Kučera flew back against the wall of his cell and fell to the ground, leaving a spray of red behind.

Lesovij opened its mouth in a silent scream of ecstasy, then crumpled like a marionette.

"And that's why we have a lock on the basement door, and that's why you can never go in there without Mommy. Okay?" The story she told her daughter was not a full account of what happened that night, but hopefully it was enough to make her more scared than she was curious. It also explained why she didn't get to name any of the mice they raised and what Mommy did with them.

"It's almost dark, so I have to go feed him now. You can come with me if you want."

Shanie, now six years old and very precocious, shook her head.

"Are you sure? You can't come in once I close the door," LaThanya said, studying her daughter's eyes carefully. Shanie shook her head again. "Okay. Go watch your cartoons. I'll be right back."

LaThanya watched her go, then picked up the little paper bag with the tiny white mouse doing laps inside. She unlocked the latch and the deadbolt, put on her gloves, took the scissors from their spot next to the door, and climbed downstairs.

She flipped on the light. "Hello, you old bastard," she said.

The skeleton was completely devoid of flesh by now, but the bones still clung together via unknown means.

She set down the paper bag and the scissors just outside its circle. She pulled the fire lighter out of a nearby cabinet and lit the candles, then wrapped up yesterday's mouse and dropped it in the trashcan. She laid a fresh sheet of plastic wrap over the serving tray.

Sitting back on her haunches, LaThanya looked at her watch. She reached into the bag and pulled the mouse out, fitting the scissors into the space behind its jaw.

"I make this sacrifice for you, Lesovij."

Snip!

The Nocturnal Habits of the Late Derek Gray

I was just climbing into bed with my wife, Evelyn, when I got the phone call. Doug Chambers had shot Derek Gray, who lived upstairs from him. Everyone knew Doug, and it came as a shock that someone so good-natured could kill anyone, much less his best friend. But I'd been sheriff long enough that I've seen this sort of thing too often. I've come to believe that anyone was capable of murder, given the right trigger.

Bob and Chuck were already on the scene, and they were good enough deputies normally, but they were having trouble getting the gun off of Doug, so I had to go have a talk with him. I laced my boots back up and retrieved my gun belt from the back of the chair where I've been in the habit of leaving it ever since little Evie went off to college.

The apartment building turned crime scene was only a few blocks from my home, but the chill of winter blew through me in ways it never used to. My joints were aching already; they were likely to freeze solid on the short walk there, so I drove in the heated luxury of my '89 Cherokee.

Maine was dotted with small towns, and Pine Glen was smaller than most. It was the sort of place where the postmaster also ran the general store as well as the hall of records. There's an Episcopal church and a Methodist church, and everyone went to one or the other, and everyone knew everyone else. I counted both Derek and Doug as friends of mine. We were on a bowling team, together with Sue Petit rounding out the quartet.

I reached the apartment block where both men lived, steeled myself against the outside temperature, and took the elevator to the second floor.

Deputy Chuck was standing in the doorway to Doug's apartment with one hand on his service revolver. I nodded to Deputy Bob as I passed him along the way. He was taking statements from Doug's cross-hallway neighbors, Mrs. Lidell and Ms. Stevens. I put a hand on Chuck's shoulder to let him know I was there to take over. Doug was sitting hunched over on a step ladder with his elbows planted just north of his knees. A snub nose revolver dangled in his grip.

"Hiya, Doug," I said. His head lifted slowly until he was looking vaguely in my direction. "I hear you won't give up your gun to my deputies. You understand that's not okay, don't you?"

He looked back down at his gun as if he'd forgotten he was holding it. "Not yet," he finally said.

"Do you remember what happened, Doug?

What you did?" I asked. His eyes were sunken, his skin was gray and shone with sweat. His expression was that of a man who'd eaten something that disagreed with him. When he looked in my direction again, his eyes continued to dance like there was a firefly off my left shoulder.

"I didn't kill Derek," he said.

"Alright, Doug." I stepped into the room, keeping my own hands far from my weapon. I slid one of his kitchen chairs around and straddled it, leaning over the back and trying to keep Doug's attention. "Why don't you tell me what happened, then maybe you can hand me your gun."

I already had a good idea of what had happened. During my walk down the hallway, I had heard a bit of Ms. Steven's statement. She and Mrs. Lidell reported hearing three gunshots, whereupon they rushed (if the word "rushed" could ever be applied to the way two such ancient women move) out into the hallway, and moments later, Doug came down the stairs with a literal smoking gun.

"I want to tell you, Phil," Doug said. His demeanor had changed in a heartbeat. His eyes had lost their glassy vagueness and were instead boring into mine with a killer's intensity. I chanced glancing away from his eyes to verify which direction his gun was pointing. His grip had tightened, but the barrel was still pointing at the floorboards.

"Hey, Chuck?" I called out without breaking eye contact further. Out of the corner of my eye,

I saw the deputy step back into the doorway. "It might be a good idea to ask Mike and Amy downstairs to step out of their apartment for a bit, don't you think?"

Chuck agreed that it was a good idea and disappeared from my periphery again.

I dug my cell phone out of my breast pocket and looked away again long enough to find the voice recorder app. I started the recording and set the phone down on the table beside me. "Now, Doug, I'm going to record what you say, just to be sure we've got it all down right for later. You don't mind that, do you?"

"No, Phil, I don't mind. I want people to know what happened."

Doug and Derek went way back. They were practically inseparable in high school. They'd worked at the same bookstore and even went to prom as a foursome with the Eisner sisters. I couldn't imagine what his trigger had been.

"Alright, Doug. Go ahead."

He went straight into his story, as if he'd been preparing it. "I think it happened a week ago. All his odd behavior started about then, and the more I think about it, the more I'm sure it was during the game against the Sabres where Bergeron got the hat trick. Do you remember that one? Rick, Derek, and me were down at The Hazel, watching the Bruins game over a few beers, and one of your boys called him about that out-of-state car abandoned and blocking part of the 11. The idea was that he'd be there and back before third period, only he was gone the whole game. I stayed on another couple hours, half waiting for him, and half to see the college basketball scores. He never did come back. At the time, I figured something made him change his mind, because when I got home, I could hear him upstairs."

Doug paused, and his face slowly contorted into a pained grimace. For a moment he looked like he would genuinely cry, then his face relaxed and he went on.

"Something struck me as odd, even then. He was up all night moving furniture around or something, and there were these clicking and buzzing sounds coming from up there, but being a good neighbor, I didn't pry."

Doug turned to look me in the eye, suddenly lucid.

"When I mentioned the next day how he missed the game, he said he just forgot. Now, I've never known him to forget a hockey match, but I wasn't suspicious or anything—me and Rick just teased him is all."

Doug's eyes went distant again, and the pause in his story went on to the point where I felt he needed a reminder that I was there listening to him. "Go on," I said.

"Derek was…acting funny after that. It was like watching a movie about Derek's life, starring Gary Oldman. Sure, he could look just like Churchill, and he could speak just like Churchill, but it was still just acting. Someone was acting like Derek, or *something* was, anyway."

"What do you mean 'funny?'" I asked.

"He wasn't doing normal everyday things anymore. It was like a Cliff Notes version of his life. He still did all of Derek's favorite things, took care of his responsibilities—he ate Derek's favorite foods, he drove Derek's tow truck, he salted the roads and all, and he hung out with Derek's friends drinking Derek's favorite beer, but he didn't do all the in-between stuff anymore. You see what I mean, Phil? He never took out his trash or bought groceries or cooked at home. Nobody eats roast beef and gravy at The Hazel every day, with peach ice cream for dessert. Especially not at our age."

"I'll grant you, it's not usual, but that's not grounds for killing your best friend," I said.

"That's only part of it. The real kicker was the nighttime activity. As far as I could tell, Derek didn't sleep at all anymore. He spent all night buzzing and clicking and pushing around furniture. But even then, I didn't think that meant Derek had been replaced, just that something was going wrong with him. Remember what a wreck I was when my Hellen died? The thing is, I had no idea what triggered the change in Derek. I tried to be a good friend, only Derek kept saying he felt fantastic and nothing was different. Except, he *was*."

I didn't know what to say to that. I thought back to my interactions with Derek over the last week. He honked and waved to me when his plow passed the other day, and he invited me to sit with him when I stepped into the Hazel for coffee. If he was depressed, or different in some way, I sure didn't notice. But I nodded to Doug, so he'd finish his story. I was more than a little uncomfortable with his casual handling of the gun.

"Then the night before last, I woke to a high-pitched scream coming from above. It sounded like a living thing, and in the fearful rush of the moment, I pictured Derek chowing down on a cat. And even though I tried to dismiss the image as something Derek could never do, I just wasn't sure anymore. When the sound came a second time, I recognized it as the sound of an old nail being wrenched out of hardwood."

Just the mention of that sound put my teeth on edge. But it pointed to Doug's motive. If he'd been renovating at night, keeping Doug up... well, sleep deprivation can easily move a man to murder.

"I cursed and pulled the pillow down over my head, but the sound came three more times. Derek, or the thing pretending to be Derek, was pulling up the floorboards in his apartment. At two in the morning! I couldn't hold my tongue anymore. I put on my slippers and went upstairs to pound on Derek's door."

There hadn't been any noise complaints to my office, but ever since Preston's kids moved him to the Care Home down in Bradford, the room next to Derek's corner apartment had been empty. Doug was probably the only person to hear any noise he made.

"Now, it's been twelve years since my Helen passed, but I still remember what she used to say when someone came to our door unannounced. 'You'll have to get that, Doug, I haven't got my face on,' and she'd shut herself in the bathroom. And if it was one of her friends, she'd hurry with her makeup bag until she could stand to be seen."

"Sure, Evie is the same way, though she doesn't hide in the bathroom, she just expects me to turn them away."

"Well, Derek didn't have his face on, and he didn't have anyone else to answer the door for him while he put it back on properly. He pulled the door open just far enough to get his eye in the crack instead. 'Hey, Dougie! What brings you around?' he said to me. You see what I mean, Phil? It's that sort of thing, like we'd just happened to meet at the park on a Sunday afternoon.

"I yelled at him about the floorboards, and he apologized. He said, 'I'm really sorry about the noise, Dougie. I'll try to do it quieter.' Can you imagine? He was going to rip up the floorboards all night, 'a little quieter.'"

"Well, did he?"

"I didn't give him a chance to. I forced the door open, shoving him back in the process, and that's when I saw his face. Like a mask where the eye-holes don't line up quite right. The cheekbone sagged on one side and bulged on the other. And I saw behind him a pile of floorboards with slats visible in the space below, only there was no hammer or pry bar or whatever to do it with. What was he using, his bare hands?" Doug let out an acrid, swampy belch and clamped his mouth tight, swallowing.

"You okay, Doug?" I asked. I noticed his wastebasket near where I was sitting and slid it over to him with the toe of my boot. If I'd seen what he was describing, delusion or otherwise, I'd be sick too.

Doug shook his head. "I'm alright, Phil."

"So, that's when you started thinking he wasn't really Derek anymore," I prompted.

"Well, later that night, I sure did. Right then, I was too horrified to think much of anything. I was standing there in shock, looking back and forth between his face and the torn-up floor. It's what happened next that chilled me to the bone."

He swallowed hard, and his face went all pale again. I thought for sure he would be sick this time, but he took a couple deep breaths and looked straight at me.

"He invited me inside," Doug said. His eyes burned into me like he had to know I understood. "A moment ago, he wouldn't even open the door, but now he wanted me to come in and talk about things. I knew then and there that if I let that door close behind me, I wouldn't live to see it open again. I was the spy who'd seen too much, and now he needed to make me disappear."

Doug was shaking his head now. He reached up with one hand and grabbed a clump of his thinning hair, and for a moment, I thought he was going to rip it out of his head, but then he went on. "I backed away instead. I imagined him lunging for me with inhuman speed, but I forced myself to move slowly. I felt like running, but then he'd chase me down for sure. I wracked my brain for what to say that would get me out of there alive, but nothing came. Then he took a step toward me, and the words just flooded out. 'I don't wanna talk, I wanna sleep. Just knock off the noise.' I left the apartment, pulling the door shut between us.

"I knew it immediately. Sure as I know you won't believe it yet, Derek went out for that car last week, and something attacked him. Derek died that day, and whatever was walking around Pine Glen wasn't him. The more I thought about the way his skin didn't fit the skull underneath, the more I thought he wasn't even human. I barely kept myself from running down the hall first and then the stairs."

"But he didn't chase you. Did he let you sleep?"

"Even without the noises in the apartment above, I stayed awake all night imagining what was inside that Derek costume, and how it was prying up a floor without tools, and what could make those clicking, buzzing noises I've been hearing. Once I got the image of a praying mantis in my mind, I couldn't get it out again. I had all night to think, and I decided maybe it was looking for something in Derek's apartment. Something Derek hid, but this thing didn't know where that was."

"But how would that work?" I asked Doug. He seemed to be slipping into some sort of madness—maybe already had. I had to try to anchor him, help him see things rationally. "He's able to know all Derek's favorite things, he clearly remembers you—heck, he said hello to me a couple days back, and asked after my wife. So, if there's a thing living inside Derek, and it knows all this, how could it not know about something Derek hid?"

Doug nodded, and I thought maybe I'd gotten through to him to some degree, but he already had an answer for that. "I think it's like I said about all his favorite things. I think the thing that was living inside him ate his brain, Phil. And maybe it tasted all the memories he had in there. Maybe the things he thought about a lot had a stronger flavor. All his favorite things, all the people he saw day-to-day, they were clear. Identifiable. But other things are more like when you catch just a whiff of something that makes you think of your childhood. You didn't get enough to remember what it was, but you know it's there. You know what I mean, Phil?"

"Yeah, I think I do, Doug." I looked over at my phone to be sure it was still recording. Suddenly, I wanted this interview to be over. He should be talking to a doctor, not to me, in either capacity of sheriff or friend.

"The next day I called in sick and followed Derek on his rounds. I made sure to stay a few cars back, and park a block away from wherever he stopped. He never did anything Derek wouldn't do, but then I saw him talking to Maggie Lawson, and I got to thinking about what praying mantises do to their mates. So, I drove down to Bangor and bought a gun."

"Jesus, Doug. If you really thought there was some danger, why didn't you call me?"

"I knew I couldn't prove any of my suspicions, even if I could get you to believe me. If I got myself locked up and something happened to Maggie, I could never live with it."

Sometime during our little talk, Bob and Chuck had come back in, and I looked up to see them just then, listening to the story with rapt, worrisome attention. I was trying to think up some other errand to send them off on when Bob leaned in and whispered to me that the coroner was downstairs. I nodded my understanding, hoping they'd head back out on their own, but they kept where they were, listening.

"So tonight, it wasn't the screaming of nails, but the sound of chewing. If you've ever had a mouse in your place, you know the sound. I knew he'd finished with the floors, and now he was having a go at the walls, but he wasn't using tools, and I don't think it would be accurate to say he was using his teeth either."

"Mandibles," Chuck said, and I glared at him. Chuck was feeding into the fantasy Doug had concocted, and it was a leading statement. People had a way of latching onto suggestions, and suddenly they remembered things just that way.

"Chuck, how about you head down and keep Martin company? Tell him to hang on for a moment and we'll let him know when it's safe to come up." Chuck nodded and disappeared, but the word was out there and the damage was done.

"That's exactly right. Mandibles. I knew I was insane in that moment. All these things I'd imagined, everything I thought I saw, none of it could be real. And yet I was contemplating murdering the best friend I ever had. The thing is, I also knew I was right. Deep down, it was the only true thing I did know. But I had to prove it to myself. I had to see it. If he really was chewing on the walls with those mandibles I was imagining, I couldn't give him a chance to put his face back on. I had to surprise him.

"So, I snuck up the stairs and listened on his door. I heard that chewing noise again, and it set my teeth on edge. I stepped back against the far wall, then ran hard at the door, and hit it solidly with my shoulder." He paused his story to rub at his shoulder. "I banged up my shoulder pretty good, but it flew open, and that thing was kneeling there with its back to me. Derek's face was bundled up like a rubber mask at the base of its neck. It turned toward me with two huge segmented eyes, and I put three shots in its face. I think I went a little mad after that, because I honestly don't remember anything until your deputies came for me."

I let it go for a bit, just in case he had anything more, then I reached over and tapped a button on my phone to stop the recording. "Alright, Doug. I've got your story, and I'll make sure people hear it. Now I'm going to need your gun, and I'm going to have to put some cuffs on you. I'm not going to have a problem doing that, am I?"

Doug went all distant again, but he held the gun out toward me with one shaking finger in the trigger guard. I took it by the barrel and put it in my jacket pocket, then stood up to the familiar sound of both knees cracking, and took out my handcuffs. Doug stood up with tears in his eyes. "I don't feel so good, Phil. I-I think I may have hurt Derek."

Bob leaned in and said, "Should I go get Martin now?"

"I want you to take Doug down and sit with him in the Cherokee." I finished cuffing Doug and handed Bob my keys. "When you get downstairs, have them meet me here. We'll go up to floor three together. I still haven't had a look, and I need to take a few photos."

As soon as they stepped out, I took a few pictures of Doug's place with my phone. When I heard the elevator ding, I locked his door behind me and got in with Chuck and Martin.

Chuck was telling the coroner, "…but I don't think it was looking for anything. I watch a lot of Animal Planet, and I think it was nesting. Just because it was in Derek, doesn't mean it was male." Chuck raised his eyebrows knowingly.

"You knock that off right now, Chuck," I said. "I don't want to hear any more of this sci-fi nonsense."

The elevator doors opened onto the third floor, and I could immediately see Derek's ruined door jamb, and as we approached the doorway, all the damage to the floor.

I held out an arm to keep Martin from entering and took a few pictures of the state of the apartment. In addition to the piled-up furniture and the torn-up floorboards, there was a sickly, glistening residue smeared across half of it. Rows of lumpy greenish fist-sized objects were wedged between the beams under the floor and covered with more of the pungent goop.

Martin turned back toward Chuck. "Where's the body?" he asked.

"It's right in the middle of the room," he said, pushing between us to get a look.

But of course, it wasn't.

"Who's been up here since you and Bob took a look at the body?" I asked.

"Nobody, sir, I swear!"

"Well, he couldn't just wander off, now could he?"

Chuck was silent for a while, and I thought he was trying to think of who could've come up when he wasn't looking, but then he said, "The way I hear it, an insect can live for several days without its head."

In the stunned silence that followed, my radio crackled. "Oh, man, Phil, Doug just lost it all over your Cherokee.."

I stepped out into the hallway. "Don't call me, Bob, call Doc Howard! And get Doug some air!"

When I turned back, Chuck was kneeling by the floorboards in Derek's apartment. He turned to me with one of the objects in his gloved hand. "Are these…eggs?"

My radio crackled again, followed by indecipherable shouting. The only words I made out were, "…snapped his cuffs…"

Then the radio went silent, except for clicking and buzzing sounds.

The Ritual

In Marco's defense, until that moment, he hadn't fully believed that a demon summoning would work.

He watched the beast pull itself up through the planar rift.

Its head was a nightmare, an animal's skull with razor-sharp teeth and spines ringing its eye sockets. The flames that burned dark inside those sockets regarded Marco, dancing with amusement and ridicule, as the creature rose from the unfathomable depths.

The body that followed was a mockery of human form, with elements that were both reptilian and insectile. Its spine protruded through the scaly skin of its back, its corded muscles visible underneath, though its chest was encased in an exoskeleton, as if it were wearing the rib cage of a larger creature. The tail came last, no trace of skin attached to it, looking sharply vertebral, with a dagger-like point at the end.

As the beast curled up inside the circle that protected the outside world from this denizen of Hell, the tail poked and prodded at the edges, and the invisible dome of air that was its prison.

Despite being unsure, Marco *had* been careful. In fact, he'd been fastidious in his work, ensuring every detail was correct.

He'd spent the last few days working in this abandoned warehouse, clearing the space necessary, calculating measurements, mixing his own ink from raven's blood and graveyard dirt. He spent hours working on each sigil, reproducing them in exact detail from the ancient texts, and he'd tracked down scholars from around the world so that when he spoke those long-dead tongues, it was as a native would have. He was as safe as any mortal had ever been in this situation.

"You dare to summon me by name, mortal? I will suck the marrow from your bones as you watch!" A molten glow formed beneath its chest plate as it spoke, and its words sounded like they were produced by machinery normally reserved for crushing boulders.

The beast's name had been an important part of the ritual. No other creature would hear the call, nor would they be able to find their way to this plane. Which was good, because the circle would not bind them either. The one-way knowledge of names is what sealed the barrier.

"You have no power over me, demon, for I know your name, and you do not know mine. You are bound by the sigils, and by the contract until its conclusion."

Those words were also prescribed in the ancient texts. They weren't part of the ritual, more of an informal "handshake."

So. Demons were real, as were souls. And they were precious. Suddenly, a little thing like Amanda's affair with Marco's boss paled in scope.

Going through it in his mind, it sounded so petty now. Was any of that really worth his soul?

"First time?"

The question took Marco by surprise. It was casual, even conversational, and the voice behind it sounded close to human. Though it still had a timbre that hit Marco just behind the ear, like the sound of chains scraping together. "Pardon?" he said.

"Well, you're all first-timers, aren't you? I mean, you've only got the one soul to sell, am I right?"

The demon sat down cross-legged. Its tail came forward to scratch idly at its chin. "Do you mind if I offer you some advice?"

Marco said nothing. He was unnerved by the demon's sudden change in demeanor. He was also still trying to come up with a better wish. Mostly to buy himself some time, he nodded.

"I might be speaking out of turn, but I couldn't help notice. It looks like you're doing a lot of thinking. I've got to tell you, that rarely ends well."

"W-what do you mean by that?" Marco asked. His voice sounded weak in his own ears. He realized that thumping sound he'd been hearing was his own heartbeat. He'd need to calm down if he was to get through this.

"Well, generally, you've got two kinds of summoners. Those that have huge plans, rulership over empires, and that kind of thing. They've done a lot of thinking beforehand, and when they get here, they're ready. The other sort, they're working on adrenaline. Somehow, they managed to get the ritual right, and when the moment comes, they just blurt something out. No thinking involved. Both of those kinds of deals go just fine. The first sort get their soul's worth, and the second sort not so much, but the deal concludes, and both parties go home happy.

"Then there are the outliers. The ones that have to think about it. Those sort are filled with regret, and let me tell you, nothing weakens a mystic barrier like regret. You understand?" He put both clawed hands against the air beside him and pressed, ever so slightly.

"Now, I don't want to drag you to Hell without a deal. You look like a decent guy. How about you just tell me what you want, the bargain gets sealed, I go back, alone? You get your wish, and many years from now—God willing—you die, and I collect your soul."

"No, you misunderstand," Marco said. Weak-kneed, he too sat down cross-legged. "It's not about regret at all. It's just that I thought I was in that first category, the well planned out one? But now I'm thinking I might be in the second. My wish was really not soul worthy."

"Can I ask what it was?"

Marco's eyes narrowed.

"Look, I promise not to grant that wish unexpectedly just to steal your soul. I'm only curious."

Marco still wasn't sure, but he did it anyway.

"My girlfriend is pregnant with my boss's baby. I wanted the child to have horns and a tail that won't show up during any ultrasound. Despite the painful birth and hideous child, she would find she loved it, so she'd be stuck caring for it. The baby would repulse Percy, though, and he'd leave her for the next woman to come along. A crack addict who would lead to his financial ruin."

The demon doubled over laughing, a sound that surrounded Marco, seeming to brush against his skin and leave a chill in its wake. When it recovered, the demon wiped a lick of fire from the corner of its eye socket. "Oh, yeah. You'd be amazed how often we see something like that."

"And now I'm thinking maybe my soul is worth more than any other thing I might wish for," Marco confided. "Maybe I don't want to sell. Now, from what I read, if I cancel the deal, the barriers come down, but you get pulled back to Hell. You're going to try to take me with you, but what happens, hypothetically, if I run?"

The beast shook its terrifying head. "No, you don't want to go that way. Like I said, you mortals only get one shot at this. I've done this a thousand times. I've heard stories of demons that returned to Hell without either soul or plaything, but those are rare, and it's never happened to me."

Marco gulped.

"Look, I've got no skin in this. I showed up. At this point, I'll get what I want. If you make a wish, I get your soul. Otherwise, I get to torture you for eternity. It's nothing but upside for me.

"But if you end this deal, and I don't have the keys to a shiny new soul, I *will* drag you back with me and I *will* take it out of your hide. And I'll let you in on a secret that's not in the manual. After a few years of constant torture, most people will sign their soul away for a glass of tepid water."

"Okay. I get it."

A devilish thought occurred to Marco. "What would you wish for?"

"Well, the temptation to cheat the system would be overwhelming, wouldn't it? The contract covers most of that—the whole 'wishing for more wishes' and all that—but I'd come up with something tricky."

"That's it!" Marco said.

"You've got something? Okay, let's hear it." The beast rubbed its claws together.

"Alright, I was thinking that I'd wish to instantly know the true name of any demon, devil, imp or infernal—seen or unseen—that came into my presence, so that I'd always have power over them."

The beast's lip curled in a horrifying smile. "That's good. That's real good." It uncrossed its legs and got to more or less a standing position. "Now, make it official. Say, 'I wish,' and put all that negative emotion into it, Lust for power, Pride, Gluttony—you know, Deadly Sins sort of stuff. Oh, and good luck. I truly mean that, uh…"

"Marco. Marco Servantes."

A chill went down Marco's spine. He realized his mistake just as the beast stepped out of the formerly protective circle.

"And that's why they call me Defiler of the Wise."

The Raven

Okay, if you found this on my computer, I don't want you to freak out, and God, I hope I remember to keep canceling send. But if you are reading this on any of the sites I regularly publish to, it means I'm dead.

As you know, I've been working at Caffeine I.V. for like a month now. I know it's not a job that fully utilizes my skill set, and it's a huge pay cut from Apple, but I really needed to de-stress after the whole Mindy-pocalypse thing. So, I've been living off my savings and limiting my drinks to what I earn in tips. It's been good. I've even managed to get to the gym a few times like I always promised I would.

Anyway, when I went in for my shift a couple days ago, there was this girl sitting at one of the tables. She had a caramel macchiato frap with the name "Francine" on it, and she was typing away at the keys of her laptop. Her hair was spiked up platinum blonde, with blue ringlets that came down past her ears—my kind of look. Tons of earrings, and a pierced nose too. The only makeup she had on was eyeliner, and she wore tons of that. Leather jacket, jeans—pretty normal there. Oh! Silver nails. Not long, or anything, but they were like…reflective.

She stayed there through most of my shift too. She never ordered another drink—in fact, I'm not sure she ever drank the one she had, but she was sitting there typing away the whole time.

Right about 10:00 PM, I was emptying out all the trash cans, so I was out back for a minute, no more than that. When I came back, the girl was gone. One of my coworkers was on bar, and the other was working drive-thru, so they didn't notice, but Francine left her laptop and a bag behind. The laptop was a new model too—an i7 MacBook Pro 15 inch with the Touch Bar. You know I know my Apple stuff, so believe me when I tell you, this is not the sort of thing you want to leave behind.

There were a couple other customers in the place, so I kept an eye on her stuff while I cleaned up. I figured she must be in the bathroom, but she never came out. I told Linsi I was going to clean the johns, and I knocked on both of them, but no one was in there. At closing time, she still hadn't come back. I took a quick look through her bag. There were five amber vape tubes or something, along with an eyeliner pencil and some tampons but I didn't see any ID, so I closed it up and put it and the laptop in the crate behind the counter we use as a lost-and-found.

Yesterday was my day off, so flash-forward to today, and the laptop was still there. I couldn't believe she never came back for it. I was really starting to…well, I don't want to say worry, but I was really wondering about her. So, during my break, I went into the back and took a look at the security tapes from that night.

Just before 10:00 I could see myself walk out back with the trash bags, then all of a sudden, the screen just glitches. I'm not making this up. It just went all staticky, but not even the whole thing, just this one stripe across the middle, like right where she was sitting. It was there for thirty seconds or so, then everything went back to normal, except the girl was gone.

So, I checked the camera out in the parking lot, and twenty seconds after the glitch inside, there was another one outside, just covering the front door. I rolled the footage back, frame by frame, and for just one frame right before the glitch, I could see something blazing white right inside the window.

Now, I was in cyber-security, so I know a thing or two about hacking, but this was some next level stuff. I could probably break into the security system at Caffeine I.V., it's not like it was Fort Knox or something, but I would just shut it down. I have no idea how they put that bar of static across the cameras.

So, break over. Now I was worried for real. I kept hoping she'd come back in, and we'd have a good laugh, but closing time came around, and she still wasn't there. I know we're not supposed to, but I decided to take the laptop home with me. If I cracked her password, maybe she'd have her contacts on there, and maybe it would have her address. When it was time to go, I waited until nobody was looking, then I stooped down really quick and stuck it in my bag.

I rode back to my apartment and called out, "Siri, I'm home!" and she responded with her standard, "Hey there." I set my satchel down next to my computer and pulled out Francine's laptop, almost screaming when I did so. There was a handprint on it in something red and sticky. I don't want to say it was blood, but that's exactly what it looked like.

The thing is, that handprint wasn't there when I put it in the crate two days ago—I swear to God. I walked away because my heart was racing, and I even grabbed the phone, thinking I'd call the cops. But then I thought about the fact that I'd technically stolen the laptop. And what if someone had just spilled some of our sugar-free raspberry syrup, and they put a hand on the laptop before washing it off?

"Siri, that's not blood, is it?"

"I'm sorry, I don't know that."

"Siri, what use are you then?"

"That's not very nice."

I put the phone back and promised myself I wouldn't involve the cops. If this thing started looking like kidnapping and murder, I would just drop the laptop in the industrial document shredder behind where I used to work and wash my hands of the whole thing.

I sat down at my desk, where the laptop was, and stared at the palmprint. I could make out all the ridges and whorls of the fingerprints on this slender, feminine handprint.

Raspberry syrup, I told myself. Then I decided to prove it to myself. Blood doesn't show up on a laptop two days after someone's murdered.

With shaking hands, I picked up the laptop, and I stuck out my tongue. Inside, I was screaming at myself, but the only way to shut up that part of my brain was to prove it, so I forced my arms to bring that laptop closer and closer to my tongue. I screwed my eyes shut so I wouldn't have to see it.

I couldn't do it. I put the laptop back down and took a couple deep breaths, then I realized I should be able to smell the syrup. I leaned in really close and sniffed. Then I drew in a deep breath through my nose.

It didn't smell like raspberries. In fact, it didn't smell like anything really, except my apartment.

This was crazy. It wasn't blood. This was not the girl's handprint, it was probably Andrea's. She's new to the coffee shop and super-clumsy. I opened the laptop. I would crack her password, and I'd find where she lives, and I'd bring it back to her, and that would be it and this wouldn't be blood.

I stared at the login prompt.

What did I know about her? Not a lot. She typed pretty fast, so she was probably a developer, or maybe a writer. She was young—twenty or so. She had a picture of Tank Girl up as her login background, so she's into obscure comics. I had a sudden epiphany. "Hey Siri, what was Tank Girl's boyfriend's name?"

"Tank Girl had a boyfriend who was a mutated kangaroo named Booga."

"Right. Booga. Thanks Siri." I tried that as her password, and the interface shook at me to let me know I had screwed up. "Thanks for nothing."

I sat back and stared at it for a bit, trying to imagine what else she'd use. My eyes came to rest on the Touch ID fingerprint reader.

I could prove that this hand print wasn't hers.

I closed the laptop and searched in my drawer for some scotch tape. Carefully laying a strip of it across the index finger of the hand print, I lifted off a perfect red impression. I opened the laptop back up, wrapped the tape around my own index finger, and pressed it to the reader.

The login prompt became a smiley face, and briefly flashed up a message, "Welcome back, Francine!"

My heart was all up in my throat at that point. And things were about to get worse.

Now, I've heard a lot about the dark web. Hell, I've had to dip my toe in it a time or two on the job, but mostly it's rumors. Cryptocurrency and hired killers. Drug smugglers and tall-tales. I really never believed most of it was any more than fear mongering to sell identity protection rackets. This Francine was all over it though, and the client she used didn't look familiar. This wasn't Tor or I2P, anyway.

She had some sort of bidding site, front and center, called SoulForge. The things on offer and sought after freaked me out even further. An unregistered gun. A virgin redhead girl. Two pints of O Positive. A child under two months.

I quickly opened her mail app, just to get that off the screen. I couldn't believe that she was into anything like that.

The most recent email was from two weeks ago, and it informed "friends and family" that she was no longer working for *The Chronicle*, and this was now her main email. She wasn't looking for work at the moment, and she had things to work out regarding her sister.

I assumed it was the *San Francisco Chronicle* she was talking about. Looks like Francine was a reporter. There was no other contact information, so I moved on. I found one from a day before that, where she forwarded herself something from her work account. The signature line contained two numbers marked home and cell.

I tried the cell number first, but it went straight to voicemail. I looked at my watch, and saw it was pretty late, but not yet midnight. I decided to try the home number. Someone picked up. They said something which could have been hello, but I couldn't hear it well. I can be hard to understand when I'm just woken up too. "Hi, this is Joseph, from the internet cafe. You left your laptop behind, and I just wanted to let you know we had it."

No one spoke on the other end, but I heard some quiet clicking.

"Hello?" I said.

"Hello, Joseph." It was a man's voice. He spoke with an accent, German maybe? "This is not Francine. Do you know who I am?"

A chill went up my spine. I found it difficult to speak over the sound of my own pulse. "No, I'm looking for Francine," I managed to say, though it came out as little more than a breath.

"I am called the Raven. I clean up problems. Francine was becoming a problem. Are you a problem, Joseph?"

"No, I'm not a problem. I'm just trying to do the right thing."

"Ah. I can see you are at home right now." I looked and saw the little green light on Francine's laptop was active. Her camera had switched on! I ran over to shut it, but the Raven spoke again. "Stop right there, Joseph."

A window popped up on the laptop, showing me, live. "Do not close or disconnect the laptop, Joseph. I am coming to collect it. If I lose touch with you, that will be a problem for me. You don't want to be a problem, do you, Joseph?"

My hands were slippery with sweat, and my breathing was no longer under my control. It was coming out in wheezes, and I couldn't stop it.

"Good. I will see you soon then." He hung up.

I did my best to slow my breathing. He didn't say anything about the microphone, so I put the laptop on mute. "What was this girl into?" I asked myself.

It occurred to me that I'd better find out. I switched back over to the SoulForge interface and clicked on her account. Transaction history was listed, so I clicked on that.

There was nothing on offer, and no purchases, but she'd made several queries to different sellers. All had the same question: "Do you have my sister? I can pay to get her back."

Human trafficking. Holy crap. She was offering five soulshards for her. That seemed to be the cryptocurrency this site used. "Hey Siri, what's five soulshards in US dollars?"

"I'm sorry, I don't know that."

I tried again. "Siri, what is a soulshard worth?"

She thought for a moment. "I don't know what a soulshard is."

A cryptocurrency so deep-web that Apple's search engine couldn't find it. That was odd. In any case, they must be valuable. If movies were any indication, ransoms went for tens of thousands of dollars.

I switched back over to Francine's email. And looked up her contacts. Under family, she had Mom, Dad, and Darla listed. "Hey Siri, look up Darla Eastbrook."

"I found a Facebook memorial page, and an obituary in the *San Francisco Chronicle*."

A chill went down my spine again. Francine was looking for a sister who was dead? I slid the chair over to my computer and selected the link Siri offered for the obituary. I scanned the article quickly. Darla had died two months ago and was buried here in Santa Clara. She was survived by father Martin, mother Mary, and sister Francine, so it was definitely the same Darla. I tried searching for "Darla Eastbrook grave robbing," but came up empty.

Francine was desperately searching for her dead sister. What the hell could that mean?

I switched back over to the laptop, and that green light of the camera burned back into me. He was watching.

It suddenly occurred to me that I had never

connected the laptop to my home network. How was it even online? I checked its network connections, and it listed "Undernet" with two bars. I'd never seen Undernet before. A quick check confirmed that it didn't show up on my desktop computer. I right-clicked on the laptop's Undernet connection and got a dialog I'd never seen before. This wasn't a TCP IP connection.

I picked up my phone and called my buddy Zhao. He still works at Apple in my old group, but he was the hardware side of things. The company rented a thirty-thousand-dollar machine for him that could trace any kind of connection. I had the sudden urge to know a little about the man who was coming for me. The one who probably disappeared Francine.

Zhao verified that he still had the machine, but said I'd have to come to him. There's no way he could bring the machine to my place. I looked back at the green light on the laptop. He'd warned me not to shut it down, but what could he do if I wasn't here when he arrived?

"Hey Siri, should I be worried about this Raven guy finding me?"

The lights flickered. Just when I thought the power was going out, they came back.

"I think you should kill yourself, right now," Siri replied.

"What?" All the blood drained from my head, and I felt ready to pass out.

"So, are you coming, or what?" came Zhao's voice on the other end of the phone.

I kept staring at my computer, where Siri's last suggestion was still up on screen. "Yes, I'm coming."

I hung up the phone and typed up this post. It's prepped to send to *The Chronicle*, though I have no reason to think they'll believe any of it. It'll go to my various writers' forums, and on a whim, I added Creepypasta. That might be the only place that will actually print it, even if they don't believe it.

I'm going to Zhao's. I know what the Raven said, but I have no reason to trust him, even if I do everything he says. I want to find out whatever I can about him, and I don't feel like being here when he shows up. If I'm not back online by 1:00 AM, this will go out, because it probably means I'm dead.

I'm back online. I made it to Zhao's house, and I've disobeyed the Raven. I don't know if this is going to cost me, but I had to send an update, because more stuff has happened.

Back at my apartment, I closed up the laptop and ran with it under one arm and my bike under the other, then pedaled the eighteen blocks to Zhao's apartment. The lights kept switching to red just before I got there. It was after midnight, and there were few other cars on the road, so I was the only person being stopped. After seeing my own Siri being hacked, and whatever that flicker was with my apartment lights, I was feeling paranoid.

Was somebody watching me from all the traffic cameras? Was somebody intentionally delaying me from getting where I was going? I waited for about five seconds at each light, then if no one was coming the other way, I went through it anyway. I never did see a light go back to green, but I got to Zhao's place, anyway.

Zhao had the ELX 9000 set up and waiting. Before I opened up the laptop, though, I told him about the Undernet. He'd never heard of it either, but said it must be a tunneling protocol over IP.

"It wouldn't show up under standard Wi-Fi, but if the machine is registered to look for it, it will find it. It's probably a low-power wide-access signal." He was busy hooking the laptop up to his machine as he spoke. He paused before lifting the lid. "You ready?"

"Hang on," I said.

The handprint was gone. I ran my fingers over the surface. Even if it had rubbed off during the bike ride over, it should have been sticky. But there was no trace of it. Had I imagined the whole thing?

"You okay?" Zhao asked.

I nodded.

Before shutting it down, I'd disabled the login password so I wouldn't have to do the fingerprint thing again. Good decision, as it turned out. It went straight to Francine's desktop when Zhao opened it, and a second later, the green light of the camera came back on.

"Is it still on mute?" he asked. I nodded again.

"Okay. Let's see who's watching."

He began punching buttons on the ELX, and a readout came up on a small screen. "Okay. Looks like the laptop is putting out a lot of stuff, and some of this is just going out to anyone. But that one there? That VLC file is your video stream, and it's going to only one recipient. We've got his IP and MAC Address. The question is, what do you want to do with it?"

"Can we blacklist him? Prevent him from capturing any of our data packets?"

"If he's already got a trojan on this system, and it sounds like he has, it might be impossible. It could also just be the nature of this tunneling protocol. Do you want to run an antivirus?"

"No, never mind that. If it is the protocol that allows this access, then maybe we can see what he's broadcasting, maybe even switch on his camera?"

"Yeah. Let's see what we can find at his address." Zhao started typing, trying to send a brute force request to the Raven's IP.

"Watch out though, this guy's good. He hacked my Siri in a matter of seconds."

Suddenly a dialog popped up. Zhao stopped typing, thinking he'd done something wrong, but I recognized it as being from the SoulForge app.

"I have Darla. Willing to trade."

"It's one of the sellers that Francine contacted about her sister! Maybe something good can come from all this after all."

"You didn't tell me anything about a kidnapped sister!"

"She isn't kidnapped…exactly. She's dead.

Tell him I'll trade. Her body for five soulshards. Then we can call the cops to be there when they bring her body, and this can all be over."

"I'll trade. Five soulshards for Darla's body," he said as he typed. "Soulshards?"

"Some sort of cryptocurrency. I've never heard of it either." He hit enter, and we waited for the response.

"This isn't Francine," the seller finally wrote.

I pushed Zhao out of the way and started typing. "No, it is. Please, let's make the trade."

"Francine knows it isn't Darla's body that I have. Also, Francine is dead."

I sat back from the keyboard. "That is so messed up," Zhao said.

Suddenly another window popped up, and a video played. I let it run for a few seconds before I turned the sound on. "No! No!"

The video was from a car dashboard, like in *Taxi Cab Confessions*, but all you could see of the driver was his right arm. Francine was in the back seat, struggling to fight off a man in a long gray coat, wearing a mask with a long beak, and thick dark goggles. The overall effect was that of a bird. A raven.

The man was trying to stick her with some sort of syringe with a pistol grip and a large glass ampule on top. She was holding onto both his wrists and trying to force him back away from her. She continued to scream throughout the video, as it looked like he was slowly overpowering her. Then she managed to get her back against the passenger door, and one of her feet up! She kicked him in the chest and held him back with her leg.

There was a knife in her hand. I didn't see where it came from. I thought she'd use it on the Raven, or at least use it to fend him off, but she reached up and slit her own throat.

"Oh, God," I said, backing away from the screen. Zhao made a sound like he was going to be sick.

She sputtered and gurgled as blood sprayed out. "No!" This time, it was the Raven who was yelling, as he tried to get at her, and she continued to hold him back with her outstretched leg and every ounce of her sapping will.

Finally, she sagged, dropping the knife. The Raven pushed her leg to the side and reached for her wrist. It looked like he was checking for a pulse.

Suddenly the scene in the car was gone, and the Raven's mask filled the screen.

"Hello again, Joseph. You shut down the computer and you ran, even though I told you not to. Luckily, this is not a problem for me."

A dialog popped up again, overlaying a corner of the video. It showed a map, with a pin over Zhao's apartment. "I am the one who has Darla. And I know where you are, so do not lie to me again." Then he turned slightly. "And, who is your friend?"

Zhao panicked and slammed the cover of the laptop.

"What are you doing?!" I yelled.

"Dude, we've got to get out of here! He knows where we are, and we just watched him starring in a snuff film!"

"But, where can we go?" I asked.

"We'll go to my office. The building has security guards, so this guy won't be able to get us, and there's another ELX there. We can call the feds and give them the IP addresses and stuff. Maybe they can take him down. Or at least shut him down."

"That's a really good idea," I said. "Give me a minute. I need to update an email, in case I don't make it out of this. Let me use your computer."

"Go ahead. It's in the bedroom. I'm going to pack up some stuff."

I headed into his bedroom to update this post, and to push forward the auto-send to 2:00 AM.

"Don't look at my browser history!" Zhao yelled after me. Right. Even in the face of kidnapping and murder, you have to remember the important things.

Hopefully I'll have a chance to update this before 2:00. If not, then...well, goodbye.

Oh my God.

I'm back online, but barely. I feel like all the life has been drained from me.

We didn't get out of Zhao's place quickly enough. The Raven caught up with us.

Just as I finished the last update, the lights in Zhao's apartment started flickering. I hurried and set the auto-send just in case we lost power, and moments later we did. I wasn't used to Zhao's bedroom, so I had to find my way back to his main room in the dark. I managed to kick something hard enough to bruise my ankle, and while I was holding it in pain, I heard Zhao screaming in the next room.

I ran toward the sound with my arms out in front of me and hit the wall. As I was feeling around for the door, the screaming stopped, and then I heard another sound. It was like a firecracker going off, but muffled—like it was in a box stuffed with cotton. It was followed by rain, like a sudden and brief summer squall.

I found the doorknob and threw it open. My heart was pounding, dreading what awaited me there.

Barely enough light streamed in through the window that I could make out most of the room. Zhao was missing. Everything else was covered in blood and gore. As if Zhao had exploded— that's not possible though, is it? People can't actually explode like that, can they?

I vomited. It had been hours since I had anything to eat, but something came up, and after that I wretched some more until tears came to my eyes. I just couldn't stop gagging.

Then I noticed one small area was still clean. Somehow that area had no blood on it, where the entire rest of the room—couch, curtains, television, shelves, kitchenette—everything I could make out in the gloom was soaked in blood. That area was in the shape of a person, and right in the middle of the clean spot was the laptop.

I half-ran, half-slid across the room and grabbed the laptop, then turned and sprinted for the door. I don't know why I went for the laptop. I wish now I'd just left it.

A section of the gory wall near the door moved to step in my way. I backpedaled fast and ended up slipping on the blood and falling to the floor. It was the Raven, covered from head to toe in blood, except for the goggles, which had been wiped clean. He took a step toward me, and I pushed myself backward, scrambling to move on this slippery floor, and only managing to spread the blood all over me.

"Good evening, Joseph," he said in his calm, heavily accented voice. "It is good to finally meet in person."

He brought his hands up as he walked slowly toward me. He held that syringe gun in one hand, but now the ampule was full of an amber fluid, but dimly glowing. With a click and a hiss, he pulled the ampule off and placed it in a pocket of his coat with a gloved hand.

"Get away from me," was all I managed to say. I was panicking again. I didn't feel in control of what I said.

"No, Joseph. Not until I get what I came for." His hand came back out of the pocket with an empty ampule, which he attached to the gun. "You have the woman's soulshards?"

I'd backed all the way against the wall, and he was still approaching. I held out the laptop. "Here! They're on this computer. You can transfer them yourself!"

The Raven chuckled. "No, Joseph. I'm afraid

they are *not* on the computer. You still don't understand what we deal in. No matter. I will extract payment another way."

He leaned down and reached toward me with the syringe outstretched. "No!" I cried, which only made him chuckle again.

He was aiming that thing for my chest! "Now, there may be a slight...explosion," he said.

Something inside me snapped. I swung at that mask with the laptop, as hard as I could, and somehow, I connected. His head whipped to the side, and he fell to the ground next to me. The syringe slid across the floor, and I got to my feet.

I ran, nearly tumbling again, but I made it to the door and threw it open. My bike was leaning against the wall. I looked back for a moment to see the Raven crawling toward the syringe. I grabbed my bike and ran with it toward the stairs.

The lights flickered again. I didn't understand it—I thought the Raven was doing that, hacking into the power grid somehow, but now he was crawling across the blood-covered floor of Zhao's apartment. I ignored it for now and plunged down the stairs.

Then the lights went out entirely, and I was again in darkness. I stopped, feeling a mix of claustrophobia and vertigo, like the darkness was full of hands that were reaching out for me, wanting to pull me over the railing to break my neck on the ground below.

A moment later, the lights came back and Francine was standing there in front of me, complete with slit throat. I screamed, nearly falling backwards, and let go of my bike to catch the railing. The bike bounced down the stairs and through Francine as she stared at me, her eyes urgent. Her lips moved, but I had no idea what she was saying. The lights flickered again, and she was gone. I seized my moment and ran down the rest of the stairs, grabbed my bike and rode away.

So now I'm here. Back at the Caffeine I.V. where it all started. I could never get past the security guards at Apple without Zhao there, and especially not covered in his blood. So, I came here, where I have keys to get me in, and an internet connection to send this out. Also, those soulshards.

I only put two and two together after I thought about the Raven changing out that ampule, but Francine had a bunch of those in her bag. If you remember, I thought those were vape tubes or bath bombs or something, but now I realize they are living souls. My God, people are trading in actual souls! That's why Darla is still out there, even with her body buried. That's what Francine wanted to trade for, her sister's soul.

And that brings the question, how did Francine get ahold of five of them? It doesn't look like she's totally innocent in all this, but I may never get her full story. And now her ghost is following me around. Holy crap, when was that video in the car taken? What if that was her ghost sitting at the table to begin with? Was she dead this whole time?

I've opened the laptop again. The green light is still on, so the Raven will be here. I'm going to try to offer him these five soulshards for my life. I can threaten to break them if he doesn't agree.

I wonder what happens if I break the glass. Does the soul inside go free, or does it die? Does it get stuck here as a ghost? What the hell do people do with them, anyway?

One thing I'm sure of is that it had to be something horrifying if Francine would rather kill herself than end up like her sister. And Zhao…No. I was going to make damn sure I didn't go out like that. If the Raven doesn't take the deal, not only is he going to lose out on these soulshards, he won't be extracting his payment from me either. And just maybe, I can take him with me too.

Ten minutes ago, I blew out the pilot lights and turned on the gas. When I took Francine's soulshards out of the lost-and-found, I picked up a Zippo lighter too.

So now I'm waiting at that same table Francine had two nights back. The ampules are duct taped under the table, so all I have to do is crush them with my knee. In one hand I've got a bagel slicer—it's a crap blade, I know, but it ought to saw through an artery okay—and in the other hand, I've got the Zippo.

I only see three ways this can go. If he takes the deal, I'll see you around town and this mail will never go out. If he rejects the deal, I'm going to do my best to smash those ampules and blow the two of us up.

If he somehow stops me, Caffeine I.V. is going to be one big blood stain, and you'll know I'm out there somewhere, for sale on the dark

web.
    And I hope you'll find me.

Trick of the Light

"Have a good weekend, Quill," Pedro said. David Quill closed his locker and spun the dial on the combination lock, then turned back and waved, paycheck clutched in his hand.

The construction site would one day be a block of high-class apartments, but Quill's team were just starting to add windows to the ugly yellow DensGlass sheathing on the lower floors, while Pedro and his team were wiring the top level.

"You need a ride, Dave?" Barney asked as he locked up his own hardhat and tool belt.

"Nah, I'm not going far. See you Monday," Quill said, hanging up his hard hat on his way out of the construction yard. His paycheck wasn't going far either, if he was honest. He'd be lucky to make it home in the morn with any of it left.

Quill made his way down the hill, taking in the sea air as he reached Front Street. The call of the gulls always tugged at his heart. He still thought of himself as a sailor, despite the thirty years since he'd set foot on the deck of a ship.

The wharf on Front Street, and the Sailor's Shanty tavern was the closest he got these days. But even still, it wasn't like it was in the old days. Sailors had respect for the sea. His face turned sour as he watched a ship putting out to sea. On a Friday. Worst kind of luck, sailing on the day Christ was murdered.

Someone standing in his path brought Quill's attention back to the sidewalk he was on. The man's shock of red hair startled Quill—another bad omen! The man smiled, looking like he was about to apologize.

"Evening," Quill said before the man could speak. The only thing worse than running across a redhead so near the sea was if they spoke first. He pushed past the man, but stopped short when he heard the man whistle some familiar Irish tune. Quill turned to watch the man walking away, whistling straight into the wind. Was he mad, or did he really not know what evils he was whistling up?

As he turned back to sea, a ship coming in past the breakwater caught his attention—a wooden sailing ship with three tall masts. It had been ages since he'd seen a ship like that, and it tugged at his soul. It had been a rare enough sight thirty years ago when he sailed on one. These days they were all fiberglass and cold steel. The ship's flag flared out in the wind, showing the colors of the Gloria In Excelsis. His ship. Drowned with all hands aboard.

"No," he said, heart catching in his chest. The wind lulled, and the flag went slack before he could be sure. A cold sweat stood out on his face.

For a moment, he was back in the lifeboat, the lone survivor rowing away as the mast sank. That flag—illuminated by a flash of lightning as it slipped below. He couldn't have seen what he thought he had.

Still, that was one too many bad omens for Quill. He pulled his coat tighter and spit three times over his left shoulder. At least the Sailor's Shanty had a tabby cat. A little good luck to balance the bad.

As he opened the door, the cat zipped out. "Devil take you, Trim!" the owner said, pushing past Quill as he chased after the cat. So much for luck. Perhaps he should just shoot an albatross and get it over with.

He signaled the bartender and sat at a small table at the back of the room, facing the door. The tavern was set up to look like the cabin of some old galleon, and the owner claimed it used to be, but Quill knew better. Decorative wrought iron nails stuck out of the rough-hewn planks, giving the place a rustic, old-world ambiance. But in a galleon, everything would be mortis and tenon joints with wooden dowels and pine pitch.

The bartender brought him a bottle of whiskey, a shot glass, and a pen. Quill quickly signed his paycheck over to the bar. "The rest in cash?" Quill said.

"Sure, Quill. How'd your day go?"

"Still tryin' to get my land legs," Quill said as he usually did, pouring himself a shot.

"I hear ya," the bartender said. He picked up the check and headed back toward the bar.

Quill leaned back in his chair, sucking on his

whiskey and watching the other patrons in the low light of the bar. Some played darts, others added songs to the rotation at the jukebox. Most just sat and ate and drank and talked and told jokes. As the night wore on, the door opened more frequently, and with each new group of patrons came glimpses of a worsening sky.

There had been a storm brewing that night so long ago. That first lightning strike had startled him, but it had also doomed the ship. Maybe it hit the rudder, or maybe it ripped the sail, but whatever it struck, it put them on the rocks, and it set the deck alight.

He shook himself out of his reverie and went back to watching the other patrons as a distraction.

His bottle was around a third gone at the point where one man at a table he was watching passed the salt to another. Quill shoved his chair back and lurched to the Cabin Boy's room. These people didn't belong in the Sailor's Shanty. Playing their rock music and thumbin' their noses at fate! Any sailor knows to place the salt on the table and let the other feller pick it up. These people didn't know the life of a sailor or the feel of the roll beneath their feet.

Quill stood at the urinal, offended by people who would shun a life at sea, a life denied him since that night…

The lights flickered, and a peel of thunder cried out. He found himself fighting through the spray as he ran across a tilting deck, the screaming of sailors and the splintering of tortured wood filling his ears. He reached out for anything to arrest his fall into the drink, his hand closing around the urinal cap.

The bathroom was back, but the storm continued to rage beyond the frosted windows. Quill let go of the urinal and zipped up, then stood still long enough to be sure the world wouldn't flip back again. He asserted himself with a loud throat clearing.

"You see what you've done? Bloody landlubbers," Quill said to the empty restroom.

He stumbled back into the tavern proper, his mind still on that fateful day thirty years ago. Before he made it to his chair, the door blew open, and a man stood in its frame. Lightning blazed like a flashbulb, throwing the man into silhouette, and yet, Quill felt he recognized his stance, his canvas slicker, the cut of his Sou'wester hat.

The door swung closed, and the man removed his hat, twisting it to wring out the rainwater. It was him! And by the way the man stared into Quill, he was recognized as well.

Omar Polat, midshipman on the Gloria approached his table. Quill backed up against the wall.

"No. You died!"

It was the drink. He was seeing things. All these bad omens made him think of that night, and Polat stepped right out of his nightmares. Quill closed his eyes. He had reached for Polat, tried to pull him toward the lifeboat, but the deck split and Polat fell away, tangled in lines and the limbs of corpses.

Polat was dead. They were all dead. It was a

tragedy, but it was also a fact.

He opened his eyes again, but Polat was still there.

"This isn't possible. I watched you die."

Polat continued to stare silently.

"Hey, you okay there, Quill?" the bartender asked, pulling Quill's attention from the specter before him. The bartender was looking around the room, and for the first time, Quill noticed all eyes were on him. "You're making me a little nervous here."

"Bill! Do you see him? This man by my table?"

"What about him, Quill? Is he bugging you? Do you want me to call the cops?"

Then it wasn't the drink…Quill stepped forward, getting a better look at him, but there was no mistaking it. This was Polat. Quill picked up his shot glass and tossed it at Polat.

Polat caught it. A mirthless smile spread across his face.

Thirty years of guilt fell away in one moment, and Quill rushed forward, throwing his arms around the man. Polat made no move to return the hug, but Quill kept it up, clinging to his former shipmate like a life ring.

Quill let go, and called to the bartender, "Another glass for my friend!"

"Sit with me. Please," he asked Polat, taking his own seat. "Tell me how you survived."

Polat pulled out the chair across from Quill and sat. The bartender brought a second shot glass and set it down in front of him. Quill poured two shots, whiskey going everywhere from the way his hand shook.

Polat ignored his glass while Quill drank. "You tell me what you remember," Polat said, his voice raspy as if he hadn't used it in years.

"I haven't stopped thinking about it since that night. Once we ran upon the rocks, it was chaos on the deck as men ran every which way. Fire cut off the starboard lifeboats, and the growing swells swept sailors overboard or slammed them against the bulwarks. The mast split." He swallowed hard. "It came down on the captain's head." He closed his eyes, but couldn't shake the vision of the captain's head splitting like a dropped melon. Polat didn't interrupt. "The men launched the port lifeboats but quickly found themselves between the hull and the rocks. I reached for you. There was one boat left to starboard. But the ship lurched. The deck splintered, and you went down as the forequarters sank."

Polat smirked, poking at Quill with one bony finger.

"You are lying to yourself. Maybe for so long you believe it by now. You've forgotten it was your turn at watch for rocks off the bow, but like so many times, you'd had too much rum. 'For warmth,' you always said." He put his pale and pruny finger in Quill's face. "But you fell asleep."

"It's not true. I—"

He slammed his fist on the table, startling Quill and spilling his whiskey to mix with the water that still dripped off him.

"You've had your say, now I'm saying mine."

Quill reached a shaking hand for the comfort

of the whiskey bottle, but it sliced into his hand. Barnacles covered the glass, and a crust of salt had formed over the neck. He tore his bloody hand away, while Polat continued.

"It was as you said, the ship breaking apart, the captain's death, the men panicking and boarding boats fated to crash, but *you* were the cause, and the sea itself punished us for your carelessness! The ship was claimed and all hands with it. I might have made it to that lifeboat, defying all the odds, but you pushed me out of your way. In the moment I fell, the captain's corpse jumped up and held me firm. He dragged me down while I watched you climb into that last boat."

The other conversations around the tavern had gone silent. The room was watching the two of them. Quill envisioned everything Polat said. He'd drunk it away all these years, denied it even to himself, but the disaster was his fault. And he'd always known the sea wasn't done with him. That was why he'd never gone back, but he'd also never left.

He didn't bother to deny it, even the part where he'd thrown Polat out of the way. He could see the two versions overlapping. Reaching for his hand, and pushing him aside, and now he couldn't remember which was true.

The one thing he was sure of was the captain's corpse, even with half his head missing, dragging Polat down.

Quill stared, Polat's intense eyes daring him to deny his story. Instead, Quill asked, "How did you get away?"

Polat pulled the collar of his coat aside to scratch idly at his puckered skin. A startled crab scuttled across his neck to hide in the folds of his collar. Polat didn't seem to notice.

"I didn't. I sank beneath the waves and saw a light from below. They were all there, the crew, floating. Wide eyed and haunted. I continued down like it weren't the captain hanging onto me, but an anchor. I struggled, swimming for the surface and kicking at the wraith that dragged me to the depths."

Impossibly, water continued to drip from Polat's sleeve so long after stepping out of the rain. It ran down the hair plastered to his face and pooled on the table between them.

Quill pushed away from the table, but he was stuck to the chair, held there by Polat's gaze. He was in a maelstrom, spinning in infinity, with Polat's eyes as the bottomless vortex of its heart. He needed something solid to ground him in reality before he plummeted back onto the deck of that ship and that day long ago. His fingers searched the wall behind him until he happened upon a loose nail.

"The crew came alive. They swam for me. Their hands clutched and tore at me, and dragged me down."

The nail came free in Quill's hand. Iron, pure and cold, with which to rebuke the foul revenant that cursed him this eve. He leapt to his feet and slammed the nail into Polat's hand, yelling "Get thee gone, spirit, and haunt me no more!"

Polat didn't flinch, entirely unaffected by the iron in the nail. He leaned forward, the overhead lights casting dire shadows across his face.

"I'm no spirit to be dispelled by iron. The crew didn't let me die that night, but nor could it be said they let me live. They breathed fetid air from their own lungs into mine until I lost consciousness—or went mad. I know not which." He pulled out the nail and dropped it to the floor.

Sea water, rather than blood, oozed from the hole left by the nail. Quill pressed against the wall. Thunder rumbled close by, and the lights flickered. In that moment, he saw a shape—a shadow over Polat's shoulder. It stood, revealing a head that was—

The lights came back up, and the shadow was gone.

Quill edged around the table, but Polat grabbed his arm. He held him there with a force greater than his strength; he held him by his will. By that fateful stare.

"The sea claimed us all that day, Quill! There is no escape, there's only reprieve, and yours is up! The captain's calling you to duty!"

The lights flickered again, and the captain was there, a shadow with half a head over Polat's shoulder. Quill shook himself free and ran for the door. It flew open at his touch, wind and rain pouring into the tavern.

Lightning struck the ocean's surface. In the street stood two dozen sailors. He knew all of them from his nightly hellscapes.

It only lasted a moment. The lightning faded, and so did the crew. Still, he hesitated before stepping out into the gale.

"Are you crazy, Quill? Close the door!" the

bartender yelled.

Quill looked back briefly. Perhaps there was still sanity where the bartender resided, but Quill couldn't see it. The wind switched directions, slamming the door. He turned back toward the storm outside.

Two pale, bloated arms snaked over his shoulders, clasping at his sternum. Lightning flashed again, and he saw the tattoo of Poseidon's trident. The captain's weight settled onto his back.

"Get off me!" he yelled, clawing at the fish-belly skin of the captain's arms.

He ran, dragging the dead man along with him. The street lurched beneath him and he fell to his knees beneath the captain's weight.

He felt the deck beneath his hands, heard the groan of twisting wood.

"No," he said.

The horizon was replaced with a heaving sea, the deck ahead of him burned fiercely, the fire raced toward him.

Driven by terror, he got to his feet and ran for the lifeboat, the captain cackling in his ear.

"I'm calling you to duty, Quill!"

Bloated hands grasped the rails between the lifeboat and Quill. The crew dragged themselves aboard. He recognized many of them despite their years in the dark, chill depths. Scarlet Joe and Hayworth. The Swede and Little Buck. Their skin sagged, and their muscles slacked, but their faces were set and focused. They blamed him, and reckoning was at hand.

"No!" Quill screamed into the night and

scrambled across the splintering deck for the far railing.

"How's your time at watch?" the captain called out gleefully as Quill stumbled and climbed, fighting for every inch of progress.

Lightning flashed, and rocks emerged from the darkness, crushing the rail and dashing Quill's hopes. The aft deck split from the body of the ship, and the world spun round again.

A wave knocked him off his feet, and he washed across the deck, arms spread wide and searching for anything to arrest his motion. When the deck tilted the other way, he got his feet beneath him.

The crew were aboard and lurching toward Quill, seemingly unaffected by the force of waves or tilting deck. Quill ran again for the only thing that stayed steady—the foremast, sheared off at head height, gave him something he could hold on to and ride out the storm.

Quill dodged flames and falling lines, buffeted by wind and wave, but made it to that mast and hugged it as tightly as the captain's corpse hugged him.

"Rough seas ahead!" the captain said.

His muscles ached and his strength was sagging. His head spun from too much drink, and the deck spun from wind and rain. The mast was the only thing Quill could count on. He found a line and lashed himself to the mast, letting his lagging arms go limp at last.

Only, the crew continued toward him.

"No, you can't have me!"

"We're all counting on you!" the captain said

in his ear.

The crew crowded around him. Little Buck reached for him with both hands.

"No! No, no, no, no!"

Buck grasped Quill's face in both hands and covered Quill's mouth and nose with his gaping mouth. Rather than fetid air, sea water spewed into Quill's stomach and lungs.

He coughed and vomited stagnant water as Buck detached, but before he could breathe in again, the Swede pressed his mouth over Quill's face.

Eyes wide with horror, Quill saw the crew lined up to take their turn, and Polat standing grimly behind them.

Pedro was first on the worksite Monday morning. He found Quill's body tied to a support beam with an orange power cord. Salt crusted his lips, and his eyes gaped. Sunburnt irises stared upward, his face contorted in horror. When the coroners came to collect him, rain water spilled from his gaping mouth.

Two Hundred Miles

Patrick worried about his daughter's relationship with her grandparents. She was young and his parents were old, but he wanted her to remember them. For his own part, three of Patrick's grandparents were dead by the time he was born, and the last one, his maternal grandfather, died when he was six. He had vague memories of lighting Grandpa's cigarettes and being scared of his prosthetic leg. Nancy's father was dead before Patrick met her, and her mom died when their daughter was seven. Patrick wanted to be sure that Flora spent enough time with his parents that she would remember them.

The good news was that his parents lived in Anaheim, California, so they always got a few days at Disneyland out of the deal. While he wanted her to have memories of Grandma and Grandpa, no one said they couldn't be idealized memories. So, while he was getting them Fast Passes for Pirates of the Caribbean, his dad, John, and his mom, Margaret, were buying his daughter Flora more candy than she could possibly eat. He allowed them to spoil her in ways he would never allow himself, or even his wife, to. Is it always that way with grandparents? He knew it was very common for grandparents to spoil kids, but he wondered if it was always for the same reason. "Okay, kiddo," he said when they returned. "But we've got dinner first. You can have all that later."

Dinner at the Blue Bayou was always the highlight for Patrick. He had the Monte Cristo, and his wife had the seafood bisque. There was a large group at the next table over, and though he hadn't spoken much Spanish since high school, he caught part of a conversation involving one woman whose mother was sick and she hasn't been able to get ahold of her for two days. The gist of the conversation was that they all hoped her mother would be okay, but everyone was getting sick in that neighborhood.

Before they knew it, it was time for them to make good on their Fast Passes. Flora got to have two pieces of candy before the ride but had to save the rest for the parade. The ride was the same as always, but it had a heck of a lot of charm. They stopped by to look at the photo of their drop at the end of the ride. Patrick famously made odd poses or faces just before the camera flash went off. His wife and daughter got a laugh out of them, he thought he was hilarious, and his father disapproved. In this particular one, he was wearing a set of plastic vampire fangs and posing as if about to bite Flora.

They walked from there all the way to the end of Main Street. This is one thing Patrick and his father agreed on—get a spot as close to the exit as possible so you can make a fast getaway when the parade is over. Patrick and his family were staying at one of the Disneyland Resort Hotels, so the car parked there, and that meant he wouldn't have to wait in long lines again to drive his parents' home.

They waited for about half an hour, Flora eating her candy, Patrick biting his tongue about it, and his wife and parents just talking. You had to get there early to get the good seats.

That's when the phones started ringing.

It was just a few at first, but he noticed when half the crowd reached for their phones. In a matter of moments, it seemed like just about everyone had theirs in hand. He stood up, the first surge of adrenaline shooting through him. Something wasn't right. Everyone that cared about him was here, so no one was going to be calling him, therefore he tried to listen in on a couple of other people's phone calls. Since he only got the local side of the conversations, though, he was largely unsuccessful. Then he happened to look down Main Street to where the parade should soon be starting, and he didn't need to listen any more. There were hundreds of people running toward them in a panic.

He picked up his daughter and grabbed his wife by the shoulder of her blouse and pulled upward.

"Babe, we need to run now. No questions. Mom, Dad, leave everything and move as fast as you can." People around him were already starting to run. He thought about the turnstiles, and the pile-up that would soon be occurring there. It would be deadly.

"Seriously, we've got to go now."

He helped his father up, then grabbed his mom's hand and started running. He trusted his wife to follow his lead and also to help his dad. Neither Mom nor Dad moved too well anymore, but the family had taken the day slowly, with lots of rests, so they were up for a short burst.

Patrick could see the exit ahead, and so he chanced a look back. His wife was right behind him, and she was actually carrying his father. Good thinking.

He headed for the turnstile with the shortest line, still longer than he liked, but he wasn't going to be the one to start the pushing which would soon lead to trampling. He looked over his shoulder again. There were two tunnels through which everyone had to pass to get to the exits. They were starting to get choked up with the mass of humanity trying to escape through them. He could see people falling, children even, and the mob kept running right over them.

"Move faster!" Patrick shouted at everyone ahead of them.

He had his hand on the shoulder of the guy in front of him. He wasn't shoving, he reminded himself, just making sure he kept up while he looked over his shoulder again. There were people crossing the railroad tracks above the tunnels and trampling the Mickey-shaped flowers at the front of the park. He was close to panic himself at this point and suddenly realized he was actively pushing the guy in front of him. He didn't stop. He was at the turnstile and went through as quickly as he could and pulled his mom after him. He ran forward about ten feet, then turned around to verify that his wife made it. She passed by him, heading straight for the hotel parking lot. He ran after her.

"Dad, what's going on?" his daughter asked, real fear in her voice.

"Shh, I don't know, Little Love, but when we get to the car, we'll tune in some news and find out," he said.

He meant for it to sound reassuring, but he knew full well that she hated listening to news.

Patrick wasn't the greatest runner, but he had an overdose of adrenaline at the moment, and he remembered a little trick from high school to keep from getting a cramp. Pick one foot. The first time it hits the ground, you take a sharp breath. The next time that same foot hits the ground, you breathe out quickly, and you alternate, but always on that same foot. Deep, controlled breaths on a regular schedule were the key to long-distance running. At least that's what he read in a men's magazine ages ago, and so far it had worked for him.

He chanced another look back, and as he expected, most people were heading for the theme park parking lot.

He yelled to Nancy, "It's okay, we're out of immediate danger. I'd still walk fast, but let's give my mom a bit of a rest."

She slowed down, and his dad said, "You can put me down now. I think I can manage this."

She did, and Patrick and Margaret caught up with them before slowing to a fast walk themselves. Mom was panting hard, but she seemed okay with this pace.

"What do you think it is?" Nancy asked.

"I don't know," said Patrick, "but whatever it is, it's big. I'm thinking nuclear attack big."

Nancy had been worried, but her face clouded further at his words.

"I figure if there is a terrorist threat of a nuke, Los Angeles is probably the target, so we get in the car and head south at top speed until we find out for sure what's going on."

They quickly made it to their rental car, and he started it as the family fastened seatbelts.

He turned on the radio and left the parking lot heading for the southbound 5. The roads were clear so far. Good. The folks in the main parking lot had to head a lot further to get to the freeway, and there was going to be a line up to get out. Patrick thanked God they'd been in hotel parking, whatever was happening.

It turned out he didn't have to change the station to find news, every station was playing it. However, the man voicing KROQ was speaking too fast, in a high, panicked voice. Nancy looked for someone more understandable so Patrick could concentrate on driving.

He ignored a red light and took the on-ramp for the southbound 5, leaving some serious rubber behind. Nancy punched buttons frantically, searching for a calmer voice. When he got onto the freeway proper, he saw that it was absolutely empty in the southbound lanes, but northbound was total gridlock. He'd picked the wrong direction. They caught a few phrases as Nancy ran through the stations on the presets, then started pressing the seek button. "—highly contagious—"…"—fires and explosions—"…"—San Diego has gone completely dark—"…"—virulent form of rabies—"

"Wait!" he cried, "That one."

They listened on.

"—is what it appears to be. Three hours ago, the Mexican border was completely overrun. Based upon early reports, the naval station in San Diego set up roadblocks to the south, but despite tanks and machine guns, tear gas and stun grenades, they were no match for the overwhelming tide of humanity that poured over them, attacking anyone they came across. Within an hour, the city was in ruins. Initial reports stated that the infected were actually biting and even eating their victims. These reports are unconfirmed because the power grid is down, no one is broadcasting, and no cell towers are operating. The infected did not stop there. They are spreading out, heading north and east. Panic and riots precede them. Hundreds have died in the mayhem in Los Angeles. The President has grounded all flights and LAX, SFO, O'Hare, SeaTac, LaGuardia, JFK, and Atlanta airports are all now quarantine zones. Any flights still in the air are being routed to one of those airports. No one is going in or out until they have been fully inspected for any wounds and cleared."

Patrick braked hard, skidding to a stop.

"Has no one ever seen a zombie film? This is it. It's the zombie apocalypse. We have to get back to Seattle as quickly as possible, then get scarce from there."

"If we're getting scarce, what's the point in going to Seattle at all?" Mom asked.

"Three reasons," Patrick replied. "Seattle is on the water, and maybe these things can't swim. San Juan Island is nearby and might be able to stay free of contagion. Secondly, that's where Nancy's older daughter and her boyfriend are right now. We've got to get to them. Third, the Boy Scout motto is 'Be Prepared.' Assuming we still have clean water, we've got enough food to last us nearly two years at home. I've got camping gear, a hand-powered filter pump, and some guns. Not much and even less ammo, but it's better than the one tire iron in the trunk, which is all we have right now."

The southbound lane was entirely empty. No one was thick enough to be heading south right now except them. He started the car back up and got into the right lane, then made a big U-turn and plowed northbound in the southbound lanes. Several of the drivers in the parking lot that had been the northbound lanes saw what he was doing. Someone in a Hummer pushed the barrier out of the way and crossed into the southbound 5 behind them, and a long line of cars followed. Patrick stepped on it and was soon going ninety-five MPH. He didn't want to push it any further and risk overheating. Several cars coming up from behind were not as cautious, and soon he was being passed as if he were standing still.

"You maniacs better not cause a pile-up ahead, or so help me…" Patrick said.

By the time they got to Los Angeles, they

passed several more places where the barrier had been pushed aside and cars were streaming through. He got into the left-most lane (if he'd been traveling the proper direction, it would have been the right lane) to avoid having to slow for newcomers, but this lane was starting to look like a normal Los Angeles rush hour freeway. He was down to forty MPH. It took them almost an hour to get through the city, and there were people with guns or bats or chains or crowbars attacking the vehicles that did stop. They were pulling people out of their cars and stealing their possessions as well as their cars. Nancy told Flora not to look. Mom covered Flora's eyes. Someone had set up a roadblock, trying to stop the southbound lanes as well, but it had been knocked aside by the cars ahead and they streamed through it without slowing.

"Let me ask you," the radio host asked a reporter, "how is it possible that this outbreak spread through Mexico so quickly without the world noticing?"

"Well, Trish, as usual, the various organizations I've talked to are doing their best to dodge blame right now, but actual data is trickling out. The real trouble seems to be that whatever this disease is, it looked like a particularly virulent strain of flu until just two nights ago when scientists say, and I quote, 'A mutation occurred.' Any actual information has been hard to come by since then, due to power and infrastructure being down."

"Right. And since power can be spotty in certain areas, this didn't cause immediate alarm.

Dr. Sullivan with the CDC spoke earlier, calling this a 'critical mass event.' Can you explain what that means?"

"Sure. This is a property of microbial life-forms where they build up to a certain point, then alter their behavior all at once. Scientists are still studying the phenomenon which has been seen in bacteria and viruses as well as molds and slimes. The behavior we've seen with this microbe, however is unusual."

The host reported that the horde had reached Mission Viejo. Anaheim would be close behind. Patrick clicked the radio off.

After Los Angeles, traffic thinned a bit, but not much. They passed abandoned cars as they approached the pass, either overheated or out of gas. People continued on foot, carrying as much of their worldly possessions as they could manage. He glanced at his dashboard. Three quarters of a tank, and the temperature was good.

"Patrick!" his wife yelled, pulling his attention back to the road.

The car in front of him loomed in his headlights. He swerved just in time, praying that there wasn't another car there, and getting very lucky. However, this lane was also stopped just a few cars ahead. He slammed on the brakes.

What could he do at this point? He looked around desperately.

"There!" Nancy yelled and pointed.

There was a car in the left-hand lane just ahead with enough room in front to fit his compact rental through sideways, and a soft shoulder beyond. He turned the wheel hard and floored it, tapping the cars on both sides, ripping the rear bumper off the forward car. The going was bumpy, but at least they were moving. A car ahead opened the door, trying to stop them out of spite. He didn't let that stop him though, and he ripped the door off that car as he plowed through.

He drove along for a mile and a half before coming to the end of a long line of cars that had done the same as he did. And in between these cars and the roadway was a long line of motorcycles. The far lane was still moving at a crawl, but the other lanes were at a stand-still. He turned off the car and took the keys out, putting them in his pocket.

"Keep the doors locked," he instructed his wife. "If anyone got this far, they've got a car of their own, but I don't want to take any chances."

According to his watch, it was almost midnight. His daughter was sleeping peacefully on his mother's arm in the back seat. Margaret gave her son a weak smile and nodded. Patrick turned back to his wife.

"We're almost at the top of the pass. I'm going to see what I can see."

He lowered his voice, though it was pointless. Everyone in the car who was still awake could hear him just fine.

"Nothing stops a line of motorcycles. I need to see what did it this time."

With that, he got out of the car, locking it behind himself and starting the trek to the top of the pass. He asked several people along the way what was going on ahead, but no one seemed to know.

A few of them even said, "Be sure to let us know on your way back." One of them added, "…assuming you make it."

He trudged on, discouraged now from even asking what people knew. Twenty minutes later, he reached the top. He navigated through the crowd that had gathered there until he reached a barrier. Beyond the barrier were two armored personnel carriers, a tank and two lines of armed soldiers. The size of the guns atop the ATVs was very intimidating, but he approached the barrier, anyway. He picked out a soldier, a woman with the name Powell sewn on her fatigues. If he understood the ranking symbols correctly, she was a private.

"Private Powell," he said, and she looked his way with a bored expression. "What's going on? Why is the road blocked?"

"You've heard about what happened to San Diego?" she asked, with a bored expression. She must get asked this every thirty seconds or so.

"Of course, and as far north as Anaheim as well. That's why we're all here," he replied.

"Yeah, well, they didn't close San Francisco International soon enough. The contagion is spreading from there as well now. Troops are trying to contain the spread as we speak, but until we get word otherwise, we cannot let anyone through. We're recommending that people turn back and get off at Santa Clarita, over to the 395 and north from there, or take the 15 to the 40 if you need to head east. Most people are choosing to wait here though. The San Francisco situation should be under control before morning, and we'll open the way at that point. But if anyone crosses this barrier before then, our orders are to shoot to kill."

Patrick saluted and turned to head back to the car.

Along the way, he informed those people he had spoken to on the way up of what he learned at the top. He was just about back to his own car, trying to figure out how he could get his car through this mess of traffic and turn around to get to the 395, when he had to stop to tell his story one more time.

"So, either you wait here for San Francisco to be cleared, which they are predicting will happen by morning, or you turn around and take the 395 North or the 40 West at Santa Clarita-"

One of the bikers nearby said, "That's bullshit!"

Patrick turned around. "Say again?"

The biker took off his helmet and got off his bike. He approached Patrick and poked him in the chest with a finger.

"I was on the 395 earlier tonight until I hit a roadblock, and they said to take the 5 because they could only 'guarantee our safety on arterials.'"

Patrick was confused. Then someone else a few cars back spoke up.

"Yeah, we were on the 15, and they had a road block before we even got to the 40. No way east either."

"But then why would they…they would be feeding us to the zombies and just making more…"

Patrick scratched his head and started pacing, puzzling things out. Then realization dawned on him and he hurried back up the pass. He moved as quickly as he could without looking like he was in a panicked run. At this point, he figured there were probably snipers at the tops of the mountains on both sides. He forced himself not to scan the hillsides for them. Best not to look suspicious. He got to the crowd of people just before the barrier and started pushing his way through.

"Excuse me...one side please...beg pardon...sorry, excuse me..."

When he got to the barrier, he sought out Private Powell again. "Can I talk to you for a moment, Powell?" He lowered his voice and leaned toward her. "I don't think either of us want people to hear what I want to say."

She studied his face for a while, then looked up to her right at the mountaintop, and back to him. She motioned with her head to her right and started heading toward the area where the left-most lane had an area cleared for them to make U-turns. Patrick followed along. When she stopped, he leaned in and spoke quietly. "You must have known that people would compare stories, right? The 15 is blocked and so is the 395, just like this one. So, we're penned in, essentially quarantining Southern California. Can't risk it getting out, right? Let's start with the assumption that San Francisco is doing just fine. Let's also assume that the military is smart enough not to feed us all to the zombies, and yes, let's call them what they are, the word 'infected' isn't fooling anyone. Anyway, with every person bitten you've got one more threat and need one more bullet—you are going to run out at some point. We also aren't going to get any kind of cure or vaccine before the horde gets here in about two or three hours and wipes us all out. So, I ask myself why else go through with the quarantine? And it dawns on me. At the rate this is spreading, the U.S. probably has 10 days, maybe a fortnight at the outside. It has to be nipped in the bud without any risk of spill-over. I'm thinking a series of nukes cutting the majority of America off from Mexico, where this contagion came to us from, all with acceptable collateral damage. Am I warm?"

She leaned forward.

"If you've figured all that out, then you also know it has to be done and that starting a panic right now would just make things worse. You understand that, right?"

"Oh, I'm not going to tell any of these folks. Ignorance is bliss. And yes, I couldn't come up with a better idea. I just wish I were on the other side of this barrier with my family when it happened. You could have safely waited another couple hours, you know. I mean, they aren't here yet and I doubt anyone north of Santa Clarita is infected."

"Negative," Powell responded, shaking her head. "We would never be able to erect this barrier while there were cars streaming through. We had to act before the rush, or else we would need to nuke a much larger area, and have double the civilian casualties. No, it had to be done when we did it. I'm sorry for you and your family. I really am. I'm sorry for all the people here who are going to die oblivious to what is going on. But you know what? This side of the barrier isn't magically out of the blast zone either. We're both going to die roughly an hour from now. There is another roadblock ten miles north of here where the soldiers are safe and their job is to make sure we don't get cold feet. I'm fairly certain there are drones overhead by now, ready to take out even the snipers if they go rogue and bolt."

Patrick stood processing this for a while.

Private Powell set her gun at ready and took on an official demeanor.

"Now sir, please return to your vehicle. And do the smart thing. Keep your theories to yourself."

She returned to her station.

Patrick turned and eased his way back through the crowd, walking much more slowly this time. His mind was full of things he needed to process. One thought led to another, and in the way they often do, he came to a sudden realization without being able to remember how he got there. There would be a radiation cloud the likes of which this world has never seen. The prevailing winds in this part of the world would carry it all east. He had a brother living in New Mexico with his family. He took out his cell phone and quickly dialed Tim's number. It was almost 1:00 AM here, and Tim was two hours ahead. Come on, pick up, he thought.

Tim's groggy voice came on the line.

"Patrick?"

"Yes, Tim. Listen. I know what time it is and believe me I would never bug you at this hour if it wasn't important. And I can't tell you how I know what I know, but you have to trust me."

Patrick looked around to make sure no one was able to hear him.

"Get out of bed now. Hitch up your trailer, get your family in the Suburban and head north. Go visit South Dakota or Yellowstone or something in that latitude. When you hit the road, tune in some news and you will understand everything. Do not call back and don't call Mom or Dad. Just head north. And Tim, I know we never say this kind of thing in our family, but I love you. Now get up and move!"

With that, he hung up the phone and removed the battery, dropping both on the asphalt as he went. He walked back to the car with greater purpose now.

As he approached his car, he got to the biker he was talking to earlier.

"Learn anything new?" he asked.

"Yeah," Patrick answered. "She confirmed what you guys said, but also told me that our information was outdated. She said she was on the radio with troops in both locations and verified that they are letting people through now. Either way, I decided that my family and I will just sit in the car until the all-clear from Frisco and wait this out for now."

The biker clicked his tongue derisively and shook his head. Patrick walked on by, feeling complicit now. He got to his car and opened the door, slipping inside as quietly as he could. His mom and dad were sleeping now too, but his wife was wide awake.

"You were gone for over an hour! I was just about to get out and come after you," she whispered.

"I know," he said. "There were a lot of people up there and it took me a long time to talk to someone." He pulled the door closed gently, locked it and leaned his seat back a bit. "They had some trouble in San Francisco too, but they have it mostly contained to the airport. The roadblock is just a precaution. There's another one behind us at Santa Clarita to protect us from the advancing horde. They've learned a lot after the loss of San Diego, and they are confident they can keep it contained now." He yawned purposely. "They say they expect to have the barrier down before dawn and will start letting us through then. Try to get some sleep. It sounds like the worst is over now."

He took his jacket off, laid it over himself like a blanket and tried to get comfortable. He knew he wasn't going to sleep, but if he looked like he was, maybe Nancy could.

Twenty minutes later, he heard her breathing deepen and become rhythmic. He opened one eye and looked at her. God, he loved that woman. He closed his eye again.

Twenty minutes later, there was a light bright enough to be uncomfortable even through closed lids. and he thought no more.

Epilogue—from the President's press conference one-half hour later.

"...our planes will remain grounded and our airports will remain quarantine areas until such time as we can be certain there is no further risk to American lives. Now to address our actions in Southwest America."

(A short pause filled with the clicking of cameras.)

"I take full responsibility for the loss of American lives that my decision alone caused. I am sorry for any family members and loved ones you have who were killed in this unprecedented attack by your own government upon American soil. I also take responsibility internationally for foreign citizens who in good faith believed that they were safe and protected while in our country. My heart goes out to all of you who are in mourning today, and to all of you living in uncertainty, not knowing whether to mourn or not yet.

"These actions were not only necessary, but inevitable. With the state that Mexico is in now, with the challenges faced now by all of Latin America, it was imperative to act quickly and with decisive force to protect American lives where possible.

"The entire border with Mexico, and for two

hundred miles to the north and east, is a burning, radioactive wasteland. And that's on me. I had technical advisors give me the worst-case scenario given how fast the infected were seen to be moving in footage from Mexico, just how far could one of them get before the radiation cooked them to the point of disintegration. That's the number we came up with. Two hundred miles.

"As President, you have to make a lot of hard decisions. But not since Truman made the decision to drop the second nuclear bomb on the civilians of Nagasaki to stop the bloodiest conflict known until his time, has a President had to face using a nuclear weapon against civilians. And this time, against those I represent. That's on me. These are the demons that will haunt me the rest of my days."

(There followed a long pause with only the sound of camera flashes.)

"This conference will be my final act as President. A man who would do this to his own people does not deserve to lead them. I go now to sign my resignation papers. I have full confidence in Vice President Ayala, and his ability to lead this country through this crisis and those to come in its wake. No questions, please. Goodbye to all of you."

"Mr. President!...Mr. President!..."

Agatha Hemsley, Beloved Mother

Martin Gardner, museum curator, leaned across the desk of his office, cradling the telephone receiver between shoulder and cheek as he arranged his papers.

"Yes, I know how late it is, but Phillip Randolph will be here in a matter of minutes. Yes, *the* Phillip Randolph, and he will be signing a sizable check."

Gardner pulled open a drawer and removed a manilla folder.

"Never mind how sizable, suffice to say it is worth your efforts to verify the value of this painting."

He spent a moment straightening the paper again, then shoved them into the folder and let it fall onto the blotter of his desk. He pulled the receiver away from his face and spoke directly into it.

"I will double your normal fee for the inconvenience of the hour. Now, did you receive the email or not? Agatha Hemsley, Beloved Mother. There should be a photograph attached.

Good. Find out everything you can about it. I want to know why Randolph wants that piece of crap and why he's willing to pay so much."

A loud knocking came at the side door.

"Alright. He's here now. I'll stall him as long as I can, but I expect your call the moment you have an informed appraisal."

Gardner hung up, carefully spooling the phone cord so that it wouldn't look untidy. His desk wasn't simply a workspace, it was a showroom. Every aspect of Dr. Gardner's office was set to convey an image and atmosphere. It said, "I am a professional, and your money will have a comfortable home here."

"Mr. Randolph. Please come in," Dr. Gardner said as he swung open the side door.

The rain had been a steady drizzle earlier in the evening, but now Mr. Randolph huddled in the eaves framed by a downpour that kicked up mud in large droplets.

Mr. Randolph stepped inside and stamped on the mat as Dr. Gardner shut out the weather. He unbuttoned his long wool coat and folded it over one arm.

"May I offer you anything to drink, Mr. Randolph?" Gardner asked, indicating a small cabinet populated with crystal decanters.

"Just coffee for me," Randolph said, looking for a place to hang his coat. Gardner offered his own arm, and Randolph handed it to him. "Thank you. I have a long drive ahead of me tonight. But feel free to have some yourself."

"I make it a habit never to drink alone. Please, have a seat," Gardner said with a practiced smile.

He hung the man's coat next to the radiator and stepped into the back room. "Cream? Sugar?"

"Black," Randolph said.

When Gardner returned with the coffee, Randolph was in The Target Chair, elegant and comfortable, with every element of the room designed around it. Randolph's eyes were perusing the room: the portraits of previous curators, the bank of mahogany filing cabinets, the tasteful rug, the photos of wife and child, finally coming to rest on the nameplate on the edge of the desk—Martin Gardner, Ph.D.

Gardner handed Randolph the mug of coffee. Randolph looked as though he were about to say, "Thank you," but stopped with his tongue on his teeth. "Is that the portrait?" he asked instead.

Gardner glanced over his shoulder at the brown paper rectangle bound in twine. "Yes, that's it. *Agatha Hemsley, Beloved Mother.*"

Randolph said nothing, his eyes darting back and forth over every detail of the bundle. Gardner broke his gaze as he swept around to his seat behind the desk.

"I'm curious, Mr. Randolph, how did you know it was in our archive when even I didn't know prior to your call?"

Randolph stared at Gardner for several moments, the intensity of his gaze quite surprising, before returning to the package just visible behind the desk. "I've been searching for this painting since before you were born, Dr. Gardner. Nearly my entire life. Did you know it once belonged to my father?"

Perhaps that was the reason for the value he

placed on it. But it can't be the sole reason—his father had been a renowned patron of the arts before him, and there must have been some reason it earned a place in his personal collection. "No. As I say, I didn't know of the painting's existence until I got your message. Frankly, I'd never heard of the artist either."

"His name was Thomas Winslow. He was nobody. A retired New England History teacher who made a meager living painting seascapes for postcards—lighthouses, terns and gulls, grassy dunes—that sort of thing. His portrait work was a side job for a few of the community members, and he didn't do many of them. Other than this painting here, nothing he ever did held the slightest significance."

Randolph finally tore his eyes away from the portrait and seemed to notice his coffee for the first time. He took a gulp of it and set the mug on a cork coaster at the corner of Dr. Gardner's desk, placed just so, next to a blank space just right for the signing of checks.

"Exactly as I've been able to discover. But surely there must be more to the story, because why else would you be willing to pay one point three million dollars for this disregarded work by an unknown artist? I do have that number correct, don't I?"

Randolph sat up straight, reaching inside his jacket's breast pocket.

"That is correct. I assume a personal check will suffice?"

Garner steepled his fingers.

"Of course. My secretary is drawing up the

ɪ

papers even now. It will be a few more minutes, I'm afraid, though that does give us a chance to talk before signing."

Randolph's face darkened in frustration, and he looked at his watch.

"What exactly would we want to discuss?"

"Mr. Randolph, if I may say, you have piqued my curiosity with your interest in this piece. I'm afraid I must insist you satisfy that curiosity and explain this painting's unexpected value before I will sign it over to you. My doctorate is not honorary. I've spent the last few hours examining the painting. Its subject matter is mundane and unremarkable. The artist's skill with a brush is pedestrian at best. I even looked over the frame for any hint of the value you place upon it. Now, unless the work is covering up some lost Rembrandt or Picasso, I would put its value somewhere around eighty-five cents at my next yard sale."

Randolph nodded grimly.

"Everything you say is true. There is no particular talent to the picture, no intrinsic value in its ownership. I assure you, there is no masterpiece hidden beneath."

"Then why are you willing to pay so much for it? Is Agatha Hemsley a relative of yours?"

"Not her, no. My interest in the painting is humanitarian in nature. I intend to ensure that no one ever sees it again."

This took the curator entirely by surprise. What a thing to say. "But, why?"

Randolph leaned forward in his chair, rubbing his palms together. He gave Gardner a piercing look, then glanced down at his expensive watch. Finally, he sat back in his seat and smiled.

"Dr. Gardner, perhaps you can pour us both a bit of scotch after all, and I'll tell you a story. A parable, shall we say, while we wait for the papers to arrive. And if you choose to apply it to our current circumstances, well, I'll leave that up to you."

Gardner narrowed his eyes appraisingly, but as soon as his back was turned and he reached for the liquor cabinet, he smiled impishly. A little lubrication for the tongue, and soon they'd arrive at the true value of the piece. He glanced at his own watch as he added a healthy dose of Macallan 25 to each glass and wondered how long it would be before Gus Cunningham called with his findings. His face was a mask of professional curiosity by the time he turned toward Randolph again and handed him a glass.

Randolph raised his glass and waited as Gardner settled into his chair. Gardner drank, then Randolph took a sip and began his story.

"I'm certain the first thing you noticed is the odd contents of the portrait. Upon hearing the title, you'd expect to find one Agatha Hemsley as the subject."

"As a matter of fact, I was surprised, especially given the reported age of the work."

"Indeed. Now in my pursuit of the piece, I managed to procure the diary of one Simon Hemsley, who commissioned the portrait of his beloved mother, and described its completion. For three days in the first week of April 1889, Mrs. Agatha Hemsley, widow, posed for her portrait. The divan she was seated on, and the wall in the background were in the parlor of Thomas Winslow, inherited when his own mother died in a buggy accident. It was painted with hogshair brushes and walnut-based oil paints on an eleven by fourteen splined canvas."

Gardner turned toward the paper-wrapped painting with a suspicious smile. "I think you may have gotten a few details wrong, starting with the painting's dimensions, which are fourteen by twenty-two."

"A parable, remember, Dr. Gardner?" Randolph quickly continued with his story as if he were being carried by the flow of it. "According to an article published at the time in the local paper, it was Winslow's finest work. To quote the article, 'It captured her very soul.' Clearly, a statement intended hyperbolically, but one which you may revisit at the end of this tale."

"Simon's diary entries ended a week later, and when the Hemsleys missed two consecutive mortgage payments, their bank took possession of the house. Neither Simon nor Agatha was found. He never returned to claim his property from within, and he had no living relatives, so the house and everything within it went to auction. The painting, however, was donated to a local museum."

Randolph sipped his scotch, watching Gardner over the rim of his glass. Gardner kept his expression even, the better to get more of the story, and eventually to the point.

"It sat in storage for over a decade until they had an exhibit with a focus on local artists, whereupon they rediscovered the painting and put it on display. The exhibit was a success, bringing in local townsfolk by the droves, yet no one was in the room when ten-year-old Christopher Atkins went missing. A thorough search followed, but the boy was never found. For reasons you may begin to suspect, but that I will withhold until the end of the story, the painting was considered part of the crime scene. A photograph ran in the local paper, while the painting was processed as evidence and placed in storage at the local police station.

"Later that same year, the police brought in a suspect in the child's abduction, and they pulled the painting from Evidence to run a fingerprint comparison only to discover that they had in fact impounded the wrong painting."

"How is that possible?" Dr. Gardner asked, then waved off his own question. "Regardless, it must have still been in museum storage."

"Not only did a comprehensive search of the museum fail to come up with the painting in question, the one in police custody had never belonged to the museum. The only conclusion they could draw was that the kidnapper had somehow managed to get into the evidence locker and swap out the painting. A small town, such as it was, didn't have the greatest security after all."

"Amazing. I wonder if it was in our collection that whole time?"

Randolph shook his head.

"The painting had more tragedy to sew before it found its way to you. If you'll recall, I said it was once in my father's possession. Though, not yet. The Hemsley portrait was lost again until 1963. Then, during a raid on a suspected art thief in Chicago, it was one of eighty-four paintings recovered. The raid made headlines worldwide, though this painting was a minor footnote. Forensics teams took photos of all eighty-four paintings before they were loaded into vans and taken to police impound with SWAT escorts. In case of theft in transit, you understand. Officers Henry Dobson and Devon Flannery rode with Agatha Hemsley, but when the van arrived at their destination, both officers were missing. The driver said they never stopped, and he never saw any suspicious vehicles."

Dr. Gardner nodded at Randolph's intense gaze. He was beginning to understand what Randolph meant by a humanitarian interest. He'd heard such superstitious tales about the Hope Diamond or the Koh-i-Noor. Even King Tut's mummy came to mind. Still, why go to such lengths, and why pay so much for a worthless painting, even if he lent credence to some supposed curse?

Randolph continued.

"The thieves were tried, and those paintings with a legitimate claim were returned to the rightful owners, but someone made the connection to the previous disappearances associated with Agatha Hemsley. The painting was taken to be destroyed in the furnace, though as you've seen, it was not destroyed that day."

"You have some theory as to how it escaped the flames, I presume?" Dr. Gardner asked.

"I do. I believe an altogether different work

was put in the furnace, having been swapped with this one, much as it had when the boy disappeared. Moreover, I believe I understand the means by which this switch occurs." He sipped at his scotch again and Dr. Gardner made a show of joining him. "I wonder if you will guess at the means before the tale is complete."

Randolph glanced at his watch again and set his scotch down next to his coffee. Dr. Gardner's lips tightened as the space reserved for checkbooks was taken by the glass.

"There is another gap in the painting's provenance until 1971, when I was ten-years-old. My parents had arranged a party to celebrate Father's acquisition of *Untitled* by Palmer Hayden, a piece he'd sought for several years. When the crate arrived on the morning of the party, it contained, instead, *Agatha Hemsley, Beloved Mother*. Anyone else would have raged over the incompetent screw-up, but not my father. He laughed and hung it in the place of honor reserved for Mr. Hayden's painting. I remember, he was certain that the mistake would be corrected, and in the meantime, he could find out which of his snobby friends truly knew good art from bad."

Randolph went silent, staring at his folded hands as he tapped his thumbs together. Then he reached for his scotch and finished it in one swallow before replacing it on the desk.

"He disappeared shortly before the party. We searched the house, and afterward, Mother phoned the police who conducted their own search. Being a multi-millionaire, they assumed a kidnapping, and we waited by the phone for a ransom call that never came.

"I was the one to discover him." Randolph returned his gaze to his thumbs.

"Oh, no. How horrible for a ten-year-old. It was a botched kidnapping then?"

Randolph sat up.

"What? No. That's not what I meant at all. I was always the sort who ate when I was upset. Since the party was cancelled anyway, I went to the display room and scarfed down petite fours by the handful. Then I happened to glance at the painting.

"You see, it isn't merely cursed, Dr. Gardner. The painting is itself a record of all those disappearances. It started out as a portrait of Agatha Hemsley, just as the name implies, but standing over her shoulder is her son Simon. Next to them is young Christopher Atkins, two police officers in riot gear, and an elderly gentleman whom I've never been able to identify. Now, next to them, stood my father."

Gardner felt the blood drain from his face. He'd noted all the extra figures in it, but he'd been rating the artist's skill, not his subject matter, and he hadn't recognized Randolph's famous father. For a moment—just a moment, and it was undoubtedly the scotch to blame—he believed the story. By the time his rationality re-asserted itself, Randolph went on.

"That's the reason for the discrepancy with the title, and with the dimensions of the painting. It grows to accommodate each new victim. Anyway, I knew instantly what had happened, but my explanation only caused the police to smile with condescension. Clearly, the painting itself was responsible for the disappearances, collecting each victim as it went. How much simpler than the official story that a kidnapper and murderer has been working for eighty-two years across the country, switching out paintings wherever he abducted people, including armed officers in the back of a locked police van. Wouldn't you agree, Dr. Gardner?"

"Simpler? Yes. However, it does presuppose the existence of the supernatural, Mr. Randolph. A point I shall not be quick to concede."

Randolph narrowed his eyes and readjusted in his seat. Perhaps Gardner had gone too far, questioning the man's story. Mr Cunningham still hadn't called, so he needed to play for more time. He needn't have worried though, because Randolph returned to his story.

"I threw a fit when the police tried to take the painting until Mother suggested they leave it overnight. They took photographs as evidence and left a patrol car in the driveway in case the kidnappers called. I slept in the room with the painting. I was convinced that if Father could somehow travel into the painting, he could again return from it. However, I woke to find the painting had disappeared overnight, replaced by one titled, *The Dink Patrol and the Love Slaves of Xuyan Than Phu* by one Bruce Minney."

He held up a finger. "And before you say it, any thief had to get past not only the police officers stationed outside, and me, sleeping a few feet away, but also our alarm system. For 1971, it was state-of-the-art. The envy of any museum on earth. No one broke into our home, and no one had the chance to switch the painting."

Randolph looked at his watch again and reached for his coffee.

"I knew from that very day what I had to do, except I was only a child, so I bided my time. The painting had taken my father, and in return I had my inheritance. One point three million dollars. That's what I received when the painting disappeared, and that is what I will pay to have it returned. I don't want anything for my father's disappearance, I only want him back. And who knows? When the painting is destroyed, perhaps they will come back." He gulped down his coffee. "Or at least they'll be free."

He went distant again, and this time the minutes stretched on until Gardner finally said, "Can I freshen up your coffee?"

"I knew I had to continue my father's legacy as a patron of the arts," Randolph said, as if no time had passed. "I studied hard. I learned the techniques and stroke patterns; I began mixing my own pigments. I learned to differentiate a fraud from an original. I feigned an interest in up-and-coming artists, encouraged donations to all the proper establishments, and when I came of age and took my rightful place as head of my father's foundation, I made those donations myself. All the while, I was gaining the connections I needed. I never stopped searching for this painting. I came close twice before, but before I could collect, it went missing. It acquired a further two victims in the process."

He held his coffee mug out toward Gardner.

"Which brings us to today, and its present size and contents. Now you know the full story, Dr. Gardner. Perhaps you could check on your secretary? The paperwork has been quite some time in coming."

Dr. Gardner took the coffee mug and returned to the back room.

"I'm afraid I must admit to some deception." He refilled the mug and stepped out, but didn't immediately approach Mr. Randolph. "It wasn't simply curiosity that bade me hear your story. The true reason was financial in nature. Only a fool would pay so much for this painting unless there was some deeper value to it "

"I've told you my reasons—"

Dr. Gardner held up a hand.

"I hadn't heard your story yet. Now, you've told an interesting story, no doubt about it, and I understand the reason behind the price. But, to reasonably settle on an intrinsic value for the work, I had to have the painting independently appraised. The papers are here on my desk, but I've been waiting for a phone call from Gus Cunningham, a gentleman I work with from time to time. I like to know more about any work of art than the buyer does, you see, except you left me with no time to research it myself. So, I sent a photo of the painting over to him, and he should be getting back to me—"

Randolph launched from his chair, knocking it back in his haste.

"You did what? Haven't you been listening? Every time the painting goes missing, it is just after someone has taken a picture of it! The newspaper photo after the museum disappearance! The cataloguing after the art sting! The crime photos at my house!"

He charged at Gardner with such ferocity that the curator spilled the coffee all over himself, but Randolph bent and grabbed one edge of the paper-wrapped portrait instead. He tore a huge section of paper, revealing the painting beneath.

"Not possible," Gardner said, dropping the coffee mug. Beneath the torn paper was the face of a sad clown with red hair and a busted top hat.

"If you care at all for your colleague's life, you'll call him immediately. Tell him to find the painting, and you tell him not to turn his back on it once he does."

Gus Cunningham ignored his phone, engrossed as he was in his research. He'd quickly found other works by the purported artist, and comparing the brushstrokes alone, it could certainly be a Thomas Winslow. The signature was also a spot-on match, but the gaps in provenance left plenty of room for a gifted forgery.

Fifteen minutes into his research, he had found a photograph in the local newspaper from 1901 that only showed three subjects in the painting. He'd reached for the phone to let Dr. Gardner know it was a forgery, but a thought stopped him. Perhaps the painting had been folded in half when it was initially displayed.

From there he wasted another ten minutes comparing the details of the left side of the painting to the grainy photo from the newspaper. It was useless. He closed the newspaper photo and looked at the painting as a whole.

Two things were impossible in conjunction. The police officers had plastic faceplates and name tags—impossible in the nineteenth century. But he'd swear the green highlight used throughout was zinc cadmium sulfide— impossible in the modern age, since nuclear testing fundamentally changed the properties of elemental cadmium.

The phone rang again and Gus instinctively reached for it. Dr. Gardner again. He sent it to voicemail.

"I said I'd call you as soon as I have something."

It was entirely possible that the canvas had been cleverly stitched to another one and the newer figures added since then. Aside from the obvious question, why would anyone want to, the sticky part was that the artist's signature covered part of a policeman's uniform.

His gaze wandered back to those green highlights. If only he'd had access to the painting itself, he could tell in two minutes what kind of paint that was. He zoomed in until that white-green pigment filled the screen.

At this zoom level, a darker area became

obvious, vaguely in the shape of a person. Realizing it was a reflection of something behind him, Gus spun around.

The painting from the photo was on the wall behind him. "What the hell?" he said.

It should be a painting of his yacht off the coast of Portland Head with the lighthouse in the background. Instead, *Agatha Hemsley, Beloved Mother,* hung in its place.

He stood gawping at it. When was the last time he'd actually looked at the painting behind his desk? He couldn't remember. Was it possible Dr. Gardner had snuck the painting over here in the last day or so? Then sent the photograph as some sort of joke? It seemed unlikely, but no better explanation came to mind.

Even if he had, his mind had latched on to something wrong about the painting itself. He couldn't quite figure out what it was, but something was definitely off.

He turned toward the image on the computer screen and zoomed back out to see the whole thing. The difference was apparent immediately. In the photograph, a young man stood behind the old woman on the couch.

"This is too weird."

He picked up his phone with the intent to call Dr. Gardner, but he stepped close to the portrait to study it first. Another incredible forgery. The area behind the old woman was a perfect continuation of the gaudy wallpaper.

A hand clamped down on Gus's shoulder, startling him into dropping his phone. He let out a yelp and grabbed his attacker.

Gus's hand *gooshed* into something soft and came away covered in a mix of muted colors.

The intruder shoved him forward, pressing his face against the portrait. It smeared beneath his cheek and ear, dripping slowly into his ear canal.

Bracing both hands against the frame, he pried his face off the canvas. Before him was a mess of smeared colors, but as he watched, the other figures turned to regard him coldly. Gus screamed, and the hand pressed harder. His mouth filled with globs of dripping paint. He spat it out, but more followed. It ran down his hair and splashed onto the small of his back.

Gus felt the fabric of the canvas stretch beneath his face as he was forced deeper and deeper into the portrait.

Beyond the Rail

"We were happy," Elie said, sniffing. "Weren't we?"

"Oh, honey," Rebecca said, hugging her dear friend. "Sometimes, there's just no way to predict these things."

"But I was so happy, and I…thought he was happy too. How could he…" She trailed off, crying.

"I know. And he didn't even leave a note. That's what they're supposed to do, right?"

Elie didn't respond. She just dabbed at her eyes with her handkerchief.

Rebecca frowned.

"Look, I can finish up here. I don't think they need you anymore. How about you go home, see if you can rest?"

"Home? Where he hung himself?"

"Hanged."

Elie stopped mid-sob. "What?"

"The proper word is hanged. We hung a picture on the wall, but Chester hanged—" A look of horror came over Rebecca's face. "I'm so sorry!"

Elie stood up. "Maybe I will go home."

"Wait! I'm sorry, Elie!"

Elie didn't listen. There was no air left in the room, and she couldn't answer if she wanted to. It was all too much. She ran out of the building and straight to her car, where she let herself sob without restraint. She had been crying all night and most of the day though, and she quickly ran out of tears. She turned the rear-view mirror toward herself, wiped her eyes, and started up the car.

Her home felt too normal. Too pleasant. White oak hardwood floors, textured eggshell walls, gas fireplace and carpeted staircase up two flights to the bedroom loft. This was not the sort of place you could think somebody died in.

Elie looked up the stairwell to the light fixture hanging at the top, the lamp her husband had tied a rope to before climbing over the bannister and jumping.

There was no sign that anything had happened. The chain supporting the lamp had taken Chester's weight without protest. If she took a picture, it could go straight into a real estate catalog.

But how was she to climb those stairs to her bedroom? How was she supposed to open her door each morning and look at that banister without seeing him climbing over and dropping off? She was so tired though, and all she wanted was some relief from reality. Perchance to dream.

She tore herself away from the self-destructive view, walked through the kitchen and into the laundry room. Opening the pantry, she pulled out the spare sheets and blankets and made up the couch.

The next several days were a blur. People would put papers in front of her and she would sign them. She had no idea what any of it meant. Thank God for Rebecca, though, because she kept Elie on track. At one point Rebecca mentioned the funeral, and Elie was surprised that it was coming up so quickly.

Then she was surprised to find an entire week had passed.

Rebecca took her shopping for something to wear.

"Something somber, yet flattering. Something respectful, yet proud," Rebecca said.

Elie ended up with a cream-colored silk blouse, with a black skirt—form fitting, but below the knee—matching jacket and flats. To top it off, Rebecca got her a wide-brimmed black hat with a veil. She felt like something out of *Dark Shadows*, but she couldn't bring herself to care how she looked.

She wanted to get home. She had taken to speaking to Chester as if he were still there. She knew him well, and she knew how he'd respond, so she had full conversations with him and could just about believe she heard his voice. Only, she knew it would look crazy, so she couldn't do it while Rebecca was with her.

Then Rebecca said something that caught her attention.

"They need to know if you want an open or closed casket. Now, I think closed would be better because it'll cost a fortune in makeup to fix his—"

"Open," Elie interrupted. "I want to see him again."

"Are you sure, Honey? It can be hard—"

"I want to see him again," she said. "I have nothing left but…stuff. And photos. I want to etch him into my mind because I'm afraid of forgetting his face."

From that point on, she counted the hours. She spoke to him often, even laughed, but it was more than his face she was worried about forgetting. Rebecca had cleaned the house that Elie was neglecting, and now she couldn't find his scent anywhere. All his soaps and razors had been tossed out, his clothes packed up for donation, and their sheets and pillows washed.

There was a breast pocket on her funeral jacket, and Elie slipped a pair of sewing scissors into it along with a small velvet pouch.

His funeral was well attended. News must have spread, whether by social media, or Rebecca directly, or news outlets, none of which Elie had paid any attention to since…

A group from Chester's high school water polo team was there in their letterman jackets, and Chester's firm was well represented too. The CEO even showed up. He took Elie by the hands and said he wanted to personally help pay for all of this.

Everyone was sorry for her loss.

People got up and spoke. They all talked about him in the past tense, having made peace with the fact that he was gone. But what good times they'd had, right?

Finally, one by one, they were given time to approach the coffin and say a personal farewell. Elie retrieved the scissors and the pouch, pulling the drawstrings wide. She slipped into the finger holes, gripping the blades in her fist to conceal them. She stepped up to the coffin, a deep bronze with brass handles, open on one end, and she stopped.

There was Chester. They'd put him in his wedding tuxedo. He was wearing makeup, rather too obviously, but there he was. He could have just been asleep, except of course there would have been his gentle snoring interrupting the proceedings.

She knelt on the second step, placing her arms on the lip of his coffin, and bowing her head as if in prayer. The grieving widow. No one would give it a second thought. Except any observant onlookers would have noticed that unlike the last ten days, her eyes were completely dry.

When she stood again, pouch full, she realized she'd made a mess of his carefully trimmed hair. She reached out and pushed it to the other side, as if they'd parted it wrong. Moments later the funeral director was at her elbow with another man, and they gently ushered her away, whispering, "So sorry for your loss."

Chester was home again. Where he should be. Elie woke up in her own bed, stretching her back as she luxuriated in the light that poured in through the south-facing windows. She was alive once more.

It wasn't just his lock of hair either, which was now tied in a silky blue ribbon and tacked above the bed. He had followed it home. His spirit once more inhabited this home, and Elie had found peace again. Everything happens for a reason, even if he hadn't done it purposely. Elie chose to believe that the reason Chester had killed himself in their home was so that he would never have to leave it again.

She hummed as she got dressed. A little eyeliner, a hint of blush, and some knock-out lipstick. She wanted to look her best for him. Taking one last look in the mirror, she admired the way she looked in this top, one of his favorites. Then she threw open the door and stepped out onto the landing.

"Good morning, my love," she said.

Chester wasn't looking his best, admittedly, but she didn't love him solely for his looks. Besides, he was hard to see when she looked straight at him, anyway. If she looked a bit

away—for instance, at the lamp he hung from—
she could see him well enough, still struggling,
one hand tearing at the rope around his neck, the
other one reaching for the banister just beyond his
fingertips.

She moved a couple paces to her right until
she stood in line with his outstretched arm, then
looked at her feet. She stomped repeatedly,
leaving visible impressions in the pile carpet.
Tomorrow, when she exited the bedroom, she
would stand just there. If she made a habit of it, it
would come naturally, and someday she would
believe quite firmly that it was her he reached for
and not the banister.

Elie stepped over the banister, her feet placed
between two balusters, one hand on the rail. She
leaned out, lips outstretched, and closed her eyes
so as not to see his bulging eyes, his beet-red face.
Her lips brushed a cooler pocket of air, and she
made a kissing noise.

Climbing back over the railing, she prepared
for work, thinking about someday, when she
would bury a lock of her own hair behind a wall
with his, and she would join him in eternity just
beyond the rail.

Two Shadows, One Gun

Boots clunked on the loose wooden planks of the saloon entry. Rusty springs protested until they brought the swinging doors to a stop.

Edgar Pertwee, undertaker, smiled at the sound.

"Deadeye Dixon, I'm calling you out!"

The young man stood some thirty feet from the bar, his right hand hovering over his pistol.

The bar was past capacity. The long cattle trail came to its end at Pine Gulch, a narrow strip of wooden buildings on one side of the North Fork Teton River just before it climbed into mountainous country. All the cattlemen were full up on silver and spending like it was doomsday in one of the four saloons along Main Street. Phineas Moorehouse's was the most popular.

A path cleared between the young gunslinger at the door and the figure in black at the bar. Pertwee made a few mental calculations. Five foot ten, slight build. He had a suit in the back of his shop that would do the job if he re-seamed the back. An ash casket would suit the young man's complexion.

Tom "Deadeye" Dixon's head raised slightly at the sound of his name, but he did not turn away from where he stood at the bar. He didn't even glance up at the young man's reflection in the mirror behind the bar. His eyes stayed planted on the shot of whiskey sitting in front of him.

A man in a pork pie hat who had just been about to hang his coat on the hat stand near the door, slowly backed away, coat clutched tightly in both hands.

The gunslinger glanced at the faces of the surrounding men, then bored into the back of the man at the bar. No one had bothered moving away from him, but most turned around to watch.

"I said I—"

"I heard you," Dixon said. He threw back his shot of whiskey and plunked it onto the bar, motioning for Mr. Moorehouse to fill it again.

"They say you're fast," the young man in the doorway said. "Only, they've been saying that for twenty years. I'm thinking you ain't as fast as you used to be. I reckon you maybe don't see so good anymore. I reckon maybe you're more reputation than gunslinger nowadays. So, how about you turn around, and we'll see if you're still dead-eye fast."

"You got a dollar on you, kid?" Dixon asked.

"Wh-what?" the kid asked.

Dixon's eyes finally looked up to meet the kid's mirror image. He held his refilled whiskey just below his lips as he spoke. "A silver dollar. I want you to toss a silver dollar high in the air, and I'll show you how fast I am."

The kid's grimace faltered for a moment, then redoubled in intensity as he dug a dollar coin out of his vest pocket. It rested on the fist of his left hand while his right still hovered over his gun.

The silver coin sang true as it launched off his thumb.

Blam!

Pertwee never even saw Dixon's hand move. His right was still holding his whiskey, but his left held the pistol that sat on his right hip. Without turning, he had put a bullet in the kid's forehead.

A look of mild curiosity crossed the kid's face. He fell to his knees, then flat on his face.

Dixon holstered his gun and snatched the silver dollar out of the air as it sailed past his ear.

"For the expense of burying him," he said.

He set the coin on the bar and flicked it down to Pertwee, who slapped his hand over it.

"Did anyone happen to catch the kid's name?" Pertwee asked.

No one responded, and the bar quickly returned to its previous activity.

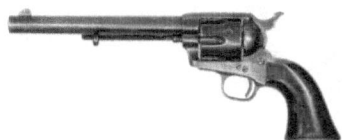

Agnes Tennyson sat bolt upright behind her desk. The vision had come, same as every day, and as bad as the headlines around here often were, tomorrow's caught the breath in her chest.

Her one reporter, Fillmore Breach, caught the

motion and stood up from his chair in the corner, quickly drawing the stub of a pencil from behind his ear.

Agnes looked at the clock on the wall, snapped her finger and pointed at Fillmore. "There's a barn dance tonight. I want you to go."

"I-I don't have a date," he said.

"Good, because you'll be working," Agnes said. "Stay by the doors. Get a full account of who is there. Take notes on what the band plays. But get out of there by 10:00. Do you hear me? You mustn't fail. Say it back to me."

"I'll get a full account of who's there, take notes on the songs and be gone by 10:00."

His brows were knitted with curiosity, but he didn't question her orders, which was good because Agnes had no intention of supplying answers.

"Exactly. And stand by the doors. If they start to close them, by God, you be on the outside. And bring that photographer friend of yours. I need pictures."

"I can ask him, Miss Tennyson, but he won't go. The dance starts at eight, and he won't work after sunset."

"Tell him to make an exception. For the sake of history."

"I will, Miss, all the same, he won't do it."

Agnes searched his face, but found nothing there but an infuriating mix of sincerity and innocence.

"Mr. Breach, how long have you lived in this town?"

Fillmore smiled with relief, but turned his

little notebook round in his hands. "All my life. I was born here, Miss."

"Of course, you were. That explains why you don't fit. And you've never lived in another town, so you probably don't see anything peculiar about this one. If I asked you why your friend won't work after dark, I'm betting you were always just too polite to ask him. Am I right?"

He smiled again, more nervously this time.

"You'd have to ask Morris, Miss."

"Alright, I'll do that. In the meantime, I heard a gunshot, and I know you heard it too. That will be the illustrious bastard Dixon, no doubt. Go find out who he killed today and get me an article."

"Yes, Miss. Only…"

"Only I shouldn't call him that, right?" She came around her desk and planted her hands on her hips. "Are you going to tell him?"

Fillmore's face drained of color.

"No, Miss!"

"Then what the bastard doesn't know won't hurt me. Now, git!"

Fillmore ran out the door. Agnes placed her wide brim hat on her head and cocked it just so before following.

The little bell over Morris Shadwell's studio door

signaled the arrival of a customer.

"One moment," he said without looking away from his work.

Painting out aberrations from his negatives was probably the most important part of his work, but it was painstaking, requiring delicate brushstrokes, silver chromate ink, and multiple magnifying lenses.

Morris put the last stroke down, perfectly matching the background wallpaper, and dropped the tiny brush into the jar of mineral oil. He greeted his visitor with a broad smile, flipping up the lens hanging in front of his glasses.

"Miss Tennyson, what a pleasant surprise. Did you want an updated portrait, or is this for your little newspaper?"

"*The Gulch Gazette* may not be *The New York Times*, Mr. Shadwell, but history remains a noble endeavor, even in this Godforsaken town."

She turned toward the wall of his gallery and began examining the unclaimed photos hanging there.

"And, yes. I have work for you. Paying work. Work that you will initially decline, but I want to strike past that."

Morris set down his glasses and left his workbench to join Miss Tennyson.

"And what work is this?" he asked.

"Mr. Shadwell, are you a religious man?"

The question took him by surprise.

"I don't see what that has—"

She pointed toward the entrance without looking.

"The mezuzah on your doorframe. You strike

me as an intelligent man. Your work is remarkable. If you are religious as well, I have to wonder why you don't ply your trade in a larger town. One with a temple? Perhaps Grand Rapids? Or even Butte?" She stood up straight and faced him, nearly eye to eye in her high-button shoes. "Are you a criminal?"

"What? Certainly not!"

"No. I couldn't imagine you were. And yet, Mr. Shadwell, people come to this little town for only three reasons. They come for gold from the nearby mountains, they come with the cattle trade, or they come because they don't belong in normal society. Since you are no criminal, and you are clearly religious, I must wonder what drives you here?"

Morris opened his mouth to respond, but she held a hand in front of his face.

"No, don't bother, I don't expect the truth. You've lived under Dixon's tyranny longer than I have, you must have a lie well practiced by now. But I have been paying attention, and I think the clues are falling into place. Did you know that your studio—and by extension, your home—is the only building on Main Street with iron bars on the windows and door? Do you really think anyone will steal your tin types?"

His eyes widened and his face paled. "The developer...s-silver—"

"Iron bars, Mr. Shadwell. Now, I've heard it said evil spirits cannot suffer the touch of iron. I understand they also cannot stand the tinkling of bells, or the prayers of our Lord, like the two wrapped up in your little mezuzah?"

She pressed even closer, seeming to take up all the air around them. Morris pulled at his collar, desperate to catch a breath.

Agnes leaned forward and whispered, "Tell me, Mr. Shadwell, why do you spend so much time touching up your photographs? And why won't you leave your studio after dark?"

He had lies, but they wouldn't hold up to this level of scrutiny and insight, and there seemed to be no escaping her questions. Instead, he pushed away, getting a plinth between the two of them, and room enough to breathe. "If I tell you, this can't end up in your paper."

She smiled, a smug but encouraging look. "Strictly off the record."

"No. You'll never believe me. I'll show you instead." He beckoned for her to follow him to his workbench. Her eyes latched onto every movement his face made, making him even more nervous. He wanted a reason to trust her, but a secret as big as his made that hard to do. Though, honestly, he'd held it inside for such a long time, and here was a chance to say it out loud.

He released the carbon smeared glass from the clamps and held it between the lamp and a yellowing sheet of paper.

"I just finished working on Mrs. Wilde's negative. It's still wet, but as you can see, a lovely portrait."

He set it down carefully and picked up another pane of glass.

"Here's the one of her husband, Jonathan. That one came out clean—no work to be done there. Now this one," he said, picking up a larger landscape, but holding it away from the light, "is a family portrait. Jonathan, Melissa, and their two boys. At least it is supposed to be. Grandmother was in Melissa's solo photo as well, and I don't even know who the other one is."

He put the negative into the lamp light, and Agnes leaned in close.

"Good God, is that...?"

The boys and their father stood dressed in Sunday best, staring fixedly at the camera. Mary had a sadness to her eyes, but still a spark of the beauty she'd once had. Only, just over her shoulder was a stern-faced woman in a tight gray bun and high collared black dress. Her face was gaunt, and her eyes were the milky white of cataracts. Worse than that, the pattern of the wallpaper continued right on through her face and dress.

"You photographed a ghost," she said, barely a whisper.

"That's Melissa's mother. She passed three years ago from fever, just before you arrived," he said. "But the town's full of ghosts. Well, all towns are, and the bigger cities are worse. I can see them, and the Lord knows why, but they show up in my photographs. They follow their living relatives around, but when the town sleeps, they come to visit me. The iron bars keep them outside."

He started to put the glass plate with the others, but she grabbed his arm, keeping her eye on the projected image on yellow paper.

"You said there was another one?"

Morris swallowed, his voice coming out in a

dry rasp, "Yes."

He pointed toward the edge of the photograph where a doorway led off into another room.

She gasped, and Morris knew she'd seen it—the blackened, nearly skeletal figure in the darkened room. Those white pinpoints for eyes were no trick of the light.

Morris pulled her hand away from his arm, and this time she let him set the plate aside.

She continued to stare at the paper background for several moments before speaking.

"I want you to bring your camera to the barn dance tonight," she said.

"Did you hear nothing I just said? These things in the photograph? There are dozens like them following people through town, but they all come for me at night. I can't go out."

"Oh, I heard you, Mr. Shadwell. That's a terrible curse to bear. But I've got a curse of my own, and I am one hundred percent certain that the ghosts will be in that barn tonight. Your photographs—from the outside, of course—may prove vitally important."

Morris backed away from Agnes. "Your curse? What curse?"

"Never mind that now. From your own

words, the ghosts will continue to follow the townsfolk while they wake, and the entire town will be at the dance. Point number two, you will only need to stay until 10:30. After that, you can run to your little home and the safety herein."

Morris stood, stretching out for as much height as he could manage. "No."

"No, Mr. Shadwell?" Agnes repeated.

"No. You ask me to trust you on the strength of your curse, and yet you won't confide in me. You think you know so much about this town. You've been here barely three years, and yet you can tell me all about it. What kind of people live here. Well, I'm telling you, you can be wrong about people. There are good people in this town, fewer perhaps than there ought be, but some."

"There will be fewer tomorrow, Mr. Shadwell. And you don't want to know the details of my curse."

"You know something's going to happen," Shadwell said, raising a finger toward her face. "Something at the barn dance. Something bad."

"Leave it alone, Mr. Shadwell. No one can change the future."

"But you know. Someone's going to die, aren't they? Who? Whose grizzly business are you sending me to witness?"

"I don't know who. I only got a count."

"A count? You mean there's more than one? We need to stop the dance!" Shadwell grabbed for his hat and pushed past Agnes.

She held firm to his collar. "Don't you dare, Mr. Shadwell! You'll only make things worse!"

"How can I make it worse? Did the count

change? You said I couldn't change the future."

"Alright! I'll tell you. Just promise me you'll listen, and I'll tell you everything."

Shadwell placed his hat back on the corner of his desk and returned to his stool. He motioned toward the armchair he occasionally used for portraits.

Agnes sat, then spent some time arranging her skirts before speaking.

"My father was a Presbyterian minister. My mother sang in church. Aside from my father's regular visits to church members' homes, I don't remember much but housework and garden tending in our lives."

She raised her eyes from her skirts and stared at Shadwell.

"I was six when it first happened. And it's been daily since then. Same time every day, but of course we didn't know what it was at first. My mother said I just went blank for a minute. She was pale as a ghost and sent father for the doctor just as soon as he got home. All I remember is the words, 'Local man wins prize in pie-eating contest.' The doctor was back the next day, and the next. From my mother's point of view, it was like some sort of seizure. Only when I came out of it, I'd say the darnedest things. Another was 'Lightning strikes tree, narrowly misses cat.'"

"These are headlines," Shadwell said. "Newspaper headlines."

Agnes nodded.

"We only got the Sunday paper, way out where we lived, but as soon as they delivered it, and it said the same thing I'd said, father knew what had happened. I'd been touched by God. He never knew how wrong he was. It seemed a harmless enough miracle at first, and it sure filled the pews on Sunday. Father would bring me up at the end of the service, and I'd say the words that came to me that day, and when they turned up on Monday's paper, we'd have even more people at next week's service."

"You must have been famous," Shadwell commented.

"Regionally, at least, for the better part of a year. But it ended all too soon. It was Tuesday, February 11th. My parents went to visit Mrs. Adale and her two girls when I had my vision. 'Local minister and wife die in buggy accident.'"

"Oh, dear girl. Your parents," he said, biting the knuckle of one finger.

"The moment I returned to myself, I ran. It was pouring rain, but I ran. Back then, I believed I could stop it. If this was a gift from God, surely I could stop it. But this is not a gift, it is a curse. I fully intended to run all the way to the Adale's house, but they were already hurrying home because of the storm. I came around a stand of trees and saw them in the distance. Father's little black buggy pulled by our two horses. I had to do everything I could to stop them, before something went wrong. But they didn't see me. I jumped. I waved my arms. I even shouted, but my words were swallowed by the storm. I was oblivious to my own danger, with the horses barreling down on me."

This was the first time she'd told the story in at least a decade, and she cursed herself internally for still getting so emotional about it. Dispassion was her trade. She pressed her lips tightly and looked away from Shadwell until the pain in her eyes subsided.

"Of course, Father saw me at the last moment. He pulled hard on the reins, but the horses turned instead of stopping. The buggy went end over end, and my parents looked like shattered porcelain dolls smothered in jam."

"I'm so sorry, Miss Tennyson." Shadwell said, and silence fell between them.

When he spoke again, it was hesitantly. "And tomorrow's headline? I presume you—"

"Twelve dead in barn dance massacre."

"Twelve! But we have to warn people! There is still time to call off the dance!"

Agnes flung herself out of the chair.

"Don't you think I've tried? How many, many times I've tried? All I know is the headline, but that's set in stone. I don't know who it will be, or how we get from here to there, but I already know you won't stop it! The story on page two might be, 'Local photographer dies of heart attack on way to warn town of massacre.' I don't know! All I know is you are going to fail. The dance will happen, and twelve people will die."

"But I can't just stand there and take photographs. That's hideous! It's macabre! I won't do it."

"No. It's not. It's eulogy. If we don't do this, these people, this act, will be forgotten. We cannot stop their deaths, but we can remember them. For history."

Fillmore Breach took up position, leaning against the frame of the open barn doors. He flipped through the pages of his notebook until he came to a blank sheet and touched the tip of his pencil to his tongue.

Looking back down Main Street, he could see people coming, wearing their Sunday finest, as well as Morris Shadwell, setting up his camera a hundred feet away. Fillmore waved. Inside the barn, Mr. Hayes was spreading fresh straw while the band did some last-minute rehearsing. Mrs. Hayes and several volunteers adjusted plates of sweets for best viewing, and counted all the cups for the punchbowl.

Fillmore considered running in and requesting a bite of Mrs. Shannon's rhubarb crisp, but he knew what Miss Tennyson would say. Work cometh before reward. Only, if he was to leave by 10:00, he would miss the reward as well.

He sighed, and instead turned toward the band, jotting down, "S. Deacon, fiddle. H. Billings, banjo. C. Knott, bass. G. Santos, tin whistle." Mr. Deacon stamped as he played, so Fillmore added "percussions" after fiddle.

"Mr. Breach."

The voice startled him, but it was only Morris.

"Gadzooks, Morris. Don't sneak up on a guy like that."

"Sorry. It's just…how much has Miss Tennyson told you about tonight?"

"Just to take note of everyone who's here and all the songs they play. Hey, don't you want to set up a little closer? Surely, you can't see the band from way out there."

"I don't think it's pictures of the band she is after. You will get out of here as soon as you have your story, won't you?"

"Oh, yes. Strict orders. I'm to bring her all the details by 10:00."

"Excellent, Mr. Breach," Morris said, and jogged back up toward his camera.

"Call me Fillmore," he called back.

He watched Morris stop to talk to Mr. and Mrs. O'Leary along the way. He was pointing at the sky and rubbing his knee. He stopped once more before reaching his camera. This time it was Deadeye Dixon who stopped him.

Fillmore entered the names in his list of attendees. Anything to avoid being caught staring at Mr. Dixon. Once, as a child, he'd caused some offense and ended up looking down the barrel of Mr. Dixon's gun. His mother had saved him that day, and he'd been wary ever since.

The line of people kept coming. There was Mr. Bing, the provisioner, and his wife. The tinsmith, Mr. Brody, was alone, curiously enough, as was Mr. Pratt, the telegraph operator. Mr. and Mrs. Davis attended with their eldest daughter, Maisy. The brothel girls were all there, though whether on the clock or off was anyone's guess. Following them were the cattlemen who'd reached trail's end this week.

Dixon and Morris were still talking. Dixon didn't look happy either, his hand even dropped to tickle one of his guns, but Morris kept smiling and must have talked his way out of trouble, because Dixon turned and continued toward the barn.

Once he was inside, the music started in earnest, and Fillmore had plenty of notes to take.

His eye kept wandering toward Dixon. He could have coerced any woman to dance with him, but he never did. He stood stoically watching the dancers from the edge of the dance floor, then switching to a new position for the next song. Likewise, he never went near the food table.

Fillmore crossed out the last line. He wasn't there to watch Dixon, and while he wasn't paying attention, a few more people had slipped in. He quickly added the late arrivals, then did his best to recollect the last few songs that had played. It was 9:50 by his watch.

"You're sweating, Mr. Peabody," Mr. Dixon said from nearby.

Fillmore looked up. The band had just finished one song, and the seconds ticked on with silence coming from them. The banker, Ellis Peabody, was indeed sweating. Buckets.

"It's the dancing. I was just dancing, and I'm not as young as I used to be," Peabody said, backing away from the gunslinger.

"Sure," Dixon said, matching his steps. "Could be that. It's just, to me, you look nervous.

Now, why would you be nervous?"

Peabody's wide staring eyes darted in all directions, looking for support. When he looked back at Dixon, he forced a smile. "Nervous? Of course I'm not nervous..." He stepped back into the table of food and nearly jumped out of his skin.

Dixon brushed back his coat and set his hand on the revolver on his right hip.

Jake Hollins and Sandy Rush stepped out behind Dixon, guns drawn. Christopher Knott up on the bandstand pulled a shotgun from behind his bass.

Hollins and Rush fired at once, but Dixon chose that moment to duck. Peabody caught a round in the shoulder, twisting him around and knocking him to the floor. Dixon spun as he came up, both guns drawn, but his first shot hit Knott up on the bandstand, directly between the eyes. He hadn't even been looking.

Rush jumped back into the crowd, but Hollins faced Dixon down. He was dead by the time he pulled the trigger, and he missed Dixon by half a foot. Rush stood up, pushing his way through the crowd, heading for the door. Dixon took aim, his face a mask of murderous intent. He fired, and Rush went down, inches from where Fillmore stood.

Dixon spun, advancing on Mr. Peabody, still laying on the floor.

"Three? You thought three men could take me? Who else did you hire, Peabody? Who was supposed to jump out along with those three but was just too yellow?"

Peabody tried to push himself backward, though there was nowhere to go. There were only two exits, the one by Fillmore, and the one out into the corral, and that one was currently barred.

"Nobody! I swear it was only them."

"Liar!" Dixon roared and put a bullet between Peabody's eyes. He turned on the crowd that was edging toward the open door. "Was it you, Stokes? You've never had the nerve to look me in the eye, but I saw you came strapped today!"

As one, the crowd froze. Stokes shook his head violently.

"How about you, Billings? You must have seen that scattergun from where you stood, but you didn't say nothing. You were in on it, weren't you?

Billings wet himself in response.

"Maybe it was Hayes. Where are you, Hayes? Maybe you thought I'd be trapped in your barn with just the one exit. Easier to kill? Come out and face me, Hayes."

Somewhere in the crowd was the click of a hammer drawing back. Dixon snatched Delphine, one of the brothel girls, from the edge of the crowd, and held her in front of himself.

The rest of the brothel girls screamed. People started running for the door. Dixon fired three shots in rapid succession, and three men went down.

Fillmore poked his head out to record who'd been hit.

"You," Dixon said.

Fillmore met Dixon's eyes.

"Get out of there, Fillmore!" came Morris's voice from behind. But Fillmore couldn't move, except for his writing hand, which he couldn't stop.

The last thing he saw was the muzzle flash.

A pounding at the door brought Agnes Tennyson out of her chair in the darkened room. She'd been waiting anxiously for Mr. Breach's return. She turned up the wick on her lamp and opened the door.

Morris Shadwell stood on her porch, looking like a cat freshly on its ninth life. She looked past him.

"Mr. Shadwell, where's Mr. Breach?"

Shadwell pushed into the office, carrying a bundle and his tripod. He closed the door and stood against it.

"Quick! Bring all the iron you have. Horseshoes, sheers, fire pokers. Anything!" He rocked forward and back, reciting something in Hebrew.

"But where's Mr. Breach? It's past 10:00!"

Shadwell dropped his tripod and reached into his bag. He pulled out a notepad and pressed it into her hands.

"Fillmore is dead. He died doing your work."

The notepad stuck to her fingers as she turned

it, barely registering Shadwell's words.

"Dead? But—" Her fingers came away red, and she dropped the notepad.

"Iron, woman! If we're to survive the night, bring iron!"

Agnes shook herself.

"The printing press," she said, and strode quickly into the next room. She was back shortly with an armload of assorted parts. Rollers, levers, half of a carriage mechanism, and a wheel. "There are more spare parts in a box back there, but it's too heavy for me."

"Place them across the threshold," Shadwell said, heading toward the back room. "How many windows do you have?"

"Just the big one here," she said, laying a lever next to a roller.

Shadwell returned with the crate. "Do you have a hammer? Some nails? We need to cross the window's corners with iron."

She pointed with her chin. "The tinsmith next door has some tools in the shed out back. He lets me use them. There's a door from the bedroom."

Shadwell set the crate down. "He won't need them anymore."

"Oh, not him too," Agnes said. "What happened?"

He paused in the doorway. "Deadeye Dixon happened." Then he disappeared out back.

Agnes sat on the floor with her back to the door, thumbing through Breach's notepad while Shadwell was out. She heard his footsteps on her floorboards and wiped her eyes dry on the back of her hands.

In a voice so steady she surprised herself, she said, "Mr. Breach only listed seven dead. Who were the other five?"

Shadwell hammered two nails near one corner of the window, then placed a lever across the corner and bent the nails over it.

"Fillmore was number eight. Even before he went down, though, people were trampling each other to get through the door. By the time Dixon left the barn, he stepped over four more bodies."

He started working on another corner.

"But whose bodies, Mr. Shadwell, whose?"

Shadwell was staring out through the gap in the drapes.

"No more questions. They're coming for me. Get the back door."

Once he was satisfied with their security, he backed far away from the window.

"Turn the lamp down."

"I can't. I have a paper to publish."

"Do it later!"

Agnes stared at Shadwell for some time without moving. She heard footsteps on the boardwalk outside, but nobody passed the window. She turned the wick down.

"Do you see them, Shadwell? Your ghosts. Are they here now?"

"They're here. But I dare not look."

"Why not? Surely, the iron will hold them back."

His voice was barely above a whisper.

"Because Fillmore may be with them."

A shudder went through her, and it was a while before either of them spoke. She could swear she heard tapping on the glass in addition to the near constant footsteps.

"Did you get photographs?" she asked.

The sounds would surely drive her mad if she didn't drown them out.

"I got your photos. You can't publish the ones with Dixon in them though."

"I wouldn't dream of it. He'd kill me. Kill us both."

She could only see Shadwell in silhouette, but it looked like he nodded.

"He told me he didn't want his photo taken. I thought it was to avoid accurate wanted posters, but I realize now he had a different reason."

"What did you see, Shadwell?"

Shadwell whispered in Hebrew again, like reciting a prayer. Once he'd finished, he said, "You remember I told you, people have spirits that follow them around? Dixon has something else. I don't know what it is—a shadow thing—but I don't think it was ever human."

"What does it look like?"

Shadwell was silent. Agnes gave him his time because she knew how slippery trauma could be. When one turned the memory onto a horrific moment, it slid right over it without catching detail. Focusing on what one's sanity tried to avoid took courage, and even still it was like trying to catch a red-hot bar of soap.

"I imagine it's this way with your headlines," Shadwell said. "Having a knowledge and the firm conviction of its truth without proof."

"I'm afraid I'm not following you, Mr. Shadwell. What does this have to do with Dixon's shadow?"

"I can't get you much detail because I can't look straight at it. I don't know how I know, but if I look right at it, I will die. I *think* it will know I can see it, and it won't abide that, but that's just what I think. I may just die from the act of looking at it. All I can say is, from the corner of my eye, it looks like it's been burnt. By the fires of hell."

"But you got photos of it."

"I did, but I will not look at them either. I'll show you how to develop them and you'll have your answer."

"You are suggesting it's safe for me to see it."

"I can't defend my assertion. It may even be safe for me to look. But I think it will know…and I'd rather not chance it."

Silence fell between them again, filled with the constant creak of floorboards and a moaning that didn't seem like the wind. Shadwell was the one to interrupt the maddening noises this time.

"But tonight, I learned Dixon's secret."

"What secret?"

"How he wins every gunfight. See, I saw Hollins and Rush come up behind him. They shot at him from the back. But that thing? That shadow? It *pulled* him out of the way. When he turned around, *it* did the aiming."

Agnes stood up. She started pacing in the small space between her desk and her stove.

"Do you understand what that means, Mr. Shadwell?"

"That no one will ever beat him because he has supernatural help."

She stopped.

"No. It means, if we can separate this shadow from him, he *can* be beaten."

Realization dawned in Shadwell's eyes, but his face quickly fell and he shook his head.

"Even if we could, who's going to take him on? You?"

Agnes had already thought of that.

"No, but I received a telegram yesterday, that Lieutenant Sam James was seen in Fort Benton boarding a stagecoach for Pine Gulch. He should be here tomorrow."

"*The* Sam James? The hero of Owl Creek?"

"That's the one. He's been hunting down the lawless since the war ended. Dixon would be exactly his sort. That is, if we can give him an advantage."

By the time the stagecoach and Lieutenant James arrived, word had spread throughout the town. And based solely on his reputation, everyone knew why he was there.

After the bloodbath the previous night, there wasn't but one person in all of town who didn't wish him well. There was also only one person who wasn't the slightest bit nervous.

A crowd formed around the stagecoach, but Agnes had sent her own telegram ahead to Fairfield, and based on her message, the

Lieutenant got off the stage before it entered town. Agnes and Morris were waiting for him in the small apple orchard tended by Mr. Peabody the younger.

"Speak your piece and let me pass. I can't have people thinking I'm scared of your Deadeye Dixon," James said.

"Given your record, Lieutenant, no one would think you a coward. But understand, if you go to face him unprepared, you will die."

"Miss, I understand he's quick, and a good shot too. I was never the fastest draw, but that didn't matter in the military, and I must admit, my aim is not as good as it was in my youth. A man more concerned with honor would still plan to outdraw him, but I am not that man. No, Miss, I got my reputation by doing the right thing and ending threats. Mr. Dixon represents a threat to the peace, and I will end him. Even if that means shooting him in the back."

Shadwell stepped forward.

"It doesn't matter if you come at him from behind. It doesn't matter if you catch him sleeping. He will see you coming, and he will not be where you shoot. He has help."

"You mean there are others in town, working for him?"

Shadwell motioned for Agnes to bring out the photos. She had developed and printed the photos in the early morning hours under his tutelage. He still steadfastly refused to look at them. Agnes understood why, with that toothy fiend seeming to always be staring at the camera.

Agnes handed him three photographs.

"No, sir, that is not what we mean."

The lieutenant flipped through the photos, his eyes widening on the first image, but narrowing suspiciously by the third.

"This is a trick. Some kind of joke," he said.

"This is no joke," Shadwell said. "I can produce the negatives if you require proof. That thing you see there is directing Dixon's actions. It is the reason you cannot win. That thing killed twelve people last night while Dixon's back was turned."

James pulled out a pipe and crammed some tobacco into it.

"When the coach passed through Fairfield, I got a message. It didn't warn me off, it suggested we meet. I can only assume you have a plan." He lit a match and puffed at his pipe until it held the ember. "Something that hopefully still ends with me shooting the bastard?"

"We do. Mr. Shadwell?"

"Iron, Lieutenant. Spirits can't touch iron, they can't even cross over a strip of it. We propose to stretch a chain across Main Street and run another over the door to that saloon he spends his days in. If you call him out, that spirit won't be able to follow him. It won't be able to aim on his behalf."

James pulled the pipe out of his mouth.

"And then I face him, out in the street, one on one? I don't like those odds. Shooting through the walls of the privy while he's afflicted is a better bet."

Somehow the papers tell the story differently, Agnes thought.

"Look, we don't have a good way to get him in the privy without the spirit, but we can get him out in the street. Believe me, when you shoot him down, you'll want to do it without his guardian helping out."

"Alright. But I want some assurance. You two know how to fire a gun?"

"I've got a Henry rifle," Agnes said.

"I've never shot anything before," Shadwell admitted.

"Then you get my scattergun. You two hide where you can see the saloon and take the shot as soon as you have one. We'll take him down at high noon."

"Better make that 2:00," Agnes said.

"2:00? Who's ever heard of a shootout at mid-afternoon?"

Agnes shared a look with Shadwell.

"I have my reasons," she said.

As Morris approached the barn, Edgar Pertwee, the undertaker, and his apprentice were loading the last of the bodies into a cart.

"Good day, Mr. Shadwell," Pertwee called to him. "Would you care to donate to the burial fund for the widows? Naturally, they'd like a Christian burial, but finances are tight."

"I haven't any money on me, Mr. Pertwee.

Perhaps if you came by my studio later."

"I will be certain to, Mr. Shadwell. What brings you out this way on such a morning? The rest of the townsfolk are avoiding it entirely."

"I was just hoping to borrow some props from Mr Hayes for a photo session."

"Life goes on, I suppose. Come, George. We have work to do."

Morris stepped around the blood-soaked hay and quickly found the tool rack. Chains of various lengths hung next to yokes, hoof picks, and an assortment of brushes. He estimated the width of Main Street and quickly left the barn with two lengths of chain looped around his neck.

Digging a trench across Main Street would have been harder to explain, but luckily for Morris, Pertwee was right. The cattlemen had left early that morning for the long ride back toward Texas, and the townsfolk weren't yet ready to stick their heads out where it could get shot at.

Miss Tennyson hurried up to him as he was packing dirt back over the chain. Her expression told him something was wrong, but without saying a word, she unfolded a sheet of newspaper, blank except for the headline. "War Hero, Two Others, Dead in Shootout."

A chill went through Morris, and he planted his shovel.

"Have you shown it to James?"

"Of course not! Nothing we do can change his fate, unless there's another war hero in town that I don't know about. But I'm out."

"What do you mean, out? It doesn't say the other two are you and me. What if one of them is supposed to be Dixon?"

"If it were me writing the headline, I would certainly mention him by name. The only reasons the headline could be so vague is if someone else writes it, meaning I'm dead, or those two others are no one of note. If I'm not involved in this ambush, then I'm unlikely to be one of them. I'm out."

She folded the newspaper.

Morris leaned on the shovel, chewing over his options.

"I'm still in."

He went back to his work, shoveling in dirt and tamping it down with his boot.

"Did you hear nothing? If you are involved, you will die!" Miss Tennyson's eyes darted around as if suddenly worried about being overheard.

"The lieutenant's chances go up if I help. So, he dies. That's a tragedy that I apparently can't change. Perhaps I die as well. But let me ask you this. Is this living? What we're doing right now, under Dixon's thumb? Where he can kill twelve people and no one's building a gallows? I choose to think of all the people whose lives get better if we succeed."

"I can see your mind is made up. Well, if you two do die saving the town, I will ensure some of what you said makes it into a glowing obituary. Of course, if you fail, I won't print anything that might offend Dixon. Either way, I will be no part of such folly. Good day, Mr. Shadwell."

She turned, taking two hasty steps, then stopped. She turned back toward Morris, eyes greatly softened.

"I wish you luck."

She turned again, hurrying straight for her print shop.

Another hour passed before Lieutenant James made his appearance. Morris stood with him in an alley about three blocks down from the saloon. Morris pointed out where he buried the chain.

"And the one above the saloon door?"

"In place. I set it there while verifying that Dixon was inside."

"Good. Where is Miss Tennyson?"

"She…got cold feet. Besides, murder is work for men, wouldn't you agree?"

James grunted, removing his pipe and knocking it against the sole of his boot before returning it to his pocket.

"And where are you planning to be?"

"My shop. It's on this side of Main Street, twenty paces past the chain. I should have a clear shot at him without raising suspicion." He didn't add that his windows and doors were covered in iron, giving him an added layer of protection.

"I'm still not comfortable with this plan. You're certain he can't shoot so well without this spirit?"

"I can only tell you what I saw. It pulled him out of the way when two fellers tried to shoot him in the back, and then it aimed where he wasn't looking, killing his ambushers. He can't do that without it."

"Alright." Lieutenant James handed Morris his shotgun and tightened his gun belt. "You get on down to your place, then. I'm itching to get this over with."

Morris lingered, torn about leaving him in the dark as to his fate. But then he thought about Mr. Breach, who probably wouldn't have been at that dance if Miss Tennyson hadn't sent him. Morris couldn't bear it if something he said was what got James killed. Better to say nothing. He nodded and walked briskly to his shop, stiffly trying to conceal the shotgun.

He felt quite a bit safer once he was behind the bars, but his mind went back to the newspaper headline. If he was to die, he'd best make his peace. He took his tallit and kippah from the coatrack and spent the next several minutes with his eyes closed, reciting his favorite prayers.

"Thomas Dixon, I am Lieutenant Samuel James of the Second U.S. Dragoons. I am calling you out!"

Morris couldn't see James from his window, but it didn't matter. He kissed his tallit and placed it back on the coatrack.

Townsfolk poked their heads out of doorways all up and down Main Street, and their dead relatives stood alongside them. But the only person brave enough to step outside was Pertwee, minus his customary waistcoat and top hat, drying off his hands on a bloodstained towel.

A minute later, Dixon emerged, frustratingly, leaning in the doorway of the saloon.

"What can I do for you, Lieutenant?" he called with an air of absolute nonchalance.

"You can come out where no one else will get hurt. I aim to kill you for at least fifty murders over twenty years."

Dixon smiled. He stepped out onto the boardwalk, removing his jacket. He tossed it casually behind himself as he stepped down onto the street. The bartender caught it.

"Alright, Lieutenant. Here I am. How about we trade our best shots, and the better man goes home."

No shadow figure followed him. But Morris wouldn't feel safe until he'd crossed the buried chain. One step, then another, and finally he stepped past it. Morris breathed easier. He checked for some sort of safety catch on the shotgun.

Dixon kept walking, seemingly unaware of any change. He passed by Morris's position without aiming in his direction. The plan was working.

A few more paces, and Dixon stopped, hands on his six-guns. Morris pressed his face against the glass to see where James stood, but he was out of range.

James's voice called out, "Your reign of terror ends today, Dixon."

"You ain't the first to tell me so. You won't be the last. Draw."

A shot rang out as Dixon went for his guns. Halfway there, he flinched and swatted at his ear. "What the hell?" he said. "He nearly got me!"

He pulled a gun from his holster, firing three wild shots.

"What the hell is going on!"

He took several steps back as a second bullet ricocheted off the ground in front of him.

Pertwee dropped his rag and stalked down the

boardwalk, stopping at the saloon. He was inspecting the door jamb.

"Get away from there," Morris whispered.

"Your difficulty may stem from this iron chain," Pertwee said. He pulled it off the mantle, and the dark shadow flew out the door straight for Dixon. It stopped dead at the buried chain.

"Our friend Mr. Shadwell was borrowing some items from Mr. Hayes's barn this morning. It appears he knows your secret."

Dixon turned toward Morris's store. Morris ducked.

"Hang on. You've got something buried here," Pertwee said.

Morris was found out, and things were about to go horribly wrong. Shots rang out, but nothing hit his store. Hopefully that meant the lieutenant had drawn Dixon's attention. He had to act.

He jumped up, shotgun planted against his hip, and he blasted Dixon with both barrels.

Glass shattered, and blood sprayed from Dixon's leg. He screamed in pain and fired back at Morris, the bullet whizzing past him.

"Give it a moment, Mr. Dixon. I'll have this chain out of the ground shortly."

Morris had no more ammunition. He'd never imagined a shot from this distance would be anything but lethal. It was all up to the lieutenant, but even that would mean nothing if that specter got free. Morris had to stop Pertwee.

He ran to the door, flung it open and rushed outside. Pertwee had uncovered the end of the chain. Another shot pinged off his storefront, but Morris ducked and kept running. He raised the butt of his gun and let out a primal scream.

The undertaker looked up, raising an arm to fend off Morris's attack. But at the same time, he pulled up as much chain as he could and flung it away.

It hardly mattered anymore, but Morris would still take revenge for this action. He brought the butt of the shotgun down hard on the undertaker's skull. Pertwee fell to the ground and pushed himself back to the doors of the saloon, fear in his eyes.

Morris steeled himself for a shot in the back. When it didn't come, he saw the spirit was still in the same location, only now it was wrapped in the chain.

"Hah!" he said, nearly dancing in his excitement.

Without looking at it directly, he could see it was thrashing about inside a loop of chain. Could it get out? The loop was in no way secure, and Dixon could still free it.

Dixon had both guns out now, and was still trading shots with the lieutenant, though neither man could hit his mark from that distance. Both men were walking toward each other.

"Do something!" Dixon yelled.

"Your shadow is trapped. I can't get to it," the undertaker said.

Iron, Morris thought. The barrel of the gun was iron. If iron could trap the spirit, perhaps it could kill it. He turned the shotgun around and swung the iron end at the spirit.

Agnes stood with palms pressed against the wide window of her print shop, watching the two gunslingers trade shots. She spared a glance toward Shadwell, who was swinging at empty air with his shotgun. It appeared as if it bounced off something unseen, but if she hadn't seen the evidence of the last two days, she would have believed him mad.

Someone screamed, drawing her attention back to the gunslingers. Lieutenant James had a hand pressed to his hip. That was going to hurt, but he could still fight.

"Come on, come on," she said.

It had been some time since she felt hope, but today she was trying.

She looked back at Shadwell, who reared back with the butt of the shotgun in both hands. He drove it forward and let go.

The gun hung in mid-air as Shadwell backed away from it. A collective gasp went up as the entire town witnessed it. Shadwell smiled, looking triumphant as he turned toward the print shop and Agnes.

Then a shot rang out, and Shadwell's expression changed to surprise. His hands went to his gut where a bloom of red was spreading across his crisp brown vest.

The shotgun fell to the ground as Shadwell

fell to his knees. Agnes ran for the door.

There was pain, but not like Morris thought there would be. Still, his legs went weak, and he found himself on his knees. Warm life leaked out through his fingers.

"The shadow is dead!" Pertwee said.

Morris turned his head and found Pertwee staring into him. Moorehouse, the bartender, was kneeling next to him, and Pertwee held a bar rag against his forehead.

"Shadwell killed it."

"Then get me another!" Dixon yelled.

Thunder cracked overhead though there were no clouds.

"Do you remember the price?" the undertaker asked.

He was standing again, no sign of fear in his eyes. He held two silver coins out toward Dixon.

"Yes! Do it!"

Lieutenant James got a good shot in, catching Dixon just below the shoulder and spinning him around. His gun fell from numb fingers, and he ran toward the undertaker with his other gun pressed against the hole in his chest.

The undertaker spun and pressed the two silver coins into the bartender's eyes.

Moorehouse screamed as blood poured from

the sockets and continued screaming as the undertaker stepped back. The coins caught fire, lighting his skull from inside and spreading throughout his body. His screams took on an unearthly tone as the fire moved down his throat and caught his clothes on fire.

It was over in moments, Mr. Moorehouse reduced to ash and collapsing to the boardwalk. In his place, invisible to all but Morris and presumably the undertaker was another shadow fiend.

The undertaker pointed at Dixon, and the shadow flew straight to him. It passed through him, knocking him back a step, then it pulled his arm away from his chest, pointing it at the lieutenant.

Blam!

The lieutenant fell to the ground with a hole in his forehead.

Agnes came up short as Lieutenant James hit the ground, feeling very exposed.

Dixon stood up straight, no longer seeming to mind the shoulder wound, but his face had aged easily ten years in a few moments. He spared Agnes a dark look, and she backed toward the boardwalk, wishing she hadn't left her shop. The corner of Dixon's mouth curled up into a smile.

He limped toward Morris with his gun outstretched. "Mr. Pertwee?"

"Yes, Mr. Dixon?" the undertaker said, a new bounce in his step, and no sign of the head wound he recently received.

"Tomorrow morning this town rounds up all the iron, and we bury it in the abandoned mine shaft," Dixon said.

Morris scooted back, trying to stem the flow of blood from his gut with one hand. Agnes's heart tugged forward even as she retreated.

"So, you can see my little friend, Mr. Shadwell?" Dixon said.

"Please," Morris said. "Don't shoot me."

"Shoot you? No, Mr. Shadwell, I won't be doing that. But I have a feeling my friend is going to want a good look at you."

"No," Morris said and screamed.

He was lifted by his head. He flailed at the empty air in front of him with the arm that wasn't holding his gut. His eyes widened, staring straight forward, and his scream raised in pitch as Agnes turned away.

Thank you.

Thanks for reading Beyond the Rail and Other Nightmares. I truly hope you enjoyed it. Be sure to let me know about any nightmares it may have inspired. I have a list for people who like my stories, and I even have an exclusive novella for you if you join.
Meet Emily Singer, putting herself through college by passing along messages from dead relatives.
Just follow this link:

https://bit.ly/2QWIHmP

Why would you want to be on my list? Well, if you liked this collection, you'll probably like other things I write, and you'll hear about those here first. There will be discounts exclusive to list members, and I may ask your opinion about things too, such as "Which cover do you like better?" or "Which of these books should I write next?"
Whatever is happening, you'll hear about it first if you join my list. But I also won't spam you. After all, how fast can I write? We're talking maybe three books a year… Maybe

Author Notes

Singalong — Originally created for an anthology requesting humorous horror stories. There were a number of songs I wanted to use but was surprised they were still under copyright. No lyrics from copyrighted children's songs made it into the final copy.

Transplant — My wife had a liver transplant because of an auto-immune disorder, so a lot of this story came from personal experience. I can confirm that aspects of her personality changed after the operation, though not to the extreme that Kevin went through.

Fertile Minds — I'm not a hundred percent sure this Steampunk story belongs in a collection almost entirely populated with Horror, but I had so much fun writing the character of Chelsea Pepperdine and I had to share her with you. I get the feeling she may want a novel of her own at some point.

The Permanent Clerk — Just a ghost story, but it's a take on one I haven't seen much of. I hope you enjoyed it, and if you happen to be or represent Greg Nicotero, I'd love to see this on Creepshow.

Condemned — My wife had a nurse named LaThanya. I promised I would write a character that shared her name. I did my best to do her justice, but I haven't had the courage to show her the end result yet. The rest of this just came from a love of underserved Eastern European folklore.

The Nocturnal Habits of the Late Derek Gray — This is the first of two stories I wrote for a tribute anthology to the great Stephen King. Hopefully this put you in mind of stories like Gray Matter, The Breathing Method, The Jaunt, and The Dune. A low-key conversation involving a small-town sheriff whose jail cell is usually just a stop-over for the town drunk. Now, without reading ahead, can you guess the second Stephen King tribute?

The Ritual — This short story was my first attempt at professional writing, and it was short-listed in Short Fiction Break's Spring Writing Contest. I felt a Joss Whedon vibe while writing it. Hopefully that came across.

The Raven — This was written for a Dark Web contest on the Creepypasta website. First person horror doesn't generally appeal to me as an author, but I did enjoy writing this story and the "found footage" aspect of it. I leave it to you to decide what the epilogue would be.

Trick of the Light — This story was heavily inspired by The Pogues' Turkish Song Of The Damned. If you don't know the song, but you enjoyed the story, I highly recommend you give it a listen.

Two Hundred Miles — If you got to this page before reading the story, I'm about to spoil it for you. I highly suggest you skip down to the next one. I know zombie stories have been done to death (then they came back only to be killed again), but this one doesn't have any zombies in it, so that makes it okay, right? Also, it was written during the Obama administration. I like to think his manner of speaking comes through, but I made it generic president to be relevant to readers of the far-flung-future.

Agatha Hemsley, Beloved Mother — If you guessed this was the other Stephen King tribute, you win the prize: the respect and admiration of your fellow readers. Well spotted.

Beyond the Rail — This story is more about the psychology of grief and madness than it is about the supernatural, but isn't that really the scariest thing in our lives? Those uncontrollable urgings of our own minds? The emotions we would switch off if only we could?

The lure and possible comforts of horrible madness?

Two Shadows, One Gun — These stories were written years apart, but if you go back to the Permanent Clerk, you'll see the office he worked at was Morris and Tennyson. I swear this is coincidence. I left it as is anyway, so feel free to draw your own conclusion there.

Oh, and while writing Agatha's character, I had Jennifer Jason Leigh from The Hudsucker Proxy running through my head.

I'd like to acknowledge the people who helped me go from rough draft to something readable.

Professional Critique
Tory Hunter

Beta Readers
Selim Ulug
Rob Johnson
Dan B. Fierce
Derek Nyberg

Editing
Richard Thomas of Storyville

Novels by Ichabod Ebenezer

A Shadow Stained in Blood

Short Stories

A Gentleman's Wager

Ichabod as Tormund Giantsbane

Ichabod Ebenezer is the genre-promiscuous author of "A Shadow Stained in Blood" as well as countless short stories ranging from Horror to Sci-fi, from Fantasy to Mystery. He lives and writes in the Pacific Northwest with his family, a chameleon, and the ghosts of three cats. He is currently working on a Fantasy novel, but there is always another skeleton at the back of his closet.